The Swallows

Kristen Clanton

Kristen Clanton

To past ghosts and present sweethearts

Thank you for everything,
Kristen

Kristen Clanton

WITCH WAY
PUBLISHING

First Edition, 2023

Witch Way Publishing
3436 Magazine Street
#460
New Orleans, LA 70115
www.witchwaypublishing.com

Editor: Tonya Brown
Copy Editor: Anna Rowyn
Cover Designer: Quirky Circe Designs

Printed in the United States of America

ISBN Paperback: 978-1-0880-0121-9
ISBN E-Book: 978-1-0880-0197-4

TABLE of CONTENTS

CHAPTER ONE
Pearl Walks Home

Pearl knew the town was dangerous. She could see it in the faces of the dead mothers, whose photos frequented the evening news. The ten-block track marooned between the black forest of Bear Mountain and the stone needles of Iron Mountain was called the Swallows by the kids who lived there, a name that rounded its way through South Dakota family lines and great American gold-rush histories. The name was said to have originated in a bar at the bottom of Carson Street, though no one alive had been there. The town's true name— the one maintained by state maps, game wardens, and out-of-towners— was Fullmouth. Though anyone who lived in the Swallows knew the town's official name was a joke, one made by the original pioneers who attempted to settle a land too shallow and rocky to seed. Even the kids who didn't know their town history knew hardly anything good came from the Swallows. Every street in the neighborhood was intimidating from beginning to end, but like magicians, the kids knew each pitfall and trapdoor, knew taking the long way around made no difference when it came to escape.

During the summer months, when fleas jumped the sidewalks freely, the problem was the population of mangy dogs. Each one was left behind in April, when the winter work of hunting and fur trapping was over, and their transient masters traveled north to board the trains that guided them back to the fishing towns and salmon boats they left behind. By the end of July, the kids were bored with their wandering, and the dogs' teeth grew brittle with hunger, snouts scabbed from scavenging. That is when the real dog days of summer began. Before they disappeared into the forest around Fullmouth, the dogs were willing to eat anything. Dead rats and pop bottles, diapers— whatever the kids would bring. Taunting the dogs was all part of the game, and if the kids got too close, there was usually a way out. On their bikes, they pedaled fast and faster, launching the curbs and cracks, laughing wildly as the dogs snapped at their sneakers. But in the fall, when most of the dogs were long gone, the fun was over. Gut instincts and measurable shifts in their mothers' behavior—from chain-smoking in bathrobes, to wearing lipstick and jeans, and trying out new recipes— told the kids to stay home. Though they never compared the happenings within their households, each kid foretold a dark stranger soon arriving at their door, divined the knock that was coming, a knock as predictable as the patterned beat of a rocking bassinet. And as winter goes, after the taverns swallowed every warmth into their blinking lights and black boxes, it was the hunters and trappers, just returned, who were spit into the streets and wanted only to devour a woman, a warm bed, and hot plate. At least until the next spring, when the women and their children were left to the Swallows, back to their bathrobes and bicycles. Angry babies left hanging on rocking hips and teats, and the mangy dogs left to the streets. Only the kids knew how to cope. In the Swallows, it was all about how fast they could move and how good they could hide. The chains were heavy, the score too far behind. And within the ruins of this desolate town, four mothers had committed suicide in the small radius of rundown rows, just since that summer, when Pearl Adler had moved into a boarding house on Mystic Avenue.

†

As Pearl walked home from Custer Day School, she thought about the suicides, but mostly in abstraction, like a scary dream. Part ghosts and goblins, part creatures rising from their graves to avenge their histories, all of it, combined with the six-o'clock newsreels, was mashed up with the purple pamphlets Miss Lippincott handed out at the final bell. After weeks of classroom conversations and a skit about a girl named Sad Cindy, sponsored by the guidance counseling office alongside the art and music departments, Lippincott finally received the administration's go-ahead for the Suicide Prevention Pamphlet. Vice Principal Richards thought the pamphlets showed weakness of character, but his hand was forced to approve the written materials. The ninth-grade students and ninth-grade teachers were locked in a war of wills. The students refused to take the awareness exercises seriously, and the teachers refused to believe comedy was how teenagers grieved. Since the Sad Cindy skit, it seemed like every ninth grader was falling to their knees, rising from the dead, or pretending to be a zombie. Even Ruby Teller mocked Sad Cindy's big line, shrieking, "I can't believe this is happening to me!", before promptly gathering her things and leaving.

In an attempt to control the gravity of the situation, herds of students were sent to Vice Principal Richard's office, their mass exodus becoming a block party right under his nose. Richards had enough of it, and Lippincott's pamphlets were supposed to close the conversation for good. But in Pearl's mind, it was only a rolling comic strip of bright dawns, dark ends, and fantastic beginnings again. On the news, suicide started with bright pills and booze, and smiling Polaroids of mothers before they were mothers, off to dances and bonfires. It was in the transition from being simple, spindly girls to ones with taut and tanned bellies, wrapped in the same bikinis they wore every season at the mountain lakes. The investigative reporters dissected the women's lives and found the instant, in all its evidence, that each began smiling into her sadness, moving deeper and deeper into the cave, where it eventually became too dark to take photos. It was these undocumented times—the ones the newsreels couldn't cover— that people like Miss Lippincott and Pastor Hall worried about.

Each Sunday since the deaths began, Pastor Hall declared the suicides by name— Cindy Stewart, Molly Boutell, Kaia Goodwin, and Maggie Teller — during confession and absolution. He wanted their names to become a canonical chant the congregation could fold into its prayers. However, the church elders were not at ease with suicide being so readily embraced by the clergy, and they were especially distraught that the suicides were repeatedly included on the list of needed prayers. They said the suicides should not be grouped with Charlie and Beth Johnson's son in Iraq or Hubert Broderick's long-drawn cancer battle, particularly because the women were not members of the church. Each Sunday, the elder's indignation grew. It started with Steve Johns and Curtis Witcham coughing when Pastor Hall began canonizing the suicide list. And by the third Sunday, the elders settled on a protest: they refused to kneel during prayer. An emergency congregation meeting was held at The Gaslight Diner, where all were on equal ground. The elders said the suicides were unwed mothers with unbaptized children, and none of them could be helped beyond Bessie Rains, God bless her soul, who had taken the children into her home. They said they could agree with Pastor Hall to pray for the orphans—who would eventually come to Christ through the guidance of Bessie Rains— but not their mothers. It was too late for them. And though Pastor Hall was greatly outnumbered, as the waitress circled the table, refilling their glasses of iced tea and hot coffee, he proclaimed God was on his side, and He alone could decide to honor the mothers' suffering. The congregation's only role was to believe in the potency of prayer on high. He felt the Holy Spirit so strongly in that moment, he pounded on the table, his fist the falling gavel of absolution.

Though Pearl knew little about what went into the making of the pamphlet, the newsreels, and ceaseless arguments, she was aware that the dead mothers disturbed the tenebrous balance of life in the Swallows. All the kids knew the trouble the dead mothers caused, and Bessie Rains' house was just part of their education.

†

Pearl listened to the dry crush sound of leaves beneath her sneakers as Benny trilled away, every other word of his singsong voice an echo in the wind. Since starting Kindergarten, Benny had mostly mastered the work of talking and walking at the same time, but when he got excited, all the energy of his body became voltaic, sparking solely from his mouth. And they were running late with all of Benny's chattering. Pearl could tell the time from the orange line, a neon glow that framed Bear Mountain and slashed through the low buildings on the East side of Main Street, making all the windows seem to yell, *Get home now!* She knew that by the time they reached the heart of the Swallows, all the tavern doors would be propped open. Conway Twitty and Hank Williams would be warbling the songs of the early crowd. There was no way Pearl could carry Benny, so she pulled him along. Guiding him across the street, the brick tenements blocked the northern winds, and she could finally hear him speak.

"—and I'm going to be a skeleton vampire!" His little voice shrieked. "With a cape and teeth and a skeleton body!" Benny jumped up and down, his giant Scooby-Doo backpack slapping the backs of his knees.

"Come on, Bens—mom's gonna be upset if she doesn't get to see us before work, and all because of your talking."

Benny was quiet then, his steps becoming hurried and determined. He looked like a tiny, long-legged bird, like an ostrich or roadrunner, the fan of his blonde cowlick transforming into bobbing feathers atop his head. Pearl wanted to laugh, but she knew he'd think she was making fun of him. And there was always the possibility Benny would stop talking altogether.

Though her mom didn't say much about it, Pearl knew Benny being mute was close to the top of her mom's list of number-one fears. When Pearl was in sixth grade, her mom cried a lot on the phone, especially when she talked to her sister in Omaha. It was always about Benny's doctor appointments and Benny's ear tests. Pearl wasn't so sure Benny was okay, but her mom just knew it to be true. The only problem was, Benny wouldn't talk. He had no interest at all. Pearl tried things too. Mostly bribes of Zebra Cakes and board games, TV shows she knew he liked, but

Benny's words were all blanks.

It wasn't until he was five years old and they went to Silver Lake for Memorial Day. Pearl's mom was dating a man who sold cars, and he showed up to their old apartment in a shiny one, all seafoam green and silver lines. Pearl thought it looked like a mermaid's chariot, not a *pussy wagon*, as the salesman said when Pearl's mom climbed into the front seat. The whole way to the lake, which turned out to be the exact same color as the car, the man went on and on about the engine and steering. Each time he patted Pearl's mom on the thigh, he said, "You're lucky you're so pretty," as he looked at the two kids in the rearview mirror. He laughed and patted her thigh the whole way there. But when they got to the lake, his good feelings ended. There were at least a hundred ducks and geese at Silver Lake. They were nesting in the grass, poking at the pebble beach, and defecating on everything. The salesman said he couldn't risk it, not with the paint job and all, but Pearl's mom refused to leave. She promised the lake on Memorial Day, and that's exactly what was going to happen. After a few heated moments, where Pearl's mom whispered through gritted teeth, the man agreed to stay because, he said, Pearl's mom owed him one. "And I'll be damned if I'm not gonna get it. Always cash on delivery," he said, laughing and pulling at the buttons on Pearl's mom's blouse.

The whole day at Silver Lake, like a sentry, the man stood next to the sea green car, chasing the ducks and geese down to the lake. Pearl's mom brought him paper plates heaped with potato salad and cold meats. She brought beer after beer, carrying away the empties, while Pearl and Benny played by the lake, where all the ducks and geese could live freely outside of the man's screams. All those corralled birds made Benny happy. By lunchtime, he'd learned to approach the geese slowly, one animal to another, with a potato chip extended from his hand. The first few chips went okay, but the last one, the one that made Benny point and yell, "Bad bird!" loudly, took off the tip of his finger. Pearl's mother was not even upset. At least not until they were headed home, and the salesman griped about Benny getting blood on the upholstery, but it was only because she couldn't hear what Benny was saying. After the first shriek, Benny never stopped talking. Though sometimes Pearl thought Benny was a deflating balloon: his words began with a blowup and endured until Benny was exhausted. Then the whole thing would go back to flat.

†

"Want me to carry your backpack?" Pearl asked.

Benny had the hangdog posture of a little boy who had walked miles and still had a little way to go. But he shook his head *no* in one quick motion, like he saw Adam West do on old reruns of Batman.

Crossing the threshold of Clifton Avenue and into the heart of the Swallows, Pearl felt the energy in her body change, like it always did. Her weight was no longer evenly taken up by each of her limbs, her head, and heart. In the Swallows, she wore it like armor. All of Pearl watched everything; her inward eyes became transfixed just below the surface of her skin, like poison darts in wait. She had millions of eyes, the egg-shaped goosebumps all over her body, hidden beneath her jacket and jeans. She moved Benny to her other side, closer to the street and away from the tavern doors, where he couldn't be grabbed so easily. It was later than she thought. John-Boy and Derry were already squatting on the parking blocks in front of Black Cat Liquor, paper-sacked bottles in each of their hands, and two more between them. John-Boy's dishwater blonde hair was tucked behind his large ears, and aside from the fact that the Black Cat parking lot was where he could be found every afternoon when Vern's Auto Repair closed, it was only those ears that made him distinguishable from any of the other short greasers who lived in the Swallows. John-Boy was a vulture on a stoop, and when he caught sight of Pearl, he let out a long, low whistle that didn't sound so much like a signal but more like the start of a horror movie—tinny and low, like the brutality to come had already been presupposed. Pearl knew it was too late to cross the street. If John-Boy and Derry thought she was scared, it would get bad— bad as what everyone said happened to Ruby Teller— and it would be even worse if Benny could tell. She tucked her ponytail into her jacket and lifted the hood over her head. She watched the sidewalk in front of her, leading Benny around the broken glass and accumulated scuzz that happened when drunks took to the street. Her legs beat faster than walking but not too fast, and a recurrent pattern developed where every third step jumped a crack.

Benny noticed the pattern of steps too, and yelled, "Oneee, twoooo, threeeee: jump!" over and over.

Pearl smiled. It was too late to worry about being quiet. She squeezed Benny's hand as they hit the jump, but she wasn't really looking at him. She wasn't really smiling at Benny. Pearl knew— as any witch or ghost— that her body was hinged. She was on the edge, bending into the blackness of disorder. Her spirit no longer walked the street freely with Benny. It was on the easement in front of

11

Black Cat Liquor. She watched John-Boy and Derry—both older than their eighteen years— stand up from the parking blocks and wipe their large hands on their jeans. She watched their eyes shift between the alley, the street, Pearl and Benny. She watched Derry say something to John-Boy, something she couldn't hear, but she felt its meaning in their dry laughs, in the way John-Boy shoved Derry toward her other self, the one with Benny, walking north on Main Street. In Pearl's head, she was standing on the easement, her face a terrifying snarl, her lips bared back behind her ears, revealing violent teeth. She watched John-Boy and Derry split up as they approached her and Benny. John-Boy fastened the few buttons still attached to his flannel shirt, and Derry pushed his long hair from his face.

They're coming. They're coming. They're coming, Pearl repeated, mirroring the words to her step.

"Pearly, pearl," John-Boy sang in a teasing lilt. "Wait up, I gotta ask you something."

She knew Derry— his height and bulk far greater than John-Boys but ten times as dumb— was about to block her path or grab her arms, which was his usual technique when it came to the start of forcing his way. To avoid Derry's hands as best she could, Pearl stopped walking, and nodded at John-Boy to speak.

"You know why your mama moved to the Swallows, right?"

Pearl heard this joke before. She had pretty much heard it on every street corner and screamed from every open tavern door since she'd moved to Fullmouth— she even heard it in the lunch line at school.

"—cause she loves suckin' the root and slurpin' the juice." John-Boy took a swig from the paper bag, gargling the liquor before he swallowed it. "But your mama's a little rode hard for me—more my daddy's speed."

John-Boy touched Pearl's cheek with a rough thumb. She didn't flinch. "But you a ripe little peach, still swingin'— and the fruit never falls far from the tree." John-Boy looked at Derry for a laugh, but Derry was too caught up in watching Pearl's legs and feet. His greasy hair fell back into his face, following the angry patches of acne on his neck and cheeks. John-Boy kicked broken glass at Derry, but he still didn't get a reaction.

"Little peach," Benny said, laughing. "Yeah! That's what you could be for Halloween!" Benny jumped up and down next to Pearl, the jarring sound of dead leaves breaking beneath his feet. Pearl thought it'd be the same sound John-Boy's thumb would make if she cracked it open. She smiled at Benny. If Pearl were happy about anything, it was that Benny couldn't really understand John-Boy's meaning. And if the conversation could stay right there, right on the edge where it was safe, not tipping in either direction, she could get Benny home soon.

†

It is a sure thing that a child's reaction to unease is directly affected by the roles lived out in the privacy of home. Pearl was seven years older than Benny, and she had lived seven years more than him— guiding him down dark streets and sneaking him into movies, helping him get dressed in the morning and brushing his teeth, wrapping Christmas presents and hiding Easter eggs— his whole life. To Benny, seven years was a galaxy, greater than his whole cosmic span. But to Pearl, there was always a *before Benny*. In Pearl's memory, the space before Benny was all short flashes of time worming into her mind through

13

endless repetition: Pearl sitting in the grocery cart, eating a free sprinkle cookie from the bakery; dancing with her mom to 45s in their basement apartment, sweaty and laughing, Christmas lights blinking; blueberry Pop-Tarts and Saturday morning cartoons, the smell of her mom's cigarettes and coffee, the laundry, all clean and new under the stale blue light of morning. Pearl protected the luxury of these memories; luxuries Benny never knew existed because they were not part of his history. They were in a hidden home, the one Pearl only thought about before she went to sleep at night, when her body was tired with work, more tired than it ought to be at fourteen. The roles Pearl and Benny lived in their family mirrored the way they coped with everything. Where Pearl led with defense and action, Benny made misdirection, chaos, and responses absurd enough to be funny, at least while he was still a little kid, young enough that any minor revelation could be amusing. Pearl mostly found Benny annoying—a pain at every point of the day, one who could hardly comprehend anything outside of comic strips and superheroes— but she was always struck by his capacity to alter the natural direction of things.

During that still point on the sidewalk between John-Boy and Derry, when Derry laughed and John-Boy didn't, Benny was either just a dumb kid, or he was good at pretending. Benny's meaning didn't matter though. What mattered was that Derry, the eighteen-year-old muscle who was at least five times the size of Pearl, was stupid as all basic things. And when Benny called Pearl a peach for Halloween, Derry thought it was funny. Funnier than anything John-Boy said and simple enough in its meaning. The Halloween peach was such a bizarre turn that Derry's body lost all its jolting intensity. His shoulders and neck slumped, his hands went to his belly as he laughed good and deep. His boots stumbled from the sidewalk and onto the matted crabgrass. With Derry bent over laughing, John-Boy lost all his force momentarily. But that's all it took. It was moment enough for Benny to squeeze Pearl's hand. It was then, five blocks from their boarding house on Mystic Avenue, that Benny gave Pearl his signal—the signal to *run!* – to run full force in a leg buckling, high-knee sprint.

†

The old woman in the pink bathrobe pushed her grocery cart down the street. Her back bent and hands knotted like the roots of Fir trees, all of her moved far too slowly. Pearl saw her as an apparition. All the details flooded in at such speed, so choked with reality, it felt like Bessie Rains, right there on Main Street, was a mirage. She was the only elder in Fullmouth who evoked both respect and fear from everyone else who lived in town. She was the only person who could get John-Boy and Derry to abandon the chase, with just her presence on the street. Pearl thought she was a figure of protection plucked from a bad dream. But Bessie Rains was there, true to form. Her gnarled hands clung to a cart wider than the sidewalk. Pearl and Benny moved quickly toward her, their sneakers beating frantic, erratic time on the concrete.

"On your left, Miss Bessie!" Pearl yelled as Benny yanked Pearl's arm, slackening their speed.

Bessie Rains paused. The gray braid curled at the base of her neck slowly shifted out of sight as she turned to look at the children. In her misshapen state, it was difficult to believe Bessie Rains had once been a ballerina. Though Pearl knew it was true. In her rotting mansion on Buffalo

Avenue, the images on the walls, wrinkled with age, showed Bessie Rains in Stockholm, London, and Paris— on stage in all the towns the trains could travel during the war. The hands clinging to the cart handle were once brilliant dreams of magic birds and daggers, but time had transformed the dancer's line into the hunched and steady posture that Pearl and Benny found in the street. Blanketed in a bright bathrobe, Bessie Rains looked like a giant worry stone, a bougainvillea out of season.

"You like to give me a heart attack," Bessie Rains said, unknotting her fingers from the cart and slowly bringing them to her chest in a pantomime of suffering. "I thought a band of wild horses finally made their way to town proper." Bessie's laugh was a throaty rasp.

"Aw, Miss Bessie, we didn't mean to scare you." Benny let go of Pearl's hand and climbed onto the side of the cart to rest his head on the metal bars. "I'm so tired."

"Those boys chasing you kids again?" Bessie looked from Benny and into the street. She narrowed her eyes, even though a milky layer shrouded the blues and prevented her from seeing anything. She settled on a shake of the head and suck of the teeth— the only act of deliverance she could meet.

"You know how it is, Ms. Bessie." Pearl didn't have to turn around to know John-Boy and Derry were heading back toward Clifton Avenue, back to their forties and parking lot stoops. She could hear John-Boy whistling again, a slow melody, one that grew more and more sluggish, losing air and speed. It was a dirge meant for Pearl, so she would know just what was waiting.

CHAPTER TWO

The Golden Image

Diane leaned against the gold Oldsmobile, the car she'd been driving west since high school, never making it all the way, though she'd almost done it twice: once with Aunt Rose and her best friend Evie, and once with Pearl's dad. She talked about the first adventure so often that Pearl felt like she was in the backseat back then, listening to Fleetwood Mac, her ponytail whipping her face. The painted train cars and long nights at all the cowboy bars along I-90, eating hot dogs in truck stop parking lots, each bite oily and sweet. The steaming concrete, making up dances and songs, the endless waiting, tanning in bikinis on the hood of the car, right in the emergency lane, where one lonely traveler after another stopped to fill their gas tank. But the second trip, the one with Pearl's dad, was more of a silent exchange. Even though it was another summer on I-90, it was always raining and the radio didn't work. There was always enough gas. Everything else beyond the bylines— one man for one baby, one woman waking up to an empty hotel room in Missoula, Montana— was a mystery.

Diane's long legs were still the same color as the car, despite the air creeping into winter. The sun was falling into its final glow right behind her head— the orange halo and wind picking up her curls, molding them into the feathers

17

of some rare and sullen bird. She could almost be the firelight image of Mary— hands open, face bent to the earth— if it were not for the grease spots on her apron, the Virginia Slim between her fingertips, and the shoes she wore to the diner.

"Why didn't you get us?" Benny whined.

"Come on now, didn't you get my message?" She looked at Pearl as she ruffled Benny's hair with her free hand, holding the cigarette to her painted mouth with the other.

"Lippincott said you couldn't make it," Pearl said.

She flicked the ash and kicked the rear tire of the Oldsmobile. "The battery died. I had to beg Henshaw to give me a ride to Vern's to get a new one, and the cheapest one was a hundred bucks. I owe him at the end of the week, and I'll be pulling doubles until then to pay it back. Never mind these bald bastards."

Benny scowled and kicked the back tire too, to emphasize her point. "Hunk a junk."

She laughed and threw her cigarette on the gravel drive.

"You got a little lipstick on your teeth, right there." Pearl pointed to the spot in her mother's mouth.

The shade of red she always wore was on a canine so long and dangerous looking, Pearl still partially believed her mother's warnings of being a werewolf, one who could fully transform if she were made angry enough. Pearl saw flashes of that transformation, when her mother got quiet and glass-eyed, her body hunched and wooden. Usually, her anger ended when she went out to the Double R with Evie. Those nights, Pearl sat in the front window and waited to see mom and Evie's shadows bobbing down the street, their heads bent toward one another, like Siamese twins or some eight-legged sea creature who made it all the way into the mountains through the endless transport of streams. Those times usually ended happy enough. Mom made popcorn and they listened to old Janis Joplin albums on low, dancing and mouthing the words so they wouldn't wake Benny. But other times. Other times Pearl couldn't predict what would happen. The last bad time, her mother broke all the dishes in the kitchen and sat in the glass on the linoleum, crying hysterically. Pearl and Benny could only watch from the rug, terror-struck by what they were witnessing. It only ended when Benny put on his galoshes and walked into the kitchen. "Let's go down to Nellie's for some ice cream," Benny said as he helped his mother off the floor. And the next morning, Pearl woke up to most of the apartment loaded into the Oldsmobile and a piecemeal plan about starting over in Fullmouth.

"It isn't all that bad." She laughed again and opened the backdoor of the car, the metallic grating of the hinges emphasizing the transition. "Come on, let's get you two some dinner and I'll check your homework between tables. You bring that math? Lippincott said you've been hiding your algebra worksheets in the back of your desk."

Pearl sighed as she climbed in. Her and Benny's heavy coats and hats were packed into the bucket seat, and Pearl pushed them to the brown carpet, worn thin against the rusted floor pan. The tension in her body collapsed as she heard her mom belt Benny in and shut the door.

Pearl opened the visor mirror to see Benny in the backseat. "Don't tell mom about those boys."

Benny looked at her in the glass. "You know she'd wanna know."

"She's got enough to worry about, and she can't do

anything but get upset."

Benny nodded at his sister's reflection. His eyes were ringed with purple, the surest sign he was too tired to keep talking.

"I've never seen you run so fast, Bens. I could hardly keep up." Pearl moved the mirror back and rested her head on the window. She closed her eyes and listened to her mother climb in next to her.

"I got the dittos," Pearl said.

"I know you had to walk, but you sure took your sweet time." She put the key into the ignition and slowly pumped the gas as the engine turned over. "Didn't think I'd catch you."

"We ran into Miss Bessie."

Their mother rolled her eyes. "She kept me near twenty minutes this morning, telling me about a pigeon that nested on her porch, feathers and poop everywhere. She thought it had a broken wing until it tried to get through her door when she headed to the grocery store, pecking its way through the screen—can you imagine? Red eyes and beak just pecking into your house? —she finally got one of the kids to chase it with a broom, but even that hardly worked. It was still sitting in the yard, just glaring at Miss Bessie. Did she tell you that one?"

†

When Pearl heard the steady crush of gravel beneath the tires, she pictured the world as she was about to see it: The Gaslight, a golden caterpillar, its giant windows curled around the building, bending into the roof. She pictured the metal wall framing the kitchen, covered in kitschy magnets, the moose head in sunglasses over the door, Rose's dark curls captured in a pink hairnet, the warm light of the world within the diner, peeling off into darkness the further it extended from the fire. When Pearl opened her eyes, what she saw was almost the same as what she pictured, but the one difference made complete continuity impossible. The goosebumps all came back. Her million-eyes fluttered at once, like bats quaking. All of her watched the islands that separated *then* from *now*, the *before* from the *after*. Pearl knew that somewhere along the drive to the diner, with her eyes closed and head resting against the glass while she listened to the familiar sound of her mother humming along to Top-40 radio, the ferryman had taken her to the wrong coastline. It reminded Pearl of the old *Voodoo Island* movie poster Mr. Hansel hung proudly at Red Rabbit Video: The Gaslight was a yellow stone sinking into an ever-darkening violence, the women inside stiff with dread, voodoo heads bulging, smiting every given light.

"Weird," Pearl's mom said as she leaned into the backseat to unclip Benny, his booster seat covering the buckle. "Never thought Rose would go in for something like this."

"It looks like a haunted house," Benny said.

All of the diner windows were painted in terrifying scenes: Macbeth's three witches bent over a cauldron, bubbling with body parts; ghosts in tattered suits and Victorian dresses sitting on their headstones; dancing skeletons, stacks of skulls, poppet dolls, the Bride of Frankenstein, electrified, and shrunken heads blocking out the faces of every living body hunched over a cup of coffee at the counter or tucked into the booths within the diner.

"The detail makes it weirder. Looks like all the eyes are moving." Pearl slung her bookbag over her shoulder and helped Benny into his while her mother grabbed their coats.

"What happened to just jack-o-lanterns' and scarecrows?" Pearl's mom asked.

"The Lutherans'll be too scared to come in without Pastor Hall performing an exorcism," Pearl said.

Diane laughed as she pushed the driver's door closed with her hip. "At least it won't cut into my tips."

"Dem bones, dem bones, gonna rise again," Benny sang as the three slowly made their way across the parking lot, gravel crunching beneath their feet.

✝

The small bells made their familiar trill when Pearl's mom pushed open The Gaslight's front door. "Happy you didn't replace the chimes with a scream box," she said loudly to Rose, who was flipping hamburgers on a skillet.

"Diane, if you don't hurry up and get to those tables, we're not gonna need a scream box," Rose yelled back as she used the handle of the spatula to scratch her head.

Pearl's mom laughed and squeezed behind the counter, stowing her purse and coat beside the ice box before retying her apron and flattening the ruffles against her plaid shift dress. She hugged Rose's shoulders by way of *hello* and began filling water glasses. "It is a little out there, Rose, even for you."

"I've heard just about enough of that." Rose eyed old Curtis Witcham, hunched over the counter, cradling his mug of coffee.

"Just isn't right," Curtis Witcham said, looking into his cup as if to discern the messages foretold on the coffee's oily surface. "And I'm not the only one who's going to say it."

"It's Halloween! When did we become a town scared

of its own shadow?"

Diane swung her hips around the counter, balancing six water glasses on a tray as she headed to the few full booths at the back of the diner, her red mouth set into an easy grin. "How ya'll doing this evening? Would you like to hear the specials?"

Rose slapped the patties on the buns, lifted the fries from the fryer, and dumped them over the open-faced burgers. She poured table salt from the big cardboard cylinder into her hand— the girl with the umbrella soggy from months of oil splatter— and sprinkled the plates before throwing the remainder over her left shoulder. She finished dressing the burgers with tomatoes, onions, lettuce, and the pickles she made herself from summer cucumbers grown in her garden each year. Rose rang the bell, yelled, "Order up!", pulled the finished tickets, and laid the plates in front of two men sitting at the counter.

"Thanks, ma'am."

"Thank ya, much."

Rose filled their coffee mugs and placed their tickets face down next to each plate.

Since Pearl was a baby, she'd sat at hundreds of restaurant counters throughout the American West, gumming crackers and cola, watching Diane work. Not once in all those years did Pearl ever see another woman move in the same way her mom did. That was until she met Rose. Diane and Rose were both duck-footed and long-limbed, even their faces matched— too much makeup applied with too little delicacy—the perfect stage masks. Their laughs were loud and raucous and tended to build off one another, but so did their physical grace. Though they both wasted words, each movement Diana and Rose made was absolute and purposeful. Pearl often watched them, happily entranced by how they fell into both the rhythm of one another and the song on the radio.

The Shangri-Las "Leader of the Pack" was in full swing. Mary Weiss and all her teenage angst moaned from the small pastel radio that hung over the drying rack, but Pearl didn't notice any of The Gaslight's soul standards. She and Benny were leaning against a booth near the restrooms, staring at the image painted on one of the rear windows. Pearl didn't see this frame from the parking lot, as the colors were not nearly as loud as they were on the other panes. The painting was done in pale golds and browns. The women's shapes were hazy, outlined in fuzzy curves of gray. There were four women, eyes closed, all wearing similar Grecian gowns and sandals, rose crowns on their heads. Most of their arms crossed over their hearts, but the first one—the one who looked like Cindy Stewart—was beckoning for the other three. One arm extended; pointer finger curled. The two women who looked like Molly Boutell and Kaia Goodwin had an arm draped around the other's shoulder, their foreheads bent toward each other like swans. And Kaia, the third woman in the row, was holding hands with the final woman, the one who looked the unhappiest, the one who most resembled Maggie Teller.

Pearl could not help but compare the cheerful snapshots of the mothers, presented over and again on the newsreels, to these painted representations. Here they were, on the other side. An image of the *after* that could never be photographed but felt truer than any image Pearl had seen before. More than the mothers— enshrined and dressed as Grecian goddesses— the painting made Pearl think of the children they left behind. Pearl imagined their children crowded into the damp rooms of Bessie Rains' house. Their small suitcases never unpacked. And one after the other, they were cut away from everything they could count on, everything that could bring them back to the side of the living. At school, the children of the suicide mothers walked the halls together, removed from every classroom and every assignment in the foreseeable future. Vice Principal Richards believed in the divide-and-conquer approach. He believed it better to separate the traumatized students from their peers, as their losses could never be readily understood by the other children, and their presence would cause even more disruption to the already chaotic classrooms.

For this reason, Bessie Rains' wards spent their school hours in the guidance office and library, hunched over old copies of *Reader's Digest* and *National Geographic*, whispering to each other. On assembly days, they gathered at the card table in Richards' office. Under the watchful eye of the school nurse, they played UNO and Bullshit, milk cartons and butter cookies spread out on the wobbly tabletop, out of the sights and minds of most every student at Custer Day. And they had been vacant from Pearl's mind too, until she woke up in her mother's Oldsmobile that afternoon on the other side of the river Styx.

†

"You kids stop acting like strangers and take a seat—keep me company while your momma does the running," Rose called to Pearl and Benny.

Pearl guided Benny over to the counter, hung their bookbags on the brass hooks beneath the bar, and boosted Benny onto the vinyl stool.

"How you doing, Miss Rose?" Benny asked as he fumbled with the paper menu placemat.

"Well, today? Today I can't complain. You want to try a Frankenstein shake?"

"Is that a dance?"

Rose laughed. She grabbed a metal tumbler and began to fill it with vanilla ice cream, mint syrup, and crushed Oreos. "It's just like my Leprechaun shake, but the face comes out a little different." Rose clicked on the mixer, and the loud *whirr* drowned out the final verse of the Shangri-Las.

"You get into all the holidays like this, Miss Rose?" Pearl asked.

Rose drew two monster faces in chocolate syrup on the inside of two tall glasses, filled each with mint cookie shake, then stacked cookie crumbles on top and used a long straw to form them into Frankenstein's zigzag hairline. She set the milkshakes on the paper menus with long spoons and a wide smile. "Now what do you think of that, Sugar?"

"Ohhhh!" Benny sat up on his heels so he could reach the top of the glass. "Could you make a skeleton vampire?" He picked up his spoon and dug into Frankenstein's face, the green decorating his cheeks and chin. "That's what I'm gonna be for Halloween, Miss Rose— already decided.

"You draw me a picture, and we'll figure it out." Rose patted his hand then turned to rinse the tumblers in the sink.

Pearl watched her mother return to the bar. The ruffles on her apron swayed to the harmonies of "Only the Lonely", her legs following the hesitant curve of Roy Orbison's voice.

"He's the big painter?" Diane pinned three tickets to

the board and looked over her shoulder. Pearl, Rose, and Curtis Witcham all turned to the back corner of the diner.

In the far booth, where the sun had already set, there was a man sitting alone. The man's head was turned to the window, looking at the scenery painted there: a dark forest, the thick trunks bent into almost complete darkness, and only one golden-eyed owl looking out. Pearl couldn't see the man's face. His long hair was the thick pelt of a black bear— the image amplified because the man hardly fit in the booth. The knees of his jeans pushed against the underside of the table. And his arms, stretched out, gave his fingers enough reach to curl around the opposite edge of the tabletop. His black wool sweater was rolled up to the elbows, revealing thick arms decorated by every paint color encasing The Gaslight.

"Don't go messing with that one," Rose warned.

Diane pulled four coffee mugs and two dessert plates from the stack. "He's got a giant red devil in his plans spread out on the table over there. Count yourself lucky he ran out of window space."

"For Heaven's sake." Curtis Witcham slammed his mug on the counter.

Rose slapped the dishrag on the sink and laughed, heavy and low. "Maybe I'll let him paint it on the bathroom mirrors. A red devil is a mighty good description of some of the people walking around this town."

"I would've done it for half of whatever fortune you paid him, and my pictures would've been more inclined to the rabble of Fullmouth," Diane said as she removed the cake knife from the utensil rack.

"I don't want to be inclined to no one around here."

"That's crystal clear, Rosie. You let him paint out the

27

sunshine. Your light bill is going to be a head-shaker come November," Curtis Witcham said.

Rose grabbed the coffee pot, topped off Curtis Witcham's cup, and filled the mugs Diane set on the serving tray. "I want to shake things up, get this town back to its center. Sometimes the only way to do that is to go too far in the other direction."

"So then— you agree. It's too far?" Diane winked at Rose as she lifted the cake plate's lid and began slicing hunks of pecan pie.

"That is as terrible an idea as I've ever heard." Curtis Witcham shook his head. "Lucky your food's so good, Rosie, or people may just stop showing up out of principle."

"Damn anyone who's running away instead of looking at what's right in front of them. This town lost some of its best girls, and I know that more than anyone. But their deaths shouldn't kill us too. We've all been too concerned with keeping quiet for too long, letting our silence cloud up, making every conversation murky and half spoke. I'm just so sick of hearing half of everything." Rose rinsed out the coffee urn and set to making a fresh pot.

"Well, I'm sure you'll hear the whole of it now." Diane set the pie plates beside the coffee mugs, heaved the tray onto her shoulder, and headed back to the booths.

Rose kept her back to the counter, busying herself with the tickets Diane had pinned to the board. Pearl watched as Rose opened the lower refrigerator and took out a platter of chicken breasts. She removed the cheesecloth from the two pans on the kitchen top and began to coat the breasts in egg, milk, and flour. She set the breasts gently into the fryer, returned the platter of raw chicken into the fridge, cleaned the kitchen top, and washed her hands. The Shirelles' "Will You Still Love Me Tomorrow?" began to play on the tiny radio as Rose poured batter into the waffle iron. Pearl could hear Rose singing along, following Shirley Owens' slow and graceful gait, as the chorus and strings filled the pauses between longing and loss. Pearl's Frankenstein milkshake remained untouched on the counter, the zigzag mouth melting into an expression that looked more worried than fearsome.

✝

When Pearl first met Rose, it was in the diner's parking lot, right after her mom's interview. Both Pearl and Benny waited for Diane in the Oldsmobile, playing Eye Spy in the August heat, stirring the thick air with takeout bags Pearl had folded into fans. Boxes and suitcases were piled high in the backseat, stacked into every free space, and Pearl was startled when she heard Rose's voice, leaning into the open window, asking them to come in for dinner. She hadn't noticed Rose approaching, hadn't heard her footsteps. But her face looked so familiar. Pearl was happy to see it. That night, while Diane waited tables in her good dress and heels, Rose stayed at the counter with Pearl and Benny, telling them stories about growing up in New Orleans, while she pan-fried the trout she had caught and cleaned earlier that morning.

"Order up!" Rose yelled as she rang the bell, drawing Pearl from her reverie. Two plates of chicken and waffles were stacked on the counter next to a warm jar of maple syrup.

"You mad at me too?" Rose nodded to Pearl's untouched milkshake, sunken into a melted mess on the counter.

Pearl shook her head and pushed away the glass. "No, Miss Rose, I just don't have much of a sweet tooth today."

"I'll eat it!" Benny said.

"You have a blueprint to make," Rose answered. "Pull out your colors and get started on that skeleton vampire."

"Yes, ma'am." Benny smiled and hopped off the stool. "You coming, Pearl?"

"She'll be round soon to start on her own work."

Benny pulled his backpack from the hook and headed to a booth surrounded by headstones. Diane ruffled his hair as he walked by her, making it stand up even further.

"That poor kid has a cowlick like a tree ring." Diane laughed. "Come on now, Rosie, don't be mad at me. I was just giving you a hard time— Hey — I think it looks great." Diane placed the platters of chicken and waffles on her tray, along with the syrup. She bent down to rifle through the condiment shelf, the sound of glass sliding across slick aluminum filling the space of the counter.

"Don't mess up my kitchen."

"Where's the honey bear?"

"Who wants honey?"

"Your painter."

Rose sighed. She went to the breakfast pantry and pulled out the honey pot. "There's honey in the waffles and the breading. This is my cooking honey."

"Man likes his honey."

"I bet he does."

Diane smirked, hoisted the full tray back onto her shoulder, and returned to the row of booths at the back of the diner.

"What do you think of all this, Pearl? Is it too much?" Rose dumped Pearl's milkshake in the wastebasket, along with the soggy placemat, and wiped the counter down.

Pearl spun around on the stool, taking the entirety of The Gaslight into her view from the central position of the counter. "It's not bad at all, Miss Rose. I like all the scary windows, especially the one with the dancing skeletons. But that gold one in the back doesn't really go with the rest."

"I figured you'd noticed that."

"They look like those women on the news—sad though, not scary like the other pictures."

Rose folded the worn dishtowel.

"What women?" Curtis Witcham leaned toward Pearl, so close she could smell the Old Spice on his collar and the days' worth of coffee on his tongue.

"God rest their souls. They came to me in a dream the night before last, clear as day. Then the painter showed up the next morning, looking to make some money, so I drew up that picture." Rose said, nodding to the window. "Came out beautiful, huh? Looks like stained glass— and I put it right where I could see it from here."

Pearl nodded. Curtis Witcham spun around in his stool, searching each window for the women.

"When I got here this morning, the rest of the windows were all finished up. I didn't have a hand in those, but I like them alright."

"Well, I'll be damned." Curtis Witcham slapped his knee and stood up suddenly. "I ran those women out of my church, and you brought them here. You'll be lucky if someone doesn't drive through and smash that window, smash all these damned windows." Arms spread wide, Curtis Witcham assumed the posture of Christ the Redeemer, but forgave nothing.

Rose looked like she'd been slapped. She curtly picked

up Curtis Witcham's mug and set it in the dish bucket. "You know better than to talk like that in front of kids."

"That's all right—I've heard worse, even just today," Pearl said, her eyes focused on the ragged edges of her fingernails.

"No excuse. Fullmouth is bad enough without hearing it from the good folks too."

"Someone needs to talk some sense into you before something bad happens—that's all I'm saying." Curtis Witcham dropped his hands to his sides but kept his eyes on the painted women.

"And I bet it'll be your old rust bucket I'll see smashed clear into the kitchen." Rose plucked Witcham's hat off of the counter— the worn rim of beaver skin facing up— and handed it to him.

"I'm your friend, Rosie, been your friend for a good while," he said, pulling his eyes away from the golden glass and setting them on Rose's heart-shaped face. When Rose said nothing, Curtis Witcham nodded and put on his hat as the doorbells telegraphed his retreat.

Pearl and Rose sat in silence, "Unchained Melody" on the radio, echoing the full weight of the conversation's end, the dead mothers buried in the cemetery, and the unrelenting battle over the relevance of their memory.

As Curtis Witcham revved the Ford's engine in The Gaslight's parking lot, Diane's laugh trilled loudly from within the diner. The brilliance of her laugh rang out against the angry engine, against the gravitational pull of The Righteous Brothers on the radio. Her laugh was in a higher octave than usual and warbled like a small mountain bird's song. When Pearl turned around to look at her mother, she was sitting in the booth with the painter, a fork full of honeyed waffles in her hand. As Pearl watched, the painter leaned into Diane. He opened his mouth slowly, an easy smirk finding its way to the edges of his lips. Then— to Pearl's surprise—the painter reached up and turned the hot bulb in the spot lamp over his head and sunk the booth into a velvet cloak of darkness.

Kristen Clanton

CHAPTER THREE

Dark Passages

Each year, Frank Turner's transit business was buoyed by the fall and winter crowds of hunters and fur trappers, kicked out of the bars at closing time. In the early morning hours, when the town shut off its streetlamps, sinking the Swallows into the thick darkness of the mountain forests, the Dial-a-Ride bus was a fluorescent bulb, highlighting the fallout of life in an impending ghost town. Investigations into the Dial-a-Ride's activities showed up on the nightly news often enough, running the range of bus brawls, stabbings, shootings, and sex trafficking. Before the bus windows became empty-paned, open-air cavities, Frank taped cardboard whiskey boxes against the shot and shattered glass. Back then, he steered his one-bus parade through town, flaunting the assembled evidence, full proof the fun did not have to end at two a.m.

Along with the local news station, the church and school warned the townspeople against patronizing Frank Turner's bus, and not just during the busy months. Albeit most of the Dial-a-Ride patrons were terrifying, Frank Turner was worse. The exploits of Frank's manhood were storied as *Great American Tales of the West*, but only if Frank or his son John-Boy were telling the tales: bar fights over mining rights, heaps of gold reaped from the surrounding mountains, and all of it lost to crooked gambling debts and bullshit court costs.

Squat and greasy, Frank Turner was never the archetypal image of the American cowboy, but he was made worse when he opened his mouth. The few rotting teeth that remained were surrounded by the black caverns of his relentless vitriol. "Weak men are killed— weak men are always killed! —but I'll be damned if their weak women don't just nuzzle up to the closest cock, when it's all said and done" was Frank Turner's famous last line, told and retold at every story's conclusion, while licking his lips and slapping backs. The relentlessness of his hateful soliloquies invariably led to the instigation of physical brutality. In his youth, Frank's known violence— those thirty-seven incidents filed away in police records— was limited to the faults of other men and blamed on public intoxication. However, as Frank Turner grew older and life came on as hard as it always had, women became the sole fixation of his savagery. Before leaving the bars, Frank delicately laid a few bills on the counter, said, "Round here, hunting women is like shooting fish in a barrel, and I'm off to load my gun," and never pretended otherwise.

For these reasons, before the church and school's steadfast emphasis on suicide prevention and bereavement took up most of their time, both entities focused on outreach initiatives to shut down Frank Turner's Dial-a-Ride Bus, or at least to severely hinder its continued success. No matter their efforts, the town council would not agree to implement many changes. Fullmouth could not support the cost of public transit, and they believed Frank Turner was filling a need. He took the drunks off the streets and kept them together to do to each other what they would inevitably do to others if given the chance. Aside from posting "Rider Beware" bulletins and telling the children to stay together and never answer back to aggressive inquiries, the overall idea was to ride Frank

Turner's bus, but ride it with extreme caution.

†

By the time the sun fell fully behind the spire of Bear Mountain, the whole of Fullmouth—both townspeople and seasonal tourists— knew about the window paintings Rose had commissioned for The Gaslight, and everyone turned up at the diner to gawk and give opinions. Even the news station was there, the camera's tripod sinking into the gravel drive, positioned directly in front of the gold window of the dead mothers.

"The Gaslight Diner, a longstanding symbol of comfort and care in the Black Mountain region, has undergone some startling changes this evening, the effect of which has only further divided a town that is already struggling to stay on its feet," Theresa O'Malley reported, her thin lips molded into a frown, for KOTA TV News.

"I've never seen anything so distasteful." The camera panned out to an old woman, her permed hair blue beneath the news camera light. "We should just let those poor women rest in peace, not turn them into Halloween decorations! It's in poor taste, let me say—Rose should be ashamed. Those poor women never had a chance, and they gave up—that's what they did— and now we're trying to make life even harder for their children. I just can't believe it." The woman turned away from the reporter, but Theresa O'Malley's hand followed her with the stick microphone. "Take me home, Buck. I just can't stand the sight anymore." The blue-haired woman reached for a tall boy's arm, her shiny black purse slapping the air between them.

"No, it's awesome!" Buck said, leaning over the old woman. "Half the year the Swallows is a party town, and

37

The Gaslight's just making sure we all remember that. It's party time! Stop whining and have a beer!" Buck gave one final laugh and whooped into the microphone—fist bumping the air— before giving his grandmother his arm and escorting her back to the car.

The diner was in as much dispute as the parking lot, maybe more, as those who made it inside were only there to prattle and drone, a coop of cawing chickens, scratching at the linoleum. Rose mostly kept her back to the counter, the barrage of questions and observations muted between the cutting board and fryer. "Werewolves of London" played on the small radio, and Rose turned the volume up high, the static emphasizing the ghoulish howls that perfectly mirrored the tone Rose wanted the window paintings to exude. The booths and counters were full, and the standing room stretched the limits of capacity. Diane could hardly move around the crowds, most of which were tight-lipped and cross-armed, though a few laughed and danced along to Rose's radio.

Diane carried her serving tray high above her head, her arms and chin arrows made of stone, her gaze wholly focused on balancing the uneven weight. During her journeys between the kitchen and the booths, some of the locals grabbed her arms and asked questions, but she quickly shrugged them off. Then the yelling started, building momentum, coming on quickly, and the front door seemed to lose its hinges, the bells chiming themselves into muteness. Pastor Hall made his way to one of the booths, waving a copy of the New Testament, the bright stone of his Ecclesiastical ring visible over surrounding shoulders. Other hands joined the high air Pastor Hall's Bible occupied, more with every "Amen!", louder and louder. Some stomped their feet. Others clapped and wolf-whistled.

A tall man with black eyes yelled, "I have exorcised the demons!" as he fell back into Diane, the four Cokes on her tray falling to the floor.

"Enough!" Diane shoved the man off her, and using the serving tray as a shield, she pushed through the crowd in search of Pearl and Benny.

She finally found them hunkered together by the bathrooms. Benny was sitting in a Penny Saver rack, and Pearl was standing in front of him, leaning on the upper frame. Diane pulled the straps of her children's bookbags over her shoulders and picked up Benny. Putting her hand on Pearl's back, she hurriedly guided them from the dining room and into the back of the house.

"You can't wait around here anymore. It's too late and too senseless— no telling when it'll calm down," Diane said as she peeked out the swinging door, scowling at the crowd.

"I know, but—"

"I'll be right back."

She left Pearl and Benny sitting on buckets next to the dishwasher. Pearl knew her mom was calling Frank Turner, and considering the immediate circumstances, it was probably the best that could be done. In the eight o'clock after-dinner lull, Diane usually had a salad at the counter and a cigarette by the dumpster, Rose swept and mopped the kitchen and bathrooms before heading home for the night, and Pearl packed up her and Benny's backpacks. Wrapped in their coats and hats, Pearl and Benny waited in the foyer for Rose to take them home. If Rose had extra side work or an old friend at the counter, Diane took fifteen minutes out of her shift to drive the kids back to the boarding house, and if The Gaslight was crippled by a startlingly busy dinner service, usually a regular could drop Pearl and Benny on the way. Only once before, during a Saturday shift on the night of Fullmouth's Opening Day Festival, did Diane underestimate the industry of the evening, and all opportunities for Pearl and Benny's safe passage home fell through. That was the first and only time Pearl and Benny had to ride Frank Turner's bus, and once they climbed down its wide steps and were safely behind their locked front door, Pearl swore they'd never ride it again. But listening to the crowd in the restaurant— the voices sounding more numerous than they possibly could have been— Pearl knew there was no real choice. Walking the night streets back to the boarding house was even riskier than taking Frank Turner's bus. Through the kitchen door, Pearl listened to the persistent sound of The Gaslight becoming the latest drama of the ever-growing spectacle that haunted the Swallows.

"I hope we get home in time for Batman," Benny said through a yawn. "The Penguin is gonna brainwash Alfred tonight."

"Haven't you seen that one a million times?"

"It's my favorite."

The kitchen door flew open, a wave of sound with it.

"Animals." Diane slouched against the tile wall and pulled at the top of her dress, trying to get air to her face. Her cheeks were almost the same color as her lips, and her curls had fallen, their dampness sticking to her neck.

"Climb the counter and spray them with the seltzer," Pearl said.

Diane laughed. "Bet Rose's already considered it."

"Send up the bat signal," Benny added.

Diane grabbed Benny's hat from the floor and helped him into his jacket. "How come you always smell like apples?"

"I wish you could come with us," Benny said.

Diane smiled. "The bus is out front. Call me right when you get home— if Rose doesn't answer, keep calling. If that phone doesn't ring, I'm calling the Sheriff."

"Mom—" Pearl hesitated.

"I'll walk you out, don't worry." Diane patted the pockets of her apron, feeling for her cigarettes and lighter. "If that bus looks better than it does in here, you take it. If not, I'll call Henshaw and see if he'll get you—but after the car battery today, I doubt he'll be up for any more favors."

"He's probably asleep anyway." Pearl put on her coat and zipped it up, tucked her ponytail into the collar, and pulled the hood over her head.

Diane pushed open the back door with her hip and propped it with a cinderblock. The side yard of The Gaslight was empty, save the few fireflies circling the dumpster and the shrieking cicadas—hundreds singing solos out of tune—occupying the immediate darkness. Diane lit her cigarette then reached for Benny's hand as they rounded the front of the building. The cameraman was packing up the news equipment into the KOTA TV News van as Theresa O'Malley shook hands and said her goodbyes. Most everyone was inside the diner, the mass of shadows obscured by the window paintings, but there were still some stragglers pacing the building. Some spent time with each window frame, studying the surface as if they were silently wandering an ancient art museum, surrounded by the romantic images of crumbling beauty and misspent youth. Others, mostly kids who rode their

41

bikes to the diner— flinging the handlebars to the gravel before running to the windows— were making scary faces and imitating the monstrous scenes.

"Double, double, toil and trouble," a girl with a thick braid croaked, her shoulders rounded and back bent, as she pretended to stir the cauldron.

"You know those kids?" Diane pointed with her cigarette. "Maybe you could walk home with them. It won't be bad if there's a bunch of you."

Pearl looked over briefly, but she couldn't make out any of their faces. "Not really."

"I'm too tired to walk," Benny whined.

"That's alright."

Frank Turner's crocodile-green and rust bus was parked on the curb. When Pearl saw it, she felt the million goosebumps again, pressing against her jacket and jeans, blinking hysterically as if to emerge from her skin and become full-fledged goblins, circling their queen. Though Pearl could tell exactly what she was getting into— the bombed-out, windowless bus kept no visual secrets, even from a distance— she knew what she could not see was forever more frightening than anything a stranger could hope to paint on Rose's windows.

"See, it's not bad right now," Diane said.

The Dial-a-Ride's front and back doors were kicked open, circling the air with smoke. Frank was at the wheel, chewing a fat cigar. A mangy beard linked the curly grey hair on his ears and chest, all of it falling in waxy clumps. The remainder was covered with a tee shirt, though coarse curlicues made their way through the shirt's worn fibers. He was wearing square-framed glasses, the lenses wide and thick, distorting the direction his eyes moved.

Along with Frank, there was one passenger on the bus, and her presence gave Pearl some hope. She was sitting in one of the last rows, surrounded by grocery bags. Her profile was set against Frank's wide rearview mirror, and with her long brown hair swept to the side, she constructed a further wall between herself and Frank Turner's gaze.

"I love you, and don't forget to call." Diane hugged Pearl with her free arm, then took the last drag of her cigarette before tossing it into the street.

Pearl helped Benny up the tall bus stairs, then she followed him down the aisle, their sneakers sticking to the grimy floor. Benny's Scooby-Doo backpack swatted the rails as he regarded each seat. He finally sat down in one of the last rows of the bus, on the bench almost opposite the woman. Benny waved at her, his hand a small claw of bent fingers. The woman grinned. Pearl stacked the bookbags on the bench and sat on the side of Benny closest to Frank, so Frank could not see Benny, and hopefully, with all the wind, Benny would not hear Frank. Over the rustling of the plastic grocery bags catching the breeze, Pearl heard her mother yell, "And don't you fuck with them, Frank."

Diane looked smaller from the height of the bus. Her head larger than her body. Hands on her hips, she grimaced at Frank Turner, who immediately flicked his well-lit and well-puffed cigar in her direction. With great accuracy, the angry mouth of the embers caught Diane's starched apron and the receipt book in her front pocket. As Frank closed the bus doors and pulled away from The Gaslight, the well-made mask of Diane's face shifted. She slapped the embers in a panic until all that remained was a blackened hole surrounded by ash.

†

While the bus pulled onto Carson Street, Pearl watched Diane through the eye of the emergency door. She looked like Alice *Through the Looking Glass*: the white bow at her back, the blue plaid dress. Her mother grew younger the smaller she became— her edges more rounded and slumped to the earth— until eventually she disappeared from Pearl's sight. The wind catapulted through the bus, causing the woman's grocery bags to slap and tremble. Their frantic music mirrored Pearl's energy, the black feeling that her mother was swallowed into a bottomless pit, and she'd never find her way back to the Swallows, back to Pearl and Benny, who were hurling into their own darkness on the Dial-a-Ride bus. Pearl blinked slowly, then opened her eyes, still looking for the speck of her mother: a wide wave goodbye, a toothy grin. But it was nothing. Through the missing windowpanes, Pearl watched the houses speed by, none of them familiar, the windows blacked out behind drawn curtains. All of them leering at Frank's rusty crocodile lurking the shadowed street.

"I wouldn't say anything. Frank's just looking for a reason," the woman whispered from across the aisle. Her eyes were gold, set off like stars in the pale and pock-marked moon of her face.

"He's a weasel, and weasels aren't scary," Benny noted.

Pearl turned her gaze to the front of the bus. The direction of Frank's stare was distorted through his thick glasses, but Pearl could see his neck stretched upwards toward the rearview mirror, the rings of dirt caught in the lines of thick flesh and fur.

"Until they bite your face off and claw out your brains," Pearl replied.

"Then you bop 'em on the head." Benny beat his fists like he was playing the whack-a-mole game at the arcade.

The woman smiled. Her teeth were small and crooked. "I'd like that just fine."

"I'd like a little more than that." Pearl drew her finger across her throat.

"And I bet there's a whole slew of women in town who'd help you out." The woman laughed, low and wispy, her voice barely audible over the rumbling bags.

Frank cleared his throat, his filthy neck still stretched to the mirror, leering at his passengers. "You got something to say, little Pearl, say it now. John-Boy and Derry looking for you— promised a handle of Old Crow if I brought you round." Frank beat his hand on the steering wheel. His laugh turned into a heavy cough that was only relieved by spitting phlegm into the bus stairwell.

"Where do you live?" The woman whispered.

"Main and Mystic," Pearl answered.

The woman nodded and rummaged through her bags. Her fingers were long and decorated with cheap silver rings. One was a unicorn. Its horn kept getting caught on the grocery bag handles. Eventually, she found what she was looking for and pulled a six-pack of Natural Ice into her lap. She plucked a few cans off the rings, returning them to the bag. She moved the shield of hair from her face, revealing large hoop earrings, and leaned toward the front of the bus. "We're all getting off together, Frank. They're helpin' out with the groceries." She shook the half-pack at the rearview mirror and set them on the seat. "You can take these."

"Like hell," Frank rasped.

"It's still early, you could use them."

"I got a lot more use for a lot of other things on this bus."

"Nothing that'll come as easy."

"You'd be surprised what I can pull from a Pearl." Frank hacked and spit again.

The woman shook her head and rummaged through her bag, pulling out the remaining cans of beer and sitting them on the seat with the others.

"You don't need to do that," Pearl said.

"Just keep quiet. It's real trouble when Frank's son is on you too—I'm sure you heard what happened to Ruby Teller."

Pearl's shoulders tensed and she tucked her hands beneath her legs. "No one's on me."

"What're you bitching about?" Frank yelled from the front of the bus.

"You should do ghost tours for Halloween!" Benny leaned over Pearl and yelled back.

"John-Boy's bad as Frank," the woman whispered to Pearl.

"You little runt." Frank shook his head. "All the bodies I buried are still in the ground, and ain't no man I put there brave enough to come back to haunt the Swallows."

"He's nothing," Pearl said to the woman.

"I've seen them! Them ghosts are wandering round, looking to eat you." Benny laughed and sat back in his seat.

"Whew, whee! The Swallows'll eat you up before any ghost gets me," Frank hollered back.

"You just don't know how bad it can be. I got a little girl at home, and I'd hope if your momma was sitting right here with her, she'd do the same." The woman leaned forward again, setting her voice above the rumbling groceries.

"You're gonna go to the bar next and buy some beer anyway, might as well take the whole pack now and save your dollars for when the night really comes on."

Frank grunted at the mirror.

The woman did not smile at Frank, but she stayed looking in his direction, her gold eyes level and unrelenting. "We're wanting Main and Mystic."

Frank pulled another cigar from the dashboard, bit off the end, and spit it at the stairwell. "Ten bucks then, twenty between you."

"That'll be fine."

Frank sucked his teeth and pointed the cigar at the mirror. "Don't get too bold, now, I wasn't asking. There ain't no changing what John-Boy got his eye on, and there's no reason for me to go outta my way for what's to be no matter what."

The woman shook her head at Pearl and frowned, then pulled the shield of her hair over her face and closed her golden eyes. She stayed that way until the bus jerked to a stop and the doors finally opened.

CHAPTER FOUR

Crystal Visions

The porch lamp was not on, but the blue glow of the living room television created enough light so Pearl did not have to worry about Diane, out there in the dark hours, trying to navigate a yard full of broken flowerpots and collected car parts. Pearl would not see her mom before breakfast, but Henshaw would wait up, asleep in his recliner until the last turn of the key. Soon he would put his work boots by the front door, lock the deadbolt and chain, and nod *goodnight* to the picture of his wife in the hallway as he carried his Bible to bed.

In her own bedroom, Pearl watched the moon through the movement of the sheer curtains, their plum shadow a bruise that churned on the moon's bright face each time the heater kicked on. In her small bed, under the quilt she'd dragged around the Dakotas since birth, she felt the soft flannel against her elbows and knees, the closeness of the heat. Despite the familiar space— her yellow desk, small and chipped, stacked with horror stories and comics, the yellow stars taped to the walls— her view of the moon was all wrong. She could swear she was seeing it from a high castle window. Too big and too close, the curtains were clouds blacking out the light between earth and sky. It was a moon from the old movies, signaling some haunted thing on its way: the carriage and horses black, the lanterns recklessly swinging light against the stone mountains, all of it creaking along to the driver's cracking whip. Through her bedroom door, Pearl heard the final bells of the late news

49

chime. It was the melody of a day's programming ended, the final call before the screen became a strange rainbow, marking the dead hours. She imagined Earl Henshaw asleep in the front room, wrapped in his dead wife's prayer shawl, his bookmarked Bible on the TV table. He was probably dreaming of the days before the cancer came, when he could still hold his wife's hand and talk about dinner and the weather, his soft snores blanking out the news chimes and all the empty days God made between him and her.

Pearl knew she was asleep then, following the television rainbow into a dream world. The rainbow stretched against the biggest sky she had ever seen, its blues a sea of white stars, vibrating all their light back to the technicolor flower field Pearl was walking through. The tall spines, full of petals, reached out just enough for her to feel their soft velvet against her fingers, before they pulled away, returning their faces to the rainbow and stars. Through the field of flowers, Pearl followed a girl in a white gown. Her steps were precise, navigating the small spaces between the brambles, only the edges of her dress brushing the leaves. The girl looked small against the rainbow, small against the blue mountain of sky. The curls of her blonde hair knotted into the bow at her waist, keeping her head perfectly straight. Pearl thought the girl beautiful without seeing her face. She thought the world warm and soft despite the sunless sky and open landscape. There was nowhere for anyone to hide. No dark edges the rainbow couldn't reach.

But all at once, the air changed, taking the light with it. A stage play reclaiming its creation, the curtain guillotined Pearl from her dream. She was returned to the blackness of her bedroom, the pale glow of plastic stars, and a moon in its place behind the plum-colored veil. Every goose bump opened its eye along Pearl's skin, the armor of scales larger and more withstanding from the shock of being awake. And though the window was locked, a great squall carried through the room, bringing the walls closer together, scraping the desk legs against the bare floor.

Pearl heard the women whispering before she could make out their shapes. Hazy and grey, they were more familiar from Rose's window painting and less like the blurry photographs in the newspapers. Though their gowns were black, not white, and the crowns on their heads were made of roses, not daisies, the women were in the same postures they assumed in Rose's dream. But this was different. It was like a diorama of *The Last Supper*— infused with all the narrative but more movement than even da Vinci's brush could expect. The curtains billowed behind Molly Boutell's head, changing the shadows on her lips as they whispered, the low and constant song breaking against Kaia Goodwin's ear. Kaia's back was straight, a figure of strength and comfort between the wilted shoulders of Molly Boutell and Maggie Teller. As Maggie cried— her chest shuddering through each nerve ending— Kaia held her hand firmly, squeezing it through the physical shocks. Unlike Rose's image of the peace and security that comes from being entombed in loving memory, these women looked like fragile survivors. Their faces were pale and tight; the grief and love between them palpable.

As Pearl realized there were only three women in front of her window and Cindy Stewart was missing, she heard an egg crack and a bird's low cackle ring. She turned to see a large crow perched on her desk, pecking at the yolk through its narrow beak. Its oily feathers bristled under the weight of Cindy's long fingers as she stroked the black wings repeatedly. She held her head high, her green eyes watching Pearl through the safety of strong cheekbones and chin.

"It isn't at all as it seems." Cindy sighed and turned to the three women, dropping her chin and eyes in a posture of prayer. "And it isn't stopping." Her eyes slowly moved across the room and cut across Pearl, shivering in her flannel blanket. Cindy pointed at the door. Her finger stiff and wrist knocking the air with repeated strikes, Cindy Stewart was the cinematic image of how she appeared in Rose's painting. "She's here too."

Pearl heard crying in the corner before she turned to look. The blue light from the living room was a beam beneath the door, highlighting the woman curled beside it, her long brown hair swept across her face, protecting the pale skin and gold eyes Pearl knew were there. The woman wasn't yet in the black gown or rose crown. She was still wearing the unicorn ring. The loose Army jacket and jeans Pearl had last seen her wearing as she left the bus. Just a handful of hours ago, the woman's arms were weighed down with bologna and Velveeta cheese, animal crackers, and all the rest of her daughter's favorite treats. Pearl asked if she could help her home with the groceries, but the woman said it was too cold. She told Pearl to go on home. Thereafter, Pearl watched her wait. She watched her wait for Frank Turner to pull the bus away from the curb, watched until he rounded the corner, then she turned her back to Pearl and Benny and headed toward Carson Street.

Pearl never met the other mothers. She did not know Cindy Stewart or Molly Boutell. She did not know Kaia

Goodwin or Maggie Teller, at least not beyond the news stories and the sad-eyed children they left behind at Custer Day School. And though she did not know the name of the woman on the bus, Pearl knew she was not the kind who would leave the world willfully. As silence returned to the bedroom and the black curtain fell between Pearl and all she had seen, she slumped further into the cave of her blanket, pulled it over her head, and cried herself to sleep.

✝

"Mama?" Deirdre Kelly asked as she slowly climbed into the bath.

Her mom sighed as she turned the spigot on extra hot, attempting to cut the chill of the heavy winds that funneled between the spires of Iron Mountain and into Fullmouth, siphoning into the apartment house and between the cracks of the Kelly's third-floor windows. There was still so much work to do. "Yeah?"

Deirdre could hear the gusts over the rush of running bathwater, so she spoke louder. "I don't really like going to Ms. Wanda's after school."

"You don't?" Deirdre's mom hunched slightly, her shoulders rounded by the day's weight, as she added two capfuls of Mr. Bubble.

"No."

She sighed again and reached into the basket by the toilet basin, retrieving Deirdre's favorite toy pony. "Why not?"

"She's just weird."

"Weird, how?" she asked, wiping her wet hands on her jeans and turning to the sink.

"Well, she always wants to talk about weird things."

"Uh-huh."

"She always asks me—" Deirdre pulled at the pony's blonde mane, twisting it between her fingers.

"Asks you what?"

Deirdre splashed the pony through the faucet's waterfall, showering the tile wall and bathmat.

"Go on," Deirdre's mom encouraged, watching her daughter through the vanity mirror.

"Well, she always asks me if I'm having my period yet."

"What? You're eight years old," her mother said, surprised.

"Mama, what's a period?"

"It's something that happens to a woman." She ran her fingers beneath her eyes to remove the smudges of black eyeliner and sighed. "And it only happens when you become a woman. You're still a kid."

"Is there blood?"

She frowned at the mirror as she tied up her long hair. "Yes."

"Ms. Wanda says she can smell the blood. She says she doesn't like it."

"Don't listen to Wanda. She doesn't know what she's talking about."

"I don't want any blood, mama," Deirdre said as her mother took off her rings, setting each silver band in the soap dish on the sink.

"We don't need to worry about that tonight, kiddo."

"She does other weird things, too."

"Yeah, like what?"

"Well, she makes these little dolls."

"That doesn't sound too weird."

"They're little girl dolls."

"That's alright."

"No, mama. They're creepy. Their eyes look like dark pits. They scare me."

"I can't believe you'd be scared of a doll."

"It's not just the doll, though."

"Well, what is it?"

"It creeps me the way she acts with them— like they're human. She talks to them and baby's them, like she wants them to be real."

"That is a little creepy, huh?"

"Ms. Wanda scares me sometimes."

"She's just weird, baby. Some women get weird when they pass the point of having babies, but she's alright."

"You know she has a big old jar of fingernails? I saw them in her room."

"What were you doing in her room?"

"Getting Frank out. She's got a lot of weird stuff under her bed."

"You stay out of Wanda's room—you wouldn't like it if she was looting around yours."

Deirdre frowned. "Can we still stay up late?"

"If I get those windows blocked up." After picking up Deirdre and putting the groceries away, Deirdre's mom tore pages from the phonebook and stuffed them between the windowpanes. Despite the weight of the winter curtains, the gale battered them against the walls, their navy skirts turning into wind sails.

"Aww, it'll be alright, like being in a tornado."

"Not what you said in Oklahoma."

"That man told you what we were getting into— but you thought he was cute."

"That old fat head." Deirdre's mom laughed, her small teeth like crooked tombstones. She had chosen the apartment in Fullmouth because of those giant picture windows and their east-facing direction. Every night before bed she referenced her battered copy of *The Farmer's Almanac*, and every morning she and Deirdre curled on the sofa beneath a velvet blanket, coffee and apple juice between them, and witnessed the exact moment the sun rose behind the thin, purple spires of Iron Mountain.

"We can put the TV in the bed—"

Deirdre's mom pressed *Play* on the small boombox that balanced atop the towel rack. Side A of *Heart's Greatest Hits* flooded the bathroom, drowning out the tail of Deirdre's ideas. Pulling up her sleeve, she checked the temperature of the water and frowned. "I'm gonna boil some water to keep the tub warm. Be right back to wash your hair," she said over the warlike guitars at the start of "Barracuda". She smiled at Deirdre then closed the bathroom door.

Deirdre smiled too. She'd been at Ms. Wanda's apartment since school let out, folding laundry while Ms. Wanda chain-smoked. When *Wheel of Fortune* came on, marking the start of suppertime preparations, Ms. Wanda had a Schlitz and Deirdre chewed the mouth of a plastic cup. The Kool-Aid was long gone, and there was nothing else to do but wait through Pat Sajak's endless jokes and stiff grimaces. Deirdre finished folding Wanda's laundry and completed her own homework. She swept Wanda's kitchen and pulled her old Tabby from beneath the bed one too many times. However terrible the hours at Ms. Wanda's were, when her mom finally knocked on the door— in that musical beat she tapped out excitedly— Deirdre knew it was going to be a good night.

✝

Deirdre knew that when her mom returned to the bathroom with the kettle full of bubbling water, she would wash Deirdre's hair slowly. She would make the strawberry suds even bigger than Mr. Bubbles and mold Deirdre's hair into a gilded crown, the peaks and arches gaining more and more height until the crown toppled from Deirdre's head and back into the bathwater.

"The Queen is dead!" Deirdre would decree.

They would sing along to Heart while her mom bathed, and Deirdre sat on the toilet seat in a flannel nightgown, combing her hair. Afterward, they would build a nest on the couch— big bowls of macaroni and cheese and a plate stacked with fried bologna sandwiches between them— and watch *The Princess Bride*. It was the nights Deirdre always anticipated. The nights of feasting that always came before the nights of fasting and its weary march to the next payday, when baths were not too warm, and dinner was canned soup and saltines.

Deirdre sang along to "Crazy on You" as she washed her pony's blonde mane and tail, then combed out the tangles with a pastel Barbie brush. She called her mom's name a few times but could not hear anything over the music, not even the wind. She built a great bubble castle for her pony. The walls were cast in countless blue stones, like Lapis Lazuli and Blue Lace Agate, all her favorite charms in her mother's jewelry box. The halls and doorways of the pony castle were wrapped in garlands of pine boughs and silver bells. She built two foam turrets and molded the peaked roofs into nearly flawless points. When the castle reached its epitome—a real prismatic beauty—it lasted only the chorus of "Magic Man" before the bubbles started to soften and melt into the water. As the crystal vision disappeared, Deirdre called again, repeatedly. She called, "Hurry, mama! You gotta see this!", setting her voice even louder than "Dreamboat Annie" played, but Deirdre could not hear any response beyond Ann Wilson's glazy verse.

And it was pretty much over by then. The castle looked like a peasant's hut. Deirdre dropped her fists through the bubbles, sinking the castle to the farthest parts of the porcelain, and moved on to braiding her pony's tail and mane, slowly, because her hands were shaking. Next, she used her fingernails to scratch the fuzzy mold framing a few of the grey bathroom tiles. She pictured each tile as a bearded face, a grizzled knight back from the war field. With the few remaining bubbles stacked on the sides of the tub, Deirdre painted smiles on the bearded squares. Each happy to be home. Happy to be back at the Queen's table.

She felt like she was going to cry.

"Mama?" she called. "Come on back."

When the boombox automatically clicked off at the end of Side A, the bathwater was cold, and the bubbles were gone. Deirdre listened for the wind, for the pots banging in the kitchen, even for the soft steps of her mother's thick socks on the linoleum floor. She tried to pick up the scent of fried bologna and cheese, but there was nothing. Under the bathroom door was a mute black line, all light and sound void. Deirdre set her pony on the toilet seat and pulled the bathtub plug. The echoes of the swirling water, the drain's large gulps, overwhelmed the little room. Too much like a guttural song, the cacophony pulled all of Plato's shadows back into the cave.

"Mama?" Deirdre shivered as she wrapped herself in a

towel and opened the bathroom door.

She heard the tea kettle calling from the kitchen and haltingly moved toward it. The high whistle sounded like a far-off train, a black engine crashing furiously through the mountain range, its angry bellow gathering all the shadows and all the light as it ripped through the tenement. The wind carried along with the whistle. The heavy shades in the living room were drawn, muting the light of the streetlamps on Carson Street. The living room was cast in a hazy blue, shadowed and dusty. Deirdre could not make out any of the photos on the wall, her mother's knitting basket, the dried roses and candles on the coffee table.

Deirdre saw none of the simple details that formed her home's history. She walked the unfamiliar space haltingly, navigating herself around effects she had never seen. The wild brambles of unacquainted objects reached from the corners and grew larger beneath the strange blue glow casting its shade upon everything. Her blonde hair knotted with the long white towel, forming a bow which kept her head from moving. Bathwater puddled into each cautious step but was wiped clean by the towel tangled up with her feet. Cold and pruned, she moved toward the kitchen sink, where the apartment's one fluorescent bulb was on, the prismed light creating an endless rainbow in all its sterile cruelty.

†

Thursday nights, the Sheriff shot darts and ignored phone calls at Fullmouth's VFW post, death and dismemberment no exception. Cash on the table and old war stories told over again, each man hung heavy on the limbs he could have lost, the remaining shrapnel more arduous the more they talked about it. And they always talked about it. Pain was a major part of their penance, paid weekly for making the boats back home and obtaining their VFW cards. As the nights shuffled on and the men moved through the set rotation of whose turn it was to shoot and whose turn it was to buy, hitches in their arms and legs became strikingly pronounced, rendering each game more comic than the last and impossible to score. Just one among his brothers in a long line of brothers before him, and not in charge of anything beyond his tab, the Sheriff considered Thursday nights holy ones, and since there was no phone in Pastor Hall's sanctuary, he did not believe there should be one in his.

Deputy Franny Stone knew this when she answered Wanda Silva's frantic phone call to the station, so she headed over without the Sheriff, despite her bad feeling. And when she entered the apartment house on Carson Street, she knew her gut was right. Nothing was as it seemed.

Wanda roosted on a kitchen stool at the top of the stairs, waiting. "Heard Deirdre screaming and ran over," Wanda yelled down the stairwell. Her wide face was shiny, a cigarette grimaced between her teeth. "It's too much— and everywhere! Got it all over my feet."

The girl was sitting on the top step, her legs and bare feet tremoring. Her hair knotted in a white towel, her skin the same chalky shade. Though the lower half of her body tremored, her head was completely still. Gold eyes wide and unseeing. She looked like a totem, marking the doorway between realities. Deputy Stone squeezed Deirdre Kelly's shoulder as she climbed past her. For a moment, the gilded star pinned to her chest beat to the rhythm of the girl's quaking knees. "Did you see anyone else in the apartment besides Ms. Kelly?"

"Didn't see Karen. Didn't go no further than the kitchen." In her hand, she rattled a short glass, the ice cubes soft and coppery.

Franny pushed her fingers further into her leather gloves as she spoke. "Did you hear anything before Deirdre screamed?"

Wanda shook her head and looked down the stairs. "Sheriff coming?"

"Stay here. I'll be right back." Franny pulled her pistol and held it low with both hands. The Kelly's apartment door was cracked open, and Franny could feel the air shifting as she approached. She pressed her weight against the hallway walls, tacked in peeling paper, the gaudy flowers too bright and innumerable within the dreary space. She breathed deeply to steady her hands and entered the dark apartment. The sound of her steps went unheard over the squall erupting between the wide front windows, flung open, and the kitchen window— which she could identify from the front door— propped open with a wine bottle over the sink. The long curtains on the front windows swung around the room furiously, blocking out the walls and furniture as they capered into different phantom shapes. Franny flicked the light switch but couldn't make out any lamps that connected to the electricity.

"Miss Kelly?" She called as her eyes adjusted to the blue haze of the room. "If you can hear me, stay where you are and call out."

The apartment was small but strange. The living room was clean: pillows and throws arranged neatly on the sofa, candles in a row on the coffee table. Everything was in its place, barring a pile of objects thrown together into a domiciliary altar at the center of the room. A dining chair on its side, sewing basket, stacks of cushions and books, magazines, family photos and keys, dried roses, a phone book. Deputy Stone advanced cautiously toward the front windows to close the panes. Behind the heavy curtains— claws gripped firmly to the frame— perched a large oily crow, its black eyes narrow and beak snapping. In one stiff jab, Franny forced the crow to the outer sill and slammed the rail. Shaking the bird from her skin, she shuddered. In the new silence, she heard the kettle whistling in the kitchen.

"Karen Kelly, you in here? Call out if you can hear me." Franny yelled again, louder this time, as she walked around the mound of totemic objects and made her way to the back of the apartment.

Much like the living room but in starker contrast, the kitchen was a reality ripped in two, right along the horizon. The dining table was polished and pushed into a corner, a small wreath of dried roses at its center. The cabinet doors and drawers were all closed, the brass knobs gleaming in the light over the kitchen sink. And the tiled countertops were bleached clean, the white grout a bright line of dead ends, all intersecting into a picture frame around the grisly pit at the bottom half of the kitchen. Just as it was in the living room, one of the dining chairs was on its side, pulled toward the oven. Felled and dragged, the chair's track highlighted the flowered linoleum pattern hidden beneath the pulpy marshes of blood.

Franny took one hand from her pistol to turn the stove off and shift the wailing kettle onto a cold burner. She pulled out her flashlight, scanning it over the lower cabinet fronts and floor. Banded into the blubbery strings of egg yolk— raw and sticking to the oven door— there was thick blood spatter. At the foot of the oven sat a whisk and a blue glass bowl. There was a small braided rug, swollen like a summer mosquito, where most of the blood was deposited. She examined the area for a visible weapon but found none. The tracks were primarily footpaths from the kitchen leading to the front door, likely Deirdre and Wanda, but also present were the narrow pitchforks of crow's feet. In the other direction, trailing into the back of the apartment, there were handprints along the floor and behind them a dragging line. *One, two, pull. One, two pull.* These were the tracks Franny followed.

When Franny was about Deirdre Kelly's age, the neighborhood boys dared her to jump from the top of the slide in Rains Park and into a snowbank beneath. It was almost supper time, but the boys called her "chicken" as they clucked and pecked at the ground, their arms folded into puny wings. In all that noise, Franny jumped. It was too late in the season, the snow too soft to hold. All her force plunged straight-legged onto the steel edge of a sandbox digger she couldn't see. The boys ran home when they heard her scream. Franny sat in the snow pile for a while, sure she had broken a leg, and too afraid to move. The quiescence of that snow was a deep cave, much like the Kelly's apartment. And all these years later, with the wind and whistle dead, the lull was anything but reliable. As a kid in the snow cave, when the sun fell and Franny stopped shivering, she knew she had to climb out or else. Through the park and two blocks home, Franny's top half was in stark contrast to her bottom half. Her arms dragged her legs. *One, two, pull. One, two, pull.* A simple song, a chant to make it to a safe space. In the Kelly's kitchen, Franny said a short prayer as she directed the flashlight's glow down the hallway— the arc of light a rainbow over the gruesome trail she had to follow— and pulled the gun's safety latch. Franny knew Karen Kelly had fallen into that survival song as she'd dragged herself to the back of the apartment, and she prayed Karen found a hole to hide in, if only until she heard Franny calling.

CHAPTER FIVE

Roosters and Snakes

In the coop across from Pearl's bedroom window, the rooster hollered just as the sun edged its way mightily from behind the stone cage of Iron Mountain. The rooster's shouting called for Fullmouth to *wake up! The king is here! There are important things to do!* And part of it was walking wholehearted into the golden hour, without fear. To shuffle feet at the river's edge of sleep, to scare the snakes away from night wanderings, so they didn't latch on and drag into day. Each morning the rooster stretched his feathers, all of him tense and purposeful against the backdrop of a red barn that only looked beautiful in the first morning light, when that bright king burst over Iron Mountain and laid his hands heavy on the Swallows.

Get up! Sleep won't change the way, the rooster called to Pearl that cold October morning, when she woke in her bed and could not remember the space in which she lived— on Mystic Avenue, in Fullmouth, in the Black Mountains of South Dakota. It all took too much time to come back. But then, in rushed the dead mothers, the crow and the wind that moved the walls of her bedroom just a little closer than they were. Pearl trundled out of her sleepy cave wrapped in her love-worn quilt and walked toward the familiar timber of daybreak: the percolator popping and milk spoons clinking against the kitchen table. The KOTA morning news team returned to Henshaw's television, the night's rainbow of dead air and hardlines pushed behind the curtain, the reporters restored, squawking and pecking at bylines gathered throughout the Dakotas. And Benny's laugh— his familiar trill the second totem behind the rooster— set the edges of the world into place and rooted Pearl to the earth. And so it was as she walked into the kitchen, wholehearted and fearless for all she remembered and all she felt was coming.

"Where's mom?" Benny asked, looking up from his Count Chocula.

"She's not here?" Pearl returned.

"Not on the porch, not in the back yard," Henshaw said as he set his mug on the kitchen table and turned to the stovetop, tending the scrambled eggs in the skillet.

Pearl pulled a coffee cup from the dishrack. "She could've gone to get cigarettes."

Henshaw sucked his teeth for a moment then replied, "Could be—but her car's not here either."

Pearl filled her mug with cream and looked at the clock above the stove. "She'll be back."

"Didn't hear her come in last night."

"She was in," Pearl avowed.

"She should've said she was going. Didn't hear her coming or going." Henshaw took a sip of his coffee, his back against the stove and eyes on the television.

Pearl walked to the front window and pulled the yellow lace aside. The gravel drive was oil spotted and empty. Pearl closed her eyes. She pictured her mother's halo of hair, her red mouth and long limbs. She imagined her mother smiling and waving, her long teeth biting into her lower lip. Pearl labored over her focus; she worked to will her mother into being. Finally, she opened her eyes again, and like so many times before, Pearl pointed to the street.

"There she is."

Diane's gold Oldsmobile idled at the curb. Her face turned to the house, eyes closed to the sun. She tapped the steering wheel to a song Pearl couldn't hear, a cigarette between her fingers.

"She's not been there long." Henshaw sucked his teeth again, turning toward the window when the morning news took a commercial break.

"Momma's back!" Benny fumbled with the locks on the door, cannonballing himself into the frosted yard, his bare feet crunching the frozen leaves.

"Get on back now, it's too cold to run outside in your night clothes," Henshaw called, but Benny was already at the street, knocking on his mother's window.

Diane smiled and turned off the engine. She stepped out of the car wearing the same blue plaid dress Pearl had last seen her in, standing in the street outside The Gaslight, wild-eyed and alone. Pearl watched as Diane grabbed Benny's hand and led him up the walk and into the house.

"Where ya been?" Henshaw asked as he dished eggs into a bowl and began walking his breakfast to the recliner.

"I went for a walk, then sat in the car to listen to some music," replied Diane.

"With no coat?"

Diane sighed. "It's a beautiful morning."

"Where'd you walk?" Henshaw plucked a fork from the drying rack, keeping his eyes on Diane.

"What's with all the questions?"

"Just a lot going on out there this morning. Did you see anything?" Henshaw forked a hunk of scrambled egg, shiny and speckled.

"There's nothing to see but sunrise and mountains."

"Not this morning." Henshaw raised his coffee mug to the morning news.

The box television was framed in photos of Henshaw's Nebraska relations and set between the two front windows so Henshaw could watch the street, the door, and the TV all at once, while his family watched him, watching everything. On the thick glass of the television screen, Theresa O'Malley stood next to a banner of yellow crime scene tape, strung tightly around the small yard of a two-floor brick tenement. Its front porch was dark green and looked soft, like moss growing into the shallows of stone the town was built upon. The second floor—where Theresa O'Malley kept pointing— had two massive oriel windows. Inside one of those windows, spotlighted by the rising sun, KOTA's camera eye projected the movements of multiple officers in their khaki uniforms and wide-brimmed hats, slowly walking the space of the room beyond. The morning sun was in Theresa O'Malley's eyes and she kept squinting. Her purple eyeshadow crinkled into corners, and her lips, painted their usual bright peach, were set into a deep, clownish frown.

Henshaw pointed his fork at the television. "That's right around the corner."

"Turn it up." Diane kicked off her work shoes and headed toward the coffee pot.

"The idyllic and out-of-the-way town of Fullmouth is little known throughout the Dakotas, not even to those who pride themselves on being born and bred in the Black Mountains."

"Hogwash," Henshaw said to the television.

"But that all changed midsummer when a series of

deaths brought Fullmouth statewide attention. Before late last evening, four women, all bright young mothers and friends of this community, were mourned for their untimely passing. And though it weighs heavy on my heart, a journalist's responsibility is to tell the truth, always. Here, on this clear and chilly October morning in Fullmouth, South Dakota— already crippled by so much human tragedy— it is my unfortunate duty to be the first to report that another name has been added to the list of strange deaths in this small town."

Pearl felt like she was suddenly standing at a great height, looking down into the small space of Henshaw's living room, dizzy from the focus of making out the separate shapes—the square windows, the square TV, her mother and Benny. Henshaw in his recliner, hot eggs and coffee mugs steaming. Her loved ones breathing and talking. The long line of Henshaws cobbled together for centuries, lining the walls and tables, all framed in dusty brass. The living mouths open, sipping and chewing. The dead ones, thin-lipped and pert, eyes on all that was coming and going. And here was a new story to add to the old history: the woman on the bus was the woman in the corner of Pearl's dream, curled and crying. She was the woman who died in that apartment building around the corner on Carson Street. Pearl knew it, even before the rest of the Swallows. Before a blurry polaroid, aged at the edges, was backlit on the nightly news. Pearl knew it was everything Cindy Stewart meant last night, when she pointed to the woman in the corner of Pearl's dream.

Pearl leaned her weight against the window, resting her forehead on the cold panes.

"You must've been walking into the sun to not notice

all that ticker tape," Henshaw concluded.

"I can't believe it," Diane exclaimed as she sat on the couch and pulled her legs beneath her, the coffee mug steaming between her long fingers.

"And you didn't see any of it?" Henshaw asked.

"Shush."

"Police are reporting that at approximately 10 PM, a resident from this apartment house on Carson Street called the station to report an incident. Details are not being released at this time, but Sheriff Barlow has confirmed that the deceased is a female in her late twenties, early thirties. With me, I have Ms. Becky Barnhardt, who lives in close proximity to the apartment house where the young woman's body was found."

The camera panned out from Theresa O'Malley to include a large woman in a pink cat sweatshirt and jeans. Her thick glasses magnified the perplexed expression in her eyes and she nervously tugged at the hem of her sweatshirt.

"You ever take her out, Earl?" Diane joked.

Pearl closed her eyes tightly. "She works in the lunchroom."

"You alright, Pearl? Look a little green around the gills," Henshaw said.

"She's nice—cuts big brownie squares," Benny added. "That's her Fun Friday sweater."

Diane snorted.

"Go get you some breakfast, Pearl. There's eggs on the stovetop." Henshaw pointed his fork at the stove.

"Pearl doesn't like eggs," Diane said.

"She likes them alright," Benny replied.

"I don't know—I live over there." Becky Barnhardt

pointed off-screen toward Buffalo Avenue, the camera's eye unfollowing. "And around ten or so, I was reading my Agatha Christie stories, and I heard a scream. I thought I was dreaming, like I'd fallen asleep reading. It happens sometimes. Maybe just imagining. I should've called at that first scream, but it took me a minute to believe it. You know? And then the screams just kept coming. I saw the flashing lights out my window right when I picked up the phone. I feel terrible about it, just sick."

Teresa O'Malley nodded, the shadow of her head bobbing behind her. "Do you have any idea who the deceased is or if she has any children?"

Becky shrugged uncomfortably. "That's not for me to say. I keep to myself and spend most of my time at the school. To hear that scream, though. I never heard anything like it. That'll haunt me forever." Becky's voice cracked, and Theresa O'Malley pulled the large microphone away from her face as the camera panned away from Becky and back to the apartment building's front window.

"There you have it, Chip. We will be closely monitoring the development of these tragic events throughout the day. Theresa O'Malley for KOTA TV News."

The station cut back to Chip Gordon, handsome and sad-eyed, carefully made up and safely ensconced in a news studio nine hours outside of Fullmouth. Gathered on the other side of all that glass, right along with Henshaw's family. Everyone in a separate box. The room rocked beneath Pearl, pitching and bowing through space as she walked to the kitchen. The visitors of last night's dream film layered on top of the morning's breakfast table. Cindy Stewart and her crow, sharing a raw egg between them while Benny slurped cereal milk from the bowl. Her mother sitting on the couch, right in line after Kaia Goodwin and Maggie Teller. Molly Boutell leaning forward, her cupped hand to Diane's ear. Diane smiling, her eyes distant and glassy. Light years, tubes and time travel, wormholes: all the dark and transient places Pearl read about in science-fiction comic books, the pages black and gummy green. The travelers were always safe between worlds. Safe before blinking. Safe before the start of questioning everything.

†

Cindy Stewart leaned against the tiled bathroom wall, smoking a phantom cigarette. Her monstrous crow was perched on the towel rack, its long claws scratching the damp fluff of Benny's Batman towel. Pearl's reflection in the medicine cabinet mirror was smudged by grimy fingerprints and flecked with toothpaste. She could not see the dead mothers in the mirror, but she could hear them behind her, lined up on the edge of the tub. Pearl filled the sink basin with cold water and plunged her face into the icy depths, pretending she was at the bottom of the Arctic Sea, looking through the deep blues of crystalized ice shelves. The polar bears and bearded seals circled the shifting glaciers as Pearl held her breath for as long as she could, searching for the Abominable Snowman. When Pearl finally came up for air, she reached for Benny's towel beneath the inky bird, and immediately felt the soft cotton pressed into her forearm by the force of another hand.

"How are you even here?" Pearl asked.

"I don't know. I didn't even know there was a here— not until last night," Cindy Stewart answered.

"We thought we were dreaming," Molly Boutell sang in

72

a low melody.

"Or in heaven. Only— the children were missing." Kaia Goodwin whispered.

Cindy shook her head. "We told ourselves they were swimming in the lakes."

"Or hiking in the mountains," Molly said.

"Little butterflies," Kaia whispered again.

"Maggie knew something was wrong before that," Cindy said.

"There weren't any stars," Maggie Teller rasped, her voice pit gravel and leaves.

"But Maggie always thinks the worst, so we didn't listen." Molly stuck her long tongue out and made a face at Maggie.

Maggie rocked her shoulder against Molly's. "Until last night."

"When she appeared," Cindy nodded toward the moon-faced woman with long hair.

"Straight out of a horror movie," Molly stated.

"I'm so sorry." Pearl hesitated. "I didn't—"

"She isn't talking yet." Cindy tapped her cigarette against the basin, invisible ash falling and disappearing against the white porcelain.

"Dear heart," Kaia whispered.

"We were terrified." Maggie stretched out each word as she clutched the skirt of her dress in two stiff hands.

"We knew something was terribly wrong when we saw her," Kaia whispered.

"All that blood!" Molly exclaimed.

Cindy sighed. "We knew we weren't in a dream."

"At least not one so lovely." Kaia's thick eyelids made her look sleepy in the blueness of the morning light.

Maggie put her fingers to her lips, pulling at her nails with her teeth. "I've never seen a color like that."

"She was weeping." Cindy pressed the end of her cigarette into the sink.

"Every time she exhaled, the blood would come," Molly said.

"She kept asking for her Dierdre," Kaia whispered.

"We tried to stop it," Cindy said, her long arms wrapped around her slim waist.

Kaia closed her eyes. "That's when we realized our kids weren't at the lake."

"That something terrible had happened." Cindy pushed off the wall and paced the small bathroom, her tall heels silent on the tile.

"I could feel the weight of the Earth on my chest—I was suffocating." Maggie wrapped her freckled hands around her throat.

"Don't be so dramatic," Molly said, leaning against Maggie.

"And we were happy the kids weren't there to see it," Kaia whispered.

"Happy as we could be," Molly uttered.

"I never had the feeling of missing them, not until last night, in your room," Maggie pressed her hands to her skirt, smoothing out the seams.

Cindy stopped pacing and looked at Pearl. "When we saw you."

"Yes. after we saw her with all that blood, we saw you," Molly agreed.

Pearl looked at the moon-faced woman with long hair, her small teeth chattering. "I met her last night, on the bus. She helped me and my little brother."

"We've been pulled into so many dreams," Cindy remarked.

"Most of them lovely," Kaia whispered.

"Until last night," Maggie said.

"And then there's now." Molly adjusted her rose crown, tilting it low to one side, the petals of one dark blossom falling across a green eye.

"I can't remember the last time I saw the sun," Maggie wondered aloud.

"You're the only one who has made us real," Cindy said.

Molly grinned at the mirror. "Real enough."

"Real enough for what?" Pearl asked.

"You pulled us from the dream," Cindy said.

"And we need your help," Kaia whispered.

"We think you need ours too," Molly said.

"What day is today?" Maggie asked.

"October 28th—Friday," Pearl answered.

"Hurry up, Pearl, I have to pee. Please!" Benny banged on the bathroom door and jangled the knob.

Pearl imagined him hopping up and down, his skinny Kermit legs goose-bumped and knock-kneed. When she abandoned the fullness of the living room for the echoed quiet of the bathroom, Pearl bolted the ancient lock and pulled the crystal knob twice to make sure it was caught. She called for a few moments of muffled static before Benny and Diane came tumbling in, all toothbrushes and hair combs. Except the ghost mothers crept through the cracks—taking no notice of the locks and bolts— and Pearl forgot about the whole living world on the other side of the bathroom door. Knock-kneed Benny and beautiful Diane were far away from the chattering of nightmares and daydreams, along with children on the other side of the veil, their mothers wishing them bright and beautiful, sun slicked and swimming in Silver Lake.

"Come on, Pearl, open up." Diane jangled the crystal doorknob like a tambourine.

When Pearl turned around from the mirror, the bathroom was empty.

✝

The leaves were wet with morning dew and stuck to Pearl's sneakers. During their walk to school, Pearl stayed by Benny's side and nodded during his meditations on fireflies, the dark side of the moon, and what happens to the frogs at Silver Lake in the wintertime. Though she listened well enough, most of Pearl turned inward— every eye wearily blinking— and tried to focus on other things. Pearl pictured how the dust caught the autumn sun in Miss Lippincott's classroom, the square slices of pumpkin pie in the lunchroom, afternoon episodes of Ken Burn's PBS documentaries, how all the teenagers were making weekend plans to smoke in the pumpkin patch and get lost in the corn maze at Friendly's Fall Carnival in Buffalo, and how fun it would be to travel in a careless pack of girls, shiny lipped and knock-kneed. Pearl listed all the best parts of an October Friday at school, but the mothers - with their long fingers and gravel voices—kept catching hold of every inward eye, their shadows marking the internal walls of Pearl's consciousness.

"Do you think if I drew a real good picture of the Batmobile, then closed my eyes and whispered *abracadabra* three times, it would show up at the house?"

"What?"

"Do you think it'd be better if I kept my eyes open? Or

if I drew me inside driving it?"

"That's a cool car—maybe too fast for you, though. If you made that happen, we wouldn't have to walk to school."

"Maybe I should draw the Batmobile in front of Henshaw's house, and I should say *abracadabra* three times with my eyes open, while spinning in a circle?"

"Why spin in a circle?"

"To get moving real fast, like the Batmobile."

"I think you need a better catchphrase than *abracadabra* - something the Batman would say."

Benny silently thought about the Batman. Pearl silently thought about the mothers. It was common knowledge that Cindy Stewart, Molly Boutell, Kaia Goodwin, and Maggie Teller grew up together. Everyone knew they struggled to grow up after high school and struggled even worse to be good mothers. They had trouble keeping jobs and paying rent. Some more cynical news reports and sneering town gossips liked to say a suicide pact was in place. But what about the woman on the bus? Pearl had never seen her interviewed on the news, never saw her in the photos they flashed across the screen during the nightly news. And Pearl was near certain that Diane did not know any of the women. Her mother's golden Oldsmobile only pulled into Fullmouth a few days before Cindy Stewart jumped from the Bancroft Building. But still. Pearl thought about the little she knew about her mother.

Where was she this morning?

"What if I said: *Here's the hope of the world!* —three times?" Benny asked.

"I like it," Pearl replied and grimaced on the inside, disparaging her own aimlessness of mind. What she needed was hours and hours of blank space. She needed time to close the door of a silent house, time to lay in bed and watch her plum curtains shift among the shadow on the wall. She needed time to focus on the story of what was happening in Fullmouth and where it was all headed. She needed to figure out why the long line of dead mothers were in her consciousness and in her bedroom. Why they spent the morning in the living room, whispering the secrets of their dark sisterhood to Diane.

At school, Pearl found the only silent place she could hope for. She looked out the window all day, watching the dust shift and sway in the sunshine as it caught the current of unknown drafts and spells. Her eyes set on the ancient oak tree in the yard, its trunk gnarled as the walls of the school. All day long, the wind picked at the tree, taking away its gold leaves. The tree was so wind-bent, its activity so constant, that no bird came along and perched for too long. The birds—two sparrows and a mountain bluebird— settled on the window's dormant air conditioner. The metal body was speckled as an egg with rust and bird droppings and slumped heavily with the years of birds jumping on its back as they talked amongst themselves. Pearl's mind was lulled by the sway of the oak's long limbs, bending to the earth only to forcefully shirk the weight of the wind and return their swaying movement upwards. The brown bodies of the branches scratched and curved, and bark white with age looked like a battle of cottonmouths, each becoming stronger— each exertion more hypnotizing— in their fall and subsequent reach. Pearl thought the birds saw the tree as an enemy, its deep hunger grasping at the window, just far enough out of reach.

CHAPTER SIX

Pale Horse, Black Moon

They were always in the street. No matter what tiny town in the Dakotas her mother steered the golden Oldsmobile—the Trojan horse, replete with haloed queen and two small sentries—Pearl and Benny always ended up in the street, their wares on their backs, the constant movement of legs and pendulum feet an incantation to keep going. Fullmouth was a different town, though. Different than Pearl had ever lived. Layered into the town's grid was the wind's furious travel along the Black Mountain spires. As Pearl and Benny trudged to the edge of town, onward to Ms. Rose's house, the wind was the sound of breath through a snake charmer's wooden flute, low in melody and slow in tempo, pulling the two children into the stasis of late afternoon.

Ms. Rose's home was a honey-colored cabin, built from Spruce trees that sprung from seeds and dug their roots into that parcel of Black Mountain soil. Rose said her Grandma June built the house and kept the trees as best she could while still getting along for herself. The cabin was tucked into the side of Bear Mountain and framed on one side by the White River, which drew closer and closer to the cabin's back door each year. The settled land was a cinematic place, ripe for movies about homesteaders and great Wild West shoot-outs. The home of a medicine woman or midwife, plucking howling babies and wet-furred creatures from the stars and into a world of rushing rivers and wind-creaked trees. It was here Rose caught the trout she served at The Gaslight, surrounded by the land she used to grow herbs, fruits, and vegetables for the lean season. The porch was low and wide as the house, wrapped around four sides, and looked upon both the immediate beauty of its surroundings and the muddy hill at the start of Rayburn Street, where Rose could watch anyone coming from half a mile up the road.

"I had a feeling I'd be getting company today," Rose called from the front porch. She was standing on a short ladder, a can of red paint beside her knee, touching up the ornately patterned trim and beaded rails.

"Oh Miss Rose, your house looks just like a chocolate cake with red frosting. I want to gobble it right up!" Benny called from the street.

Rose's laugh echoed off the mountain face as the two children walked through the front gate. "Just like in Hansel and Gretel," he whispered to Pearl.

Pearl pushed the hair out of Benny's face. "You're a funny little bird," she whispered back.

"Hey, Miss Rose. Sorry to pop in on you like this," Pearl called as she and Benny made their way past the small pumpkin patch and squash garden that framed the front walk of the house.

"Oh, hush— I'm happy to see you two. I've been so distracted today, haven't had the mind to get anything done." Rose took off her work gloves and brushed the dirt from her jeans.

"Pearl says you're the only one she can talk to," Benny said.

Pearl's face was half hidden behind long hair, her prominent cheekbone without its natural glow. The one eye peeking between the thick strands was shadow-rimmed and haunted.

Rose leaned toward Benny, resting her hands on her knees. "And what would you like to do while Pearl and I talk?"

"Can I watch TV? Henshaw is always watching the TV at home, so I usually have to watch his shows." Benny set his hand against the front door as he took off his mud-caked sneakers.

"Sure can, Sugar, but be wary of that antenna. Sometimes moving it makes the picture worse," Rose replied as she removed her own boots and led the children into the cabin. "You can put your things there by the door and come on into the kitchen, and I'll make you a snack."

†

Pearl sat at the long bench of the kitchen table, its raw wood face of knots and veins scrubbed clean and high-polished. The kitchen was a pure reflection of Rose. The cabin walls were hung with brass framed cross-stitch patterns of regional flowers and fading daguerreotypes of Rose's ancestors, their faces smudged and strong behind thick metallic glass. An antique oven captured most of the room's attention, but for the towering oil painting of the Black Mountains that hung on the wall over Pearl's head. This was one of Pearl's favorite paintings.

Along with Van Gogh's *The Church Auvers*, which looked more like a haunted house than a church, with its blue window glow and Gothic turret clock. Whenever Pearl saw Van Gogh's church, her breath caught in her throat and all the goosebumps on her body rose. It was as if her subconscious knew a spirit was waiting in the navy shadows and would soon walk past the cathedral windows.

And if Pearl stared long enough, she'd see the apparition slowly creep by.

However the reproductions of Van Gogh's church made Pearl feel, the painting in Rose's cabin created even more suspense. Its title had long been lost in the thick tomes of Rayburn family history and included no such architectures to place it in space and time. Its only identifier was a date—1933— tagged in a small sample of white paint. Though, the image itself felt more archaic, more infinite and recurring than the simple timestamp it held. Rose's painting storied the rare night of a Black Moon in the Black Mountain region, the spires' long fingers, endless and reaching through grey clouds and on toward a starless sky. The moon was formed by muted shades of black, and only its pale veins refracted some light to the world of thick shadows and stone limbs set forth by the painter's hand. The moon's spidery light was only enough to discern how treacherous the imminent trail, how sinister the stone needles were. Within the moon's weak glow, two travelers could be discerned. In the bottom corner—right above Pearl's messy hair and sleepy eyes—rooted to the road upward and into the spires' dark grasp, under the veil of a Black Moon and shadow clouds, was a lone rider. His white horse was a kind of destiny, forging its own light in the nightscape, as the rider hunched his shoulders and leaned into the darkness.

It was one of Pearl's favorite paintings because it made her think of *Dracula*, yes, but it also made her think of hope. Rose set the kettle on the range. As she peeled apples and sliced cheese, as Benny searched for crackers in the cupboard, Pearl imagined herself as the lone rider on the white horse. She understood the feeling of standing below those spires on a blackout night. Rose hummed softly while she completed her small tasks, adding a cadence to Pearl's thoughts that was full of nostalgia and sweetness.

"Enjoy having some time to yourself, and if you need anything, Pearl and I will be right in here." Rose leaned down to look at Benny squarely and handed him the snack plate.

"Oh, Miss Rose, you make me so happy every time I see you." Benny hugged her quick and tight, then took the plate, his blue socks slipping on the polished wood as he left the kitchen.

"That is one sweet kid. I don't think I've ever known a kid as good natured as that one," Rose said as she set to the task of preparing the table for tea. She stacked the gardening books and almanacs into the bench's corner and smoothed the crocheted tablecloth.

"Sometimes I worry he's too nice. Nothing ever seems to bother him."

"I would've agreed with you before this year, but this has been a hard one. Nowadays, I don't believe there is any way a person could ever be *too* nice. And Benny, he's tough in his own way. He's smart and real observant too, just like you."

Pearl nodded.

"I'm sorry to say it— because I hate when people say it to me— but you don't look too good, Sugar. You feeling okay?" Rose placed two cups and saucers on the table, along with the sugar bowl and milk.

"I'm just tired. I didn't really get to sleep last night. Me and Benny got home late, and things just felt weird. We rode Franks' bus home, so that was bad. And I had some nightmares."

"About the bus?"

"No." Pearl pulled her teacup toward her and traced her finger along its gold-plated edge. "Do you believe in your dreams?"

Rose set a plate of fruit and biscuits on the table. "You mean enough to paint up The Gaslight so everyone thinks I'm a nut?"

"Most of those pictures weren't yours, though."

"Well, they're mine now." Rose looked out the window, the White River rushing past. "How's your mom?"

"I haven't really seen her."

"Did she come home last night?"

"I think so. She wasn't there when I woke up, but she drove up a few minutes later."

Rose sucked her teeth but did not say anything.

Pearl watched her for a spell. Rose's dark hair was loosely bundled on top of her head, and her small gold hoop earrings caught the afternoon light. Rose's wide-set eyes were lined in shades of bronze and looked lovely above her full mouth, painted the color of candied peaches. Pearl thought about how Rose was the kind of person who got up every day and made a face to meet others, even if she did not plan on seeing anyone or going anywhere. She was always ready for a knock at her door.

"She put you on Frank's bus?" Rose inquired.

Pearl sighed, her shoulders hunched forward. "There wasn't much else she could do."

"That painter hung around until closing time. Seems like he and your mom really hit it off."

"I wouldn't know about that, but that's not surprising.

Lately, I've been thinking that I don't know much about my mom at all."

"That's how it is as a kid, but you're getting older. Soon you'll start asking her the right questions," Rose replied as she dried her hands on a dishtowel.

Pearl nodded, her fingers still tracing the rim of the teacup.

"But that's not what you came to talk about."

"No, not this time," Pearl mumbled at her teacup.

The kettle whistled, filling the room with the sound of a steam engine screaming into a hollow gorge.

"Sheesh," Pearl breathed.

Rose turned back to the range, unhurried. She raised her voice over the kettle's call. "This was my grandma June's kettle. That cast iron makes the whistle too loud to bear, but I swear it makes magic tea. Nothing ever tastes so good as Grandma June's tea." Rose tucked tea leaves into the pot, then swaddled a dishtowel around the kettle's belly, careful to set it on the table before taking her seat. "Did you come all this way to talk about dreams?"

Pearl crossed her arms. "You make it sound crazy."

"No, no. Not at all, Sugar. I'm just trying to get to the heart of things."

Pearl looked out the window, the river rapids audible through the cabin's thick Spruce walls. The repetitive exploration of the turtle-back shapes of the river rocks, over and over, rushing past in the same motion, gathering white caps and foam before moving on down the mountain, was hypnotizing to Pearl. Her shoulders relaxed as she leaned into Rose and the beautiful table she set.

Rose placed a biscuit on Pearl's plate then filled each cup carefully. The tea smelled of cinnamon and cloves, licorice.

Pearl wrapped her fingers around the cup and cradled it to her chin, breathing in Grandma June's magic tea. "Do you think dreams can just seem like dreams, but they're not really dreams at all?"

"Like the dreams are actually happening?"

Pearl nodded.

"Yeah," Rose said slowly, "sometimes that happens."

"Has it ever happened to you?"

"The Swallows are a strange place, Pearl—it's near impossible not to feel that strangeness scratching at you. The whole Black Mountain region is ancient holy land that was violently pillaged during the 1874 gold rush. Most of us are still out here because this is where our ancestors are buried, but there are a lot more people whose bloodlines have been here a lot longer than those we come from, and those are the ones who are angry. You bury that kind of anger in the land, things are bound to grow strange from the soil. The Swallows has been a dying town since it was founded, and that's part of its darkness too. No one was ever meant to stay here, we were just meant to wander through, respecting the silence and sacredness. But that's not what happened. The ghosts outnumber us here, Sugar, and us who've been out here our whole lives know it. We just try to get along like we don't."

"You believe in ghosts?"

"Only because I've seen them. I was going to tell you not to tell your mom or Benny I said that, but now, I just don't know. I truly believe the problem right now is that no one is talking about anything that's real. We're just pretending to know everything without actually seeking out the answers. That's what makes you so different, Sugar.

You're always looking for answers. Here you are on my doorstep on a Friday afternoon, and I know you're full of questions you haven't even asked yet."

Pearl smiled faintly but kept her shadowed eyes downcast.

"Did you see a ghost? Is that what has you so freaked out?"

Pearl slouched lower on the bench, her shoulders curled forward. "I don't even know, Miss Rose. I don't even know how to say it all, or where to start."

"Just tell it as straight as you can, we can figure out the order of it later."

"Alright, but don't think I'm crazy because I already think that's probably true, and if you say so too, then I think they'll have to put me up in a padded room."

Pearl took a sip of her tea while Rose laughed.

"Last night, there was a woman on Frank's bus who was real nice to Benny and me. Frank was threatening to take me down to where John-Boy and Derry were—because they've been looking for me—but the woman gave Frank a six-pack of beers and paid him twenty bucks to let us all off together. She said she had a little girl at home and would want my mom to do the same for her. She had all these groceries just for her daughter. She was so nice." Pearl's voice cracked. "It would've been bad for me and Benny if she wasn't there."

"John-Boy and Derry have been looking for you?"

Tears formed in Pearl's eyes, but she chewed her cheek to keep from crying. "Oh, I don't care about them. It's the woman. She was the one who died last night—the woman on the bus— they'll show her picture on tonight's news. I swear it's true. I know because she was in my room last night, right after it happened. She couldn't stop crying. They're going to say she's a suicide, but she isn't—there's no way she would've done that."

"She was in your room?"

"They all were—all the ones who died."

Rose held her teacup in front of her mouth and was silent for a moment. Then she reached to the corner where all the almanacs and gardening magazines were stacked, and pulled out her golden drawing of the four dead mothers. Rose's drawing was humbler than the painter's interpretation at The Gaslight. Her mothers were soft-lined, wearing the same Grecian gowns and braided sandals, the same rose crowns. The postures were nearly identical. There was only one difference.

"Their eyes are open," Pearl said.

Rose smoothed the drawing against the table and framed it with her hands. "They were when they showed up here a few nights ago too, but they didn't stay long—not long enough to talk anyway, which is a shame." Rose pointed to the drawing, her finger softly landing on the closest face. "Cindy was a real character— always planning little parties, she'd make anything into a little party. And you can't tell from how they talk about her now, but Maggie was a hoot, one of my favorite people to be around, especially when I was feeling low." Rose moved her finger down the line of women. "Molly was the beauty— a real straight arrow. She had a moral compass that made her play everything straight, even when you didn't want to hear it. And Kaia was kind. You'll learn that true kindness is rare. She was always the one who would show up when you were at your worst and really needed someone, and she would just know. I guess it was last February—one of those frigid lonely days, when the winter has seeped so far into your bones it makes your heart hurt. I'd been alone all day, in one of those low-down dark moods, and as soon as night was coming on, all four of them showed up like a hit parade. Cindy brought over these glitter party hats, a giant bottle of whiskey, and little jelly jars that said 'I Fall to Pieces'." Rose's eyes were glassy, like she was seeing past Pearl, imagining her friends around the table, laughing and talking. "Maggie cooked up a big pot of stew and she was such a mess—just so funny—we were rolling all night. Molly and Kaia cleaned up the whole place – I don't even know when, they were like Cinderella's little mice. Then we all sat on the back porch wrapped in blankets and watched the stars. We fell asleep—all five of us—nearly in this very posture." Rose framed the drawing with her hands again, the black mascara on her lashes starting to cake from catching her tears.

"And that's how you saw them again?"

"A few nights ago. I got home later from the diner than usual. There was fog coming off the river, and it was nice outside, so I decided to spend a little time in the garden, gathering up the squash and blossoms that were ready to come in. It was when I was done, my apron loaded up and hands full, that I saw all four of them sitting on the porch, their eyes wide open, staring at the stars."

"Did they see you?"

"I don't know. I wasn't loud, but I wasn't quiet. I guess I treated them like sleepwalkers, just afraid to wake them up and confuse everything. I don't know why I did that. I guess I was scared. It was a strange feeling, though. Like an impossible wish had come true. By the time I made it all the way up the porch, they were gone. I tried to convince myself it was just the fog, but when I was in the kitchen, cleaning up the vegetables, I saw my reflection in the window. I can't explain it, really, but at that moment—seeing my own face reflected back at me, imagining the stars and moon, the White River just on the other side of my floating face—I knew I saw them out there. I knew they'd come to see me because they were always welcome here."

Pearl set her empty teacup on the saucer. "I didn't know that."

"You three didn't get here until after they had all passed, so you wouldn't know. And I'm sure you haven't heard anything good. But this town remembers. We all know who those women really were before the town turned them into some kind of cautionary tale."

"You don't think they killed themselves?"

"When Cindy died, I was in a shock. We all were. There was no reason for her to be on the roof of the Bancroft Building. And if she really was up there, she must've fallen down. Or she was pushed. When the suicide rumors started, I knew it wasn't possible but still questioned the possibility. That's what happens with tragedy. In a lot of ways, Cindy was the one who kept our group together—we leaned on her a lot. I think all four of us felt guilty about that. Like maybe we took too much and didn't give enough. But then, when Molly died at the lake and the town cried 'suicide'—well, I knew she'd been murdered. I knew—right then—there was a killer in Fullmouth. Aside from Molly being such a straight arrow, the fact is, she could swim like nobody else. She would take little Jack to the lake all summer long, and whenever we all went out there to picnic for the day, she was in the water for at least an hour, swimming laps. There is no way she accidentally drowned, and there is no way she killed herself. She'd never leave Jack behind. If she's really gone—and I know she is because I saw here in that casket at Jefferson's— there's only one way it happened."

Pearl let out a long sigh and leaned back against the wall, the pale rider in the painting, stoic and solitary as ever. "Why do you think someone would kill them?"

Rose pressed her lips together as she spun her empty teacup around the saucer. "I've thought about that a lot. And it sounds a little crazy, but I'd say it's because they were so happy. If it is a killer—and I think it is— then their deaths were supposed to be a warning. You're talking about a group of women who were more like family than friends. They all helped each other, raised their kids together. It was beautiful, really. Tragedy is all over the place out here— we all know it. If a killer started with a lone woman, one who had no family or connections, then it wouldn't be as sensational as running the rumor about a suicide pact. And this—" Rose pointed to the drawing of her friends again— "this makes death sensational. A story that gets attention. And then to label it 'suicide'—." Rose sucked air through her teeth and paused, "Well, if it can happen to them— women who figured out how to be happy out here, then it can happen to anyone— someone who is even less fortunate than they were."

Pearl pulled the sketch toward her, looking at Cindy's bright eyes, her rigid bearing. "So you figured there'd be others."

"I thought I'd be next—the final woman of the five."

"Is that why you painted up The Gaslight?"

Rose laughed. "Probably self-preservation. If I can turn

the cautionary tale about suicide into a horror story about a serial killer, I think I may have a chance."

Pearl eyed the cuckoo clock hanging on the wall next to the table. The lattice work was elaborately carved and painted red. The shutters were the same shade, with hearts cut out of their centers. Standing precariously at the peak of the roof was a gold weathervane with a crescent moon at its highest point. It looked just like Rose's house, or how it would appear in a fairy tale. From Hansel and Gretel, maybe—just like Benny said.

"They all talked to me—last night and this morning. Last night, I had this dream. It wasn't a bad one, but it was weird. I felt like I was walking into another world. I could feel the dirt and flowers under my feet as I walked across a field toward a rainbow. I was following a girl whose face I couldn't see. When I got to the rainbow, I was back in my room. But it didn't feel like mine. It was all off, like the walls were closer together and everything had been moved. The room was shrinking. Even as I laid in my bed, I knew the walls were moving closer and closer each time I blinked. The moment I realized this, I saw them. That was the first time. Cindy Stewart had this big crow. She cracked an egg on my desk so it could eat."

"What did they say?"

"Only Cindy talked last night. She said that it was going to keep happening."

Rose sighed deeply. "A crow, huh?"

"Biggest crow I ever saw."

"Leave it to Cindy to be dramatic." Rose shook her head and smiled. "She never had a crow before—I don't think she even liked birds. But she's smart. When she was alive, she'd carry a crossword book everywhere she went, and she'd work away at a puzzle any time she had a free moment, even at this table, waiting for the coffee to brew." Rose laughed. "That crow has to mean something." With that, Rose pushed herself up from the table and left the kitchen.

Pearl could hear her muffled voice and Benny's laugh through the swinging door, and as soon as Benny's laugh died down, Rose was back in the kitchen, a thick, tattered book spread open in her hands.

"This is something else Grandma June left, right along with the kettle and magic tea." Rose moved the kettle and biscuit plate to the far end of the table, brushed the cloth off with her free palm, then gently set the book down. "You could also say it's a family journal, just a hundred or so years old, and filled in by a lot of Rayburn women folk. I learned to read from this book, by learning to read the handwriting of my ancestors. And I know there is something in these pages about crows, something about the crows out of season." Rose turned the pages.

"Here it is—'Crows and the harvest. Many crows will come each year during harvest. These birds are familiar and can be kept from crops with a simple scarecrow put together with carved pumpkins, corn stalks, and rags. The more the scarecrow appears to be dancing in the wind, the better, so work the dressings into a simple garment.'" Rose smiled. "Nothing like a woman in a field to keep the crows away. 'If a crow arrives on its own, give it mind. If it perches near the house, if it vocalizes when it sees you and doesn't leave, give it mind. If it stays longer than three days, give it mind. Crows are remembrancers of Jesus on the Cross, remembrancers of sin. However, they also mean a change is coming, by death or a great transformation. Either way, that crow has come to talk about a loss that's on your doorstep."

Rose closed the book gently. "Seems like Cindy was just saying the same thing in as many ways as she could."

"I hope I'm not the crow on your doorstep."

"It wouldn't be you, Sugar." Rose patted Pearl's hand. "What else did they say?"

"I don't know if they ever left last night because they were there again this morning. I didn't see them right when I woke up, but when mom got home, they were there too. It was one of those times you talked about, when I knew it wasn't possible but questioned the possibility. Then the news came on, and there was the new death. I knew it was her—the woman who helped me and Benny. When I went to get ready for school, the women followed me into the bathroom."

"Sounds like they were waiting to talk to you the whole time."

"Maybe."

"What did they say?"

"They all talked this time. And they finished each other's sentences. Cindy and Molly seemed less upset, I think. I mean, before last night, they didn't know they were dead, not really. They said they knew they hadn't seen their kids in a while, but thought they were just traveling in the mountains or something. When the new woman showed up—someone I don't think they knew—just out of the blue, all bloody and hysterical—it was like their memories came with her. I think they are remembering their own deaths, or at least now they know they're dead."

"Maybe so, Sugar." Rose's peach-lined mouth was small with worry. The slip of Princess Peach lipstick on Rose's fine face was the only painted ornament that survived their conversation. "But that doesn't often happen— not with ghosts. Souls still walk the Earth because they either don't know they're dead or because they're here for revenge— sometimes it's both. And if it's both, the soul is filled with a thick black hatred—usually from being killed—but it doesn't know why it carries so much hate because it doesn't know it's dead. The hatred becomes revenge because revenge is the only real force a ghost can hang on to. And that's scary because that ghost soul doesn't know who it hates so much, so it hates everyone. A ghost will haunt a host until the host is destroyed. A lot of people believe that ghosts haunt places, but that's not true. Ghosts haunt people. There are so many ghosts in Fullmouth because there is so much anger. Fullmouth is haunted by its hatred."

Pearl's face was pale in the waning sun, her lips disappearing into her face, her eyes purple fractals of shadow. "I don't know what to say about that. I guess by now I would settle on you telling me I'm crazy."

Rose smiled. "Don't worry too much, not just yet. They didn't seem hostile, right?"

"I don't know. Last night they were sad, and this morning I'd say they were less sad and more angry, especially Cindy, but with all of them talking the same sentences, it was like they were sharing a brain. So, it was probably all of them, only Cindy expressed it the most."

"Is Cindy brighter than the others? Can you see her better?"

"No, they're all pretty bright. I mean, they look alive, if not for the weird clothes and just popping in and out. If I saw them in the street, I'd think they were real."

"That's a little intimidating. Those women were a force in life, I can't imagine how it would feel to be surrounded by them in death."

"You know though, I never got a bad feeling from them."

Rose frowned. "Spirits are pretty good at manipulating their host, in the beginning. It goes along with all those demon and vampire books you're always reading."

"Those are mostly about body snatching. If you invite them in, they come in and take over."

"Exactly."

Pearl frowned. "But demons are ancient—they were never human, so they don't know what it's like— and vampires have to kill to survive. I can't imagine it'd be the same."

"Just be cautious."

"You think they'll come again?"

"There's a reason it's you."

"I wish you could talk to them."

Rose nodded. "Did they say why they came to you?"

"No."

"Has anything like this ever happened to you before?"

"Not like this. I've had dreams about stuff that was about to happen; I get feelings that turn out to be true, but I've never seen a ghost or talked to one."

Rose looked at the clock. It was nearing four-thirty, the sun beginning its sleepy routine of sinking behind Bear Mountain. Her arms were still wrapped around the Rayburn family grimoire. "Are you scared?"

"A little, but not of them, not really. Last night was scary, but after seeing this morning's news—I'm more scared that there really is a killer. That there is a killer hanging around the Swallows, and no one has figured it out yet. *That's* crazy. Five women in four months, and no one is saying anything except they're villains. I feel bad for them."

"Me too, Sugar." Rose opened the grimoire, a bookmark tucked in the page she most wanted. "What do you think about communicating with them again, but with me there?"

"Well," Pearl sighed, "If they're coming again, I'd rather you be there."

"Ever since I was a kid, we've hosted dumb suppers in this house. They've all been for our ancestors—most of who died on this land, so they're easy to draw near—but I don't see why it wouldn't work with these ghosts."

"Dumb supper?"

"It's a kind of rite for those who have passed into another realm. Right now—right around Halloween—is the best time to host a dumb supper because the curtain between the realms is thin. This may be why you just started seeing Cindy and all, why they've been able to communicate with you."

Pearl nodded. "That makes sense."

"It's going to be dark soon. I think you and Benny should sleep over. This is your mom's late night at the diner, and after last night, I'm sure Henshaw will be happy to have the house to himself. I'll drive you two home to pick up some of your things. Then we'll make a big feast. When Benny goes to sleep, we'll get the supper started."

"Sounds good," Pearl said.

"I'll talk to Benny. We'll leave in ten minutes." And with that, Rose cleared the cups from the table and left the kitchen.

Pearl pulled the hood of her jacket over her head and closed her eyes. She imagined the pale horse in the painting, the dim lantern of its strong body, willfully tasking its hooves forward, into the menacing cathedral of spires, tooth shadows and the black mouth of the mountain range. She imagined the dark rider, his face turned from the eye of God, turned toward the Black Moon and all the gloomy objects of omen. She knew the rider would keep going.

CHAPTER SEVEN

Seven Wonders

It was dusk when the flurries began. As Rose pulled her old Chevy truck into the parking lot of Big Bear Grocery and cut the engine, the miniature furies fell from the sky, catching tempests and tracing the curling wind before reaching the concrete lattice parking lot.

Big Bear Grocery looked like an old train station, with its cathedral ceilings, arched windows, and clock tower. All of the building's identifying characteristics were purposeful in its past life as the major trading post in the region during the Goldrush days. The large doors enabled horses and livestock to enter the back stalls easily, and the tall hatch windows and ventilation slats kept the air moving, even on busy trade mornings when the post was past capacity with animals, farmers, ranchers, and townsfolk from the surrounding regions. Through the summer and most of the spring, Big Bear Grocery was pleasant and dewy, the air and vegetables crisp and new. But in the fall and winter, the store was frigid, the Black Mountain wind finding its way through every slat and window crevice until shoppers could hear it faintly rolling along nearby aisles. It was in the winter months the produce froze, the ice perfectly tracing the curve of a blueberry or the crowns of a broccoli floret, permanently altering the plump and colorful harvest.

Clifford Marchand could not well afford to seal the windows and alter the genius of the grocery's initial design, so during fall and winter, he put his best effort forth to make Big Bear's atmosphere festive. The windows were framed by red awnings and painted with the weekly specials: *carving pumpkins a dollar ninety-nine, sugar pumpkins a dollar twenty-five, butternut squash fifty cents a pound.* The sliding doors and parking lot were separated by haystacks with friendly scarecrows lounging across them, pursuing various forms of amusement. Two scarecrows with matching toothless smiles and reading glasses were playing a game of oversized checkers. The large black and red pieces glued to their garden-gloved hands. Another was playing fetch with a small dog made of gourds, and a third was in overalls, a prospector's pick over his shoulders and his pockets stuffed with gold-painted rocks.

Big Bear Grocery was in the town square, directly across from Rains Park and Bessie Rains' crumbling mansion, where all of Fullmouth's newly orphaned children were taking refuge. Through the fogging windows of Rose's truck, Pearl watched the snow shift along the pine-lined paths of the park. It was just after dusk, the hazy plum sky still too bright to see the stars, but dark enough so that if one looked up, she could make out nearly all the snowy flakes descending from above. The streetlamps that lit the paths through Rains Park had not yet turned on, so Pearl could only see the spidery shapes of shadowy people when a pair of headlights passed. She tried to make out shapes that looked similar enough to John-Boy and Derry, but it was impossible. And with the snowy fog descending, she hoped her need for caution was pointless. The minor bright spots of the snowy scene were the eight street-facing windows of Bessie Rains' mansion, which glowed red and orange like candles on a cake. Here too, Pearl could see the spider limbs of shadow people as they walked across the window stage, but she did not recognize the figures.

The disconnected parts and fragmented bodies made Pearl weary. Her heart felt hard in her chest, too anxious to beat one creak of sound for fear it would give the rest of her body away. Pearl could feel parts of herself turning inward: her skin becoming shingled, all the eyes turning their scopes on the sightlines from Pearl's shoulders and face. Something was coming. Pearl could feel the footsteps, heavy and slow, circling her head. She could hear the scraping sound of fingernails tapping on glass, the creaky blink of tired eyes waking. Something was coming, but she did not know who or what it was. As Pearl climbed out of the truck, she checked again to see if John-Boy and Derry were on the grocery stoop or smoking cigarettes on the park benches. She still did not see anything.

†

The fluorescent lights inside the grocery store cast everything in a sickly green glow. The orange shades of the plastic jack o' lanterns, navel oranges, and box displays of Wheaties were greatly affected, their cheerful brightness tempered by a hospital-room stringency. Still worse off was Sandy Lane Snyder, a decrepit woman who chain-smoked on her breaks and chewed nicotine gum at the cash register. She was barely five foot five, the red smock of Big Bear Grocery like a red mouth devouring her body from the shoulders down. The stitched bear logo looked menacing in its largess when transposed upon her miniature skeleton. As Sandy nimbly punched in all the codes for the strange fruits and vegetables Rose placed on the conveyor belt, her penciled eyebrows, drawn high on her forehead in black pencil, danced like ever-changing punctuation marks, depending on the facial expressions her practiced monologues demanded.

"Old Cliff, he's always been an okay cousin. Maybe the world's okayest, just a little weird as a kid. He was always carrying around some briefcase full a clipboards and pencils." Here Sandy laughed, her eyebrows ellipses. "He moved me way out here from Arizona—I was doing alright there, doing some laundry for a nice hotel, but I hurt my back— but Cliff, he said he got me a easy job and a nice place to live. Said it like I'd have all the bells and whistles. So, I left my friends and my favorite bar and moved on up here. Come to find out, I'm a cashier, standing on my feets all day, and living in a basement apartment, in some building where no one else lives." Her eyebrows exclamation points.

Benny stood directly in front of the cashier stand, his attention fully focused on Sandy Lane's face as Rose unloaded the cart and Pearl bagged the groceries. This was how all of Sandy's storied started.

"I get so lonely down there. It's cold and there's no one to talk to. I'm not supposed to smoke in the apartment, but sometimes I do. Who's gonna know if I'm smoking?" She asked Benny. "No one there to catch me." Her eyebrows thick black parentheses. "Ain't no mice either. And my landlord, he's alright, real uptight though. I tell him I'm lonely, but he won't come over, and he won't let me get a pet."

Sandy Lane looked at Pearl, her face full of gushing regret, her eyebrows periods—small, simple dots, filling out the porous page of her face. Pearl nodded and gave a small frown as she placed three sugar pumpkins in a paper sack.

"But then!" Sandy clapped for emphasis. "I got an idea! Way to shake him up." Sandy snapped her fingers. "I says to him, 'I got a pet. It eats bugs.' He looked all worried, thought it was an iguana or a spider or something." Sandy paused to laugh at the punchline before she got there, to get the joke good and primed before it went off. Her throaty rasp-laugh turned into a deep cough. She swallowed the wad of nicotine gum in her mouth before she could continue. "He says, 'You know you can't have no pets.' I says, 'I know, I got what you call a Venus Fly Trap.'"

Her eyebrows were dashes, looking to Benny for an aside.

"You know what a Venus Flytrap is, hun?"

Benny nodded, his big eyes at their widest, the green light making the whites a pistachio shade.

"Wells, I got me one a those, and I love my little Buddy. I feed him gnats – can you believe it? Lots of weekends I go down to the lake and hunt up some gnats. Never thought I'd be hunting gnats. Used to be drinking Mai Thais by the pool in Arizona, watching Carlos on duty, now I'm out in the middle of nowhere, hunting gnats. Life's funny like that." Sandy Lane shook her head, her red hair stiff with hairspray, its contrast too cheerful for her story. "Now that it's getting cold, though, I go buy gnats from the bait shop. You believe they sell gnats? In little sacks. Buddy just loves 'em. Thirty-eight, seventy-five, please."

And at that, Sandy Lane Snyder's one-woman show ended. She popped another piece of nicotine gum from the foil wrapper. Pearl finished bagging up the flour sack and cinnamon as Rose handed Sandy two twenty-dollar bills.

"How long have you had your Buddy?" Benny asked.

"About six months."

"He get any bigger?"

"Oh yeah, hun. He's doubled in size! Eats as much as I

smoke." Sandy rasp-laughed.

"You ever seen *Attack of the Killer Tomatoes*?"

"My Buddy would be way more dangerous out on the streets than those tomatas. He didn't come from outer space, but he's what you'd call one of God's oddities. He's a carnivore—a meat-eatin' plant. That's a weird thing to put out into the world."

Benny's mouth was slack as he stared at Sandy Lane's face, considering all of what she said. "Buddy's a nice name."

"Thanks, Sandy, we'll be seeing you," Rose said as she waved goodbye and pushed the grocery cart away from the counter. "Come on, Benny."

"You think she was joking?" Benny whispered.

"Some of it was a joke, but mostly I think she just trying her best not to be sad, and that's admirable."

"That was a funny story about Mr. Marchand."

"He's a funny duck, one of those kinds who was born with everything he needed to know, so it's near impossible to teach him anything new."

"That doesn't sound too good."

"I wouldn't think so either, but in a small town, he does alright."

Rose pushed the cart across the parking lot and through the banking snow, coming to a stop at the truck. Pearl unlatched the bed and carefully opened the tailgate. As Pearl unloaded the groceries, Rose got the engine turned over and the heater working. She buckled Benny into the bench seat, then slowly and methodically pressed her foot on the gas pedal, making sure the engine's rumblings settled into a steady sound before they headed toward home.

Pearl watched Benny and Rose in the truck. With the snow and the cab's dim yellow light, the scene looked like an Edward Hopper painting. Those two bright and lovely people sitting inside all that yellow warmth, while the night outside stayed dark and heavy. Hopper always kept the night at bay, need it be through the windows of a diner or the lounge of a train car. Pearl imagined the light of the cab floating in space, a bright orb heading to unknown galaxies. How peaceful it would be to float in space with Rose and Benny.

As she wrapped a canvas tarp around the groceries to keep them dry, a low whistle interrupted her thought. At first, she thought it was the sound of the wind moving snow through the trees, but as the truck engine mellowed into a steady mumble, Pearl could hear the whistled melody changing. Low and sluggish, all the weight of buried octaves clawing through dirt and into the atmosphere— it was the horror movie soundtrack that begins too early, hinging on the precipice of *what is* and *what is about to appear* from the dark. It was a dirge meant for Pearl— tinny and low— and it was coming from Rains Park.

Pearl finished unloading the groceries and tucked her ponytail into her hoodie. She set her winter cap at an angle so she could see the periphery and pulled her coat's hood around her face. She latched the tailgate, taking care not to bang it and destroy the idyllic scene of Rose and Benny. Pearl kept her eyes down and her ears on the sounds around her. She slowly walked the cart to the stall by the checker-playing scarecrows. The lenses of their matching glasses were foggy from the furies spinning webs around them. The fingers of their gloves moved to the sound of John-Boy's song. Pearl walked back to the truck, her legs steady and strong. As she climbed into the Chevy's cabin with Benny and Rose, she yanked the door shut to catch the old latch, and Patsy Cline's sugary lament smothered John-Boy's menacing call.

✝

That evening, the constant commotion of the White River was muffled by the first heavy snowfall of Autumn. Even the long creak of Pine trees shifting in the wind was preternaturally silenced by the slush. Each hour that passed, the quiet surrounding the cabin became more and more distilling. Rose hummed and sang fragments of old soul songs, but her deep voice could not overshadow the darkness that silently tapped at the windows and doors. Eventually, her songs sounded as melancholy as the outside world appeared. But as Rose chopped and stirred, as she folded and prayed through the comfort of old melodies, the nostalgic aroma of cinnamon and maple, of roasting meats and thick soups, became the flickering candles of bygone holidays. Rose's cooking was a connection to universal histories, to cheerful timelines that reached further and further into the past and became warming orbs that lit even the darkest corners of the cabin, pushing the darkness beyond the porch, into the yard, all the way back to the row of frozen squash blossoms that never had the chance to fall from the vine.

Pearl also rallied against the gloom. As Rose cooked her dumb supper feast, Pearl sat at the kitchen table with Benny, drinking hot chocolate and magic tea, playing Gin Rummy and Crazy Eights, engaging Benny in anything he wanted to talk about. And mostly he wanted to talk about Halloween.

"You think people'll know I'm a skeleton vampire

when they see me?"

"Are you going to wear that old Voodoo skeleton suit, the one with the bow tie and top hat?"

Benny nodded. "Yep. A cape too, and vampire teeth."

"Are you going to paint your face?"

"Will you paint my face like a skeleton vampire?"

"How's that?"

"I can draw it for you." Benny stood up.

"No, no. Just play your hand and tell me."

"Well," Benny said as he laid down his cards to mime the future painting of his face. "I want this all white, ears and neck too. But my eyes'll be big black circles and my mouth'll be big with drawn-on teeth. And there'll be blood right here." Benny pointed to his cheek.

"Because that'll be how big your mouth is?"

Benny nodded.

"I can do that—if you sit still long enough."

"You think people'll know I'm a skeleton vampire?"

"I think so. And if we do it right, they'll be too scared to worry about exactly what you are. They'll just know you're some kind of monster. Right when they see you, they'll know they better run or else."

Benny finally pulled a card from the deck, his fan of cards too big to hold. "I don't know if I want to scare 'em that bad."

"Then you should be a Dodo bird or a kangaroo— not a skeleton vampire."

Benny grimaced. "I guess I'd rather scare 'em than not."

"Good choice, Bens. You'll be the best monster in town to go Trick or Treating with."

"Gin!" He grinned, his cards still strewn across the

table.

✝

While Benny ate a bowl of butternut squash soup and requested silly songs for Rose to sing, Pearl built a fire in the living room and made a pallet bed on the thick rug in front of the fireplace. Then she, Benny, and Rose wrapped themselves in quilts and watched *The Wizard of Oz* until Benny fell asleep.

"It's getting to be ten o'clock," Rose whispered, wrapping her quilt around Benny. "We should probably watch the news before we set up everything. See if it's really her."

"I don't really want to know if I'm right," Pearl said, but she turned the knob on the front of the television anyway, the static between turns sputtering sound before each pause.

"It's nothing anyone would want to be right about, but it's still the right thing to do."

Pearl found her way to the KOTA TV News desk, where Chip Gordon was buttoned up in a crisp white shirt and Western print tie. His face was superficially honest, stereotypically masculine and reliable, handsome and strong-chinned. But Pearl knew what he was holding back. Chip leaned toward the camera, his elbows on the news desk, a pained and practiced look of being nearly undone hovering around his brow but never making its way to his mouth. His face and neck were pancaked into an orange tan until it reached his collar. His ears pointier than most, the eyes globular and spider-lashed. Pearl thought his face grotesque, a monster mask. She knew what he was about to say in the way his mouth was grim. A straight red line— the dead line—only warping at the corners, working to hold back a gruesome joke, or to wait for a heinous prank to come to its full effect. Pearl could see the muddy fog of his aura hanging from his earlobes, a limp hat wrapped around his head that disclosed the sickness of his spirit. Pearl did not want to hear what he had to say, but Rose turned up the volume dial until Chip Gordon's wooden voice broke the surface of the static.

"I never know just how to begin these stories, and each time I have to tell you all something painful, something I don't want you to have to hear—" Chip turned his head at an angle, meeting the camera in close range. "— I feel like maybe this is the story that'll get me to leave the news desk and go back to cattle ranching, like my daddy did, God rest his soul. But then I think of my mama and daddy, how I was born in a Nebraska cornfield, riding back home from a cattle drive, mama giving birth to me right there in the bed of daddy's truck. And no, I don't think I'd change it." Chip paused and shook his head, a mimed consideration. "My parents taught me to be a straight shooter, to look a stranger right in the eye and tell him the truth—no matter how bad it is— just like I would anyone I'm blessed enough to sit around the supper table with. And tonight, like family, I'm going to tell you this tough news in the same way I'd tell my daddy. Tonight, I'm blessed to sit at this desk, across from you." Chip Gordon turned back to the main camera, the desk an oak skirt beneath his elegant hands. "Tonight, you're my family, and I'm here to break it to you."

If Chip Gordon were wearing a cowboy hat—which Pearl knew he regretted forgetting, as it would be the perfect prop for an evening of bad news and hard times in the great and Wild West—he'd take it off right now, maybe hold it to his chest, or set it brim-side-up on his desk. He would ask the cameraman to pass the potatoes, pull up a chair, and have little Henry come sit on his knee. But Chip Gordon could only work with what he had: the desk his steer, the camera his cow hands, the stack of papers a fire, and his tie the stand-in for his missing cowboy hat. Chip Gordon did what he could. He leaned in closer to the camera, nearly holding his fist to his chin, in a tough but romantic Clark Gable way.

"I'm sorry to tell you this, but another suicide has changed the life of another little girl in Fullmouth, South Dakota. Her mama is never coming back from the cattle drive, never coming home again, not in the same way she did before." Chip steepled his fingers and rested his head on his hands in an affected moment of silence.

"Tonight, the Fullmouth Police Department released a statement that there has been a fifth suicide in its small town." The camera panned out slightly, and a photo of the woman on the bus hung next to Chip Gordon's face. Her long hair was in a side ponytail. Her smile was wide and tiny-toothed, and her long fingers were decorated with the same silver rings she wore on the bus. The woman's thin arm hung across the shoulder of a young girl whose small face was fuzzed out. "The Fullmouth police identified the deceased woman as twenty-eight-year-old Karen Kelly. Our thoughts and prayers are with Ms. Kelly's family tonight, and especially with her young daughter, as she navigates this difficult time. God bless her and protect her."

"Karen Kelly," Rose said, looking at Pearl's pale face, her glassy eyes.

Pearl nodded as she worked to bury her sadness beneath the anger she had carefully cultivated toward Chip

Gordon. "That was too much."

Rose put her arm around Pearl's shoulder— both of them cross-legged in front of the coffee table— and hugged her. "I'm sorry you're having to go through this, Sugar. But you knew it was going to be her. All day you've been preparing yourself to see her face and find out her name, and now, maybe you can do her some good."

Pearl swallowed the tears that fell into her throat. She turned off the television and watched Benny. His breath beat along his heartline, subtly shifting the quilt across his body. The flickering light of the fire moved along his round face, pulling him in and out of shadows, making it look like all of him was moving closer and closer to the flames. Pearl abruptly reached out and put her hand on his chest. She felt his heart beating beneath her palm.

†

Pearl had not seen herself in a mirror since the early morning— when all the dead mothers were crowded into her bathroom— and that felt like so long ago. As she hung black cloth over each antique mirror— the silver ovals lined one wall of the dining room— Pearl's reflection seemed to lift its arms and tilt its head long before Pearl ever did. Her eyes looked strange too. Wider and darker, the purple caves of exhaustion made her face upturned and feline. Her long hair was pulled back into a low bun, and she wore one of Rose's black dresses, the long lace sleeves and high collar giving her a look of finality. The full expression was nothing she had ever seen in the mirror before. She was glad to shield the long line of reflective eyes from view.

The dining room was created by the same design and decorum as Pearl's solemn appearance. The legs of the long oak table looked like carved black totems in the candlelight, and the setting itself was an intricate altar. A long black crocheted cloth ran the length of the table, end to end. Rose had gathered beautiful, gold-leafed books from her library and stacked them into different heights along the table. The platter of roasted duck stood atop *The Secret Garden* and *Jane Eyre*. The tureen of butternut squash soup on *Wuthering Heights*. And the spice cake's glass plate and bell jar balanced atop *Rebecca*, *The Picture of Dorian Grey*, and *The Woman in White*. Their gold titles glowed. Surrounding the books, Rose placed sausage and cranberry stuffed pumpkins, their stalks jaunty-like fashionable hats. Three tall milk jars were filled with seven sunflowers between them and placed evenly between the books and pumpkins, their faces turned to the window. Like a winding train cutting through the scene, black candles in crystal holders rolled throughout the table, twenty-five in all, ending in a circle around a small dish of salt. A basket of bread sat at the table's end, and fat red apples were tucked between everything. Seven places were set, one for each of the mothers—their chairs wrapped in the same black cloth that covered the mirrors—one for Rose, and one for Pearl. On the edges, leaning against the pumpkins and apples, or framed between the sunflower stalks, were seven photos of the women. None of these images made it to the newsreels. Each was homed in Rose's scrapbook and reflected days at Silver Lake, a fair in Wyoming, the time they followed the rodeo to Denver. Each face in the frames was bold and self-assured, smiling and bright with nothing to hide. They were faces on roller coasters, faces eating ice cream, faces captured in the pure time of a single moment. The only photo Rose did not have was one of Karen Kelly, so she chose the best silver rings from her jewelry box and strung them on black lace next to Karen's wine glass. Seven levels in all, and each significant to the dumb supper's setting.

Rose met Pearl in the hallway and they entered the dining room together. Silently, they walked to the North corner of the room and placed a black candle and another dish of salt. In the East, they placed a second candle and a feather. South, a candle and incense. And West, the final black candle and a small bowl of water. Returning to the North corner, Rose lit the candle and called, "North quarter of Earth, I ask for your grounding power of protection, I feel you here, and I welcome you." Pearl followed Rose's slow steps as she lit the black candles in each corner of the room. Rose asked the East quarter of air for wisdom and grace, the South quarter of fire for strength and life-giving warmth, and in the West quarter of water, she asked for power and gentle cleansing. Pearl whispered the end of each prayer— "I feel you and welcome you"—as an incantation that moved through her. After the circle was cast, the room felt like it had fallen into the silence at the center of the Earth. The dining room became a submarine, all its electricity and life contained— a shifting, blinking light at the dead bottom of the sea.

The tealights on the place settings for each of the dead mothers flickered and sparked. The setting for Cindy Stewart was at the head of the table. The basket of bread at her elbow, a place for the oily crow to perch on the high-backed chair. Each spirit setting followed the date of each woman's death: Molly Boutell, Kaia Goodwin, Maggie Teller, and Karen Kelly. A place for Pearl was made next to Karen, as she was the only one who knew the living Karen, and maybe that could be a comfort. Then Rose sat next to Pearl—a sure hand to hold—and next to her was Cindy.

Rose put her arm around Pearl and they slowly walked the line of spirit chairs, stopping at each to silently pray. Pearl thought of the stories that Rose had told about each woman. And mirroring the prayers Rose made to the cardinal directions, Pearl called to each woman, focusing on their kindness and humor, their strength and understanding. After the final prayer at Karen Kelly's chair, where Pearl thanked her for her protection and prayed she could offer the same, she came to her own chair and sat down while Rose gathered the soup tureen and ladle and slowly served each dish to her guests. She began with the eldest and followed the line of youth from mothers to maidens, not one yet a crone: Kaia Goodwin, Rose Rayburn, Karen Kelly, Cindy Stewart, Maggie Teller, Molly Boutell, and Pearl Adler. The circle cast.

Pearl kept her head bowed, all her wishes tossed like stars into the black space of her mind, blinking brighter with each wish formed and flung into the wide net of skyscape. Only when she felt Rose's chair shift, felt Rose grab her hand, did Pearl focus on one star set. Closer and closer, Pearl moved toward its golden blink—the ship in space, the submarine in the sea—it was the room, the dumb supper table set. Inside the star were a hundred candles, a feast for queens. Rose's head bent, her thick velvet headband and braid. It was Cindy and Molly, Kaia and Maggie, it was Karen holding her hand. Karen was holding her hand. Pearl felt the slim fingers, the coldness of Karen's silver rings, the single horn of the unicorn poking into her palm.

When she opened her eyes, all of the women were at

the table. All of the women except for Rose.

"She's still there, don't worry," Cindy Stewart said, an unlit cigarette between her thin lips. "Rose just can't get way out here. You're still there too. I bet if you close your eyes again and do whatever it is you do, you'll get all the way back to Rose's house. There's no place like home, huh?"

"I love that movie. Deirdre and I watch it all the time," Karen said, still holding onto Pearl's hand.

"Benny likes it too. We watched it tonight."

"It's one of those movies that just sets the world back to *right*," declared Kaia.

"And Dorthy's so determined. Nothing keeps her off the yellow brick road— no witch or creepy flying monkey," Molly said.

"But you didn't call us here to talk about movies," Cindy interrupted.

"No, I—"

The massive crow cawed loudly, its guttural sound silencing the room as he scratched at Cindy's chair back. She used the carving knife to remove a piece of the roasted duck's leg and gave it to the crow, who stretched his throat and croaked it down, his head leaned back, the sharp black beak a hook at the top of his body.

Pearl shivered.

Molly rolled her eyes. "Do you know where the kids are staying? We can only seem to find them at school, and it's miserable. They're miserable. I sure do miss Jack, but Jack hated school. I'm hoping he just looks so bad because I can only see him when he's down at Custer Day."

"They're all together at Bessie Rains' house. It was the only way to keep them in town."

Maggie sobbed. Her rose crown tilted and trembled

with each wrench of her shoulders.

Kaia put her arm around Maggie's shoulder. "Don't worry, Mags, at least they're here, and they're all together. We can go see them now that we know where they are."

"None of the streets look the same. I can't find anything."

"It's different on this side of things," Molly told Pearl.

"And we definitely can't find a place we've never been," Kaia whispered.

"You're the only one we seem to be able to find," said Cindy.

Maggie wiped her face with the table lace. "Are you friends with them?" She asked Pearl.

"I'm not really friends with anybody. I haven't lived in Fullmouth too long and I spend most of my time taking care of Benny."

Cindy leaned back in her chair, the knife still in her hand. "You should go see them, talk to them, so we know they're okay. Don't tell them too much about us, though."

"But tell them something," Maggie pleaded.

Molly knocked twice on the table. "Tell them we're all together, and we're looking out for them."

"Like guardian angels," Kaia said.

Cindy flicked invisible ash from her unlit cigarette. "We don't want them to think it's some kind of party on this side of things. We don't want them to come on over."

"No—not at all. I want Jack to do all kinds of things, but that's not one of them," agreed Molly.

"Jack's obsessed with you, who knows what he'll do." Cindy set the knife down but kept the cigarette to her lips.

"Especially now that he's living with Charlie."

"Now he's a wild card," interrupted Kaia.

"No more than Jack," Molly said.

"But Charlie's way older than Jack. If anything—" argued Cindy.

"I can go to Bessie's house," Pearl interrupted. "Maybe you can follow me there."

"That would be wonderful," Maggie clapped. "I'd feel better if I could see Connor and Emma."

"And they could all use a friend like you right now," Kaia said.

"And Benny," Karen whispered.

"And Benny," replied Kaia.

"Especially Deirdre."

Kaia leaned against Maggie's shoulder. "I sure hope they've all brought her into the fold."

"I'll go see her soon—I promise," said Pearl.

Karen nodded, circling Rose's lace bracelet of silver rings around her wrist.

"Moving on," Cindy said abruptly. She pulled the unlit cigarette from her mouth and held it between her long fingers, motioning to the table. "Why did you two do all this?"

The crow was the only one eating, its forked feet pulled at the lace as it walked across the table sampling Rose's dishes.

"You didn't need to go to all this trouble. We would've just come if you called us. That's what happened anyway," Molly said.

"It's more for Rose. Remember that dumb supper we had? And we pulled out that Ouija board and drank about a gallon of coffee brandy?" Kaia recalled.

"That was a riot," Maggie said, her laugh a small hiccup.

"I sure do miss Rose," said Kaia.

"We see her. Her place isn't too tough to find." Molly clicked her fingernails against the side of her wine glass.

"She's seen you here once, on the porch," said Pearl.

Maggie sighed. "We had a lot of great nights on Rose's porch. Too bad she can't be here."

"We have her letter, though." Cindy leaned into the center of the table and plucked Rose's letter from between the pages of *The Secret Garden*. "She says she loves us."

"We love her," Kaia sang.

"And she wants to know what we remember," noted Cindy.

"About what?" asked Molly.

Cindy rocked back and forth in her chair. "Our deaths."

"We talked about that," Kaia said to Pearl.

"We don't remember anything, not really." Molly held her empty wine glass next to her heart-shaped face.

"We remember bits and pieces, but nothing that hangs together."

"I remember wind," said Cindy.

"Water," Molly mumbled.

"Rocks," answered Kaia.

"A train whistle," Maggie added.

"But nothing that means anything," Cindy said.

"Were you happy?" Pearl asked.

"Yes," Maggie said.

"I didn't know how happy I was, not until now," answered Karen.

Kaia sighed and slumped in her chair. "I feel bad about that too."

Pearl hesitated. "It's just—"

"Go on," pled Kaia.

"Did you kill yourselves?"

Cindy laughed, paused, and took a drag off her unlit cigarette.

"No."

"Never."

"No way."

"It's the only thing we know for sure," Cindy contended.

"So, every one of your deaths was by accident?" asked Pearl.

"Maybe."

"Or murders?"

"But why?"

"Right? For what? There's nothing about me important enough to kill," asserted Maggie.

"And I've never pissed anyone off that much," agreed Molly.

"Not that you know of," Maggie joked.

Kaia shook her head. "We went to work, came home, hung out, and took care of our kids. There's just no reason."

"Then they were definitely accidents?" Pearl asked.

"That's a little far-fetched, too," muttered Karen.

"Nearly impossible."

Pearl sighed. "Me and Rose think so too."

"So, if it's not accidents and it's not suicides, then it has to be murder," Cindy said.

"Damn," Karen exhaled. "I can't even imagine that."

"Well, how did we die?" Maggie asked

Molly laughed. "That's abrupt."

"We're probably ready to know."

"You okay with that, Karen?" Kaia asked. "Yours just

happened."

"I'm alright."

"I don't know about what happened to you," Pearl turned to Karen. "They haven't said yet. But as soon as I know, I'll tell you."

"That's probably a blessing, at least for now." Kaia squeezed Karen's hand.

"Alright then— tell the rest of us straight," Molly said.

Pearl took a sip of her water. "Cindy fell from the Bancroft building. Molly drowned in Silver Lake. Kaia crashed her Volkswagen into Iron Mountain—"

"Thank God Dakota and Genie weren't with me."

"And Maggie fell down her building's fire escape."

"What was I doing out there?"

"How could I have possibly drowned?"

"That's a lot to take in."

"None of it makes sense," Maggie said.

"Is that everything? That's all you know?" queried Kaia.

"How come we don't remember any of that? How could we possibly forget moments in our lives that were so brutal?" Molly asked.

"Rose says ghosts stay on earth because they don't know they're dead or because they're here for revenge, so they're real angry."

Cindy smiled. "But we know we're dead."

"Unfortunately," said Karen.

"And none of us are angry," Kaia assured.

"Not yet, anyway," contended Cindy.

"I may be a little pissed off after finding out I drowned in Silver Lake."

"Then there has to be another reason."

"Maybe it's the angel thing," Kaia said. "Maybe we're

still here for our kids."

Karen looked at Pearl. "That's the only thing that makes sense."

"You really do need to go see them," asserted Maggie.

"I will."

"And maybe try to figure out what happened," said Cindy.

"Do you know if it's going to happen again?" Pearl asked.

"Not for sure."

"But it seems likely," Molly said.

"If it were just about us, someone who just knew us, then Karen wouldn't be here," Maggie observed.

"It's something else."

"Has to be."

Kaia sighed. "Our lives were so small."

"They were. Now they're less than that," Molly mumbled.

"Gone completely," said Maggie.

Kaia yawned. "I'm getting tired. I can't stay here much longer."

"I'm beat," Molly added.

"Alright." Cindy smashed her cigarette into the dish of salt. "We will see you tomorrow, Pearl. And tell Rose this was all lovely and that we love her."

"Yes, do." Maggie yawned.

"We will come to see her again soon."

Karen gave Pearl's shoulder a squeeze as the women got up to go. The crow snatched a final piece of duck from the platter and hopped along the table, following Cindy to the door. Alone in the dining room, Pearl watched the tracks of candles halt their dancing and stand straight as sentries, the flames wide-hipped and pin-headed. She imagined the great night sky, the blinking silvers and golds. Pearl slowly left the room, her mind focused on Benny asleep by the fire, his fingers knuckled next to his face. In the room adjacent was Rose in the dining room, her head bent, a soft smile as the candles melted down and began to flicker again. Pearl imagined sitting next to Rose in matching black dresses, holding Rose's hand. She held Rose's hand.

Rose smiled and knocked on the table twice. She stood up, loosened her skirt from the tablecloth, and pulled her letter from the pages of *The Secret Garden*. Pearl stood up too. Her own letter to the dead mothers was still in her pocket. Together, they walked the line of spirit chairs in reverse. They prayed for Karen Kelly and blew out her candle. Then Maggie Teller, Kaia Goodwin, and Molly Boutell. At Cindy Stewart's chair, Rose and Pearl burned their letters in her spirit candle before snuffing the flame. They silently extinguished the candles in the corners, then those on the table. Pearl could hear the White River again. She could hear the funnels of wind breaking through the snow, gathering fury and working to find the small cracks in the logs of Rose's cabin. She imagined the cabin as a face, finally breathing, gulping the wind through the chimney and snuffing out the fire.

CHAPTER EIGHT

Night Stalker

Rose opened The Gaslight early on Saturday mornings, as it was the only place in Fullmouth that served a hot breakfast. Even if the townsfolk were upset with her over the spectacle she had made of the diner, there were still those who would travel from Wyoming or Colorado on a Saturday morning to gawk at the beauty of a Black Mountain Autumn, especially if the final destination was a town in the middle of a scandal that centered on young and dying women. A suicide town, like Hollywood without the flash or glamour. Without the reason for being. Fullmouth was the big black question mark conjured through the black box of nightly news. A question that pulled the gawkers from the comfort of their lives and homes and had them travel the dangerous, hairpin curves and needle highways of the Black Mountains to get to a town that was nearly exact to the destitution and strangeness they expected. And now, with The Gaslight painted up in all the hokey images of every hokey horror movie ever made, Rose could not pass up the crowd she knew would come. Fullmouth was a town that survived solely on the winter season of hunting and fur trapping, and no one who lived there forgot that fact. Picking the carcass of three months over a full year turned each town denizen into a desperate dreamer. Survival was made by way of the mirage: the intense focus of what could happen in Fullmouth— what was on its way, what was right in front of them. If they could only hang on. Better still if they could hang on longer than anyone else. The deaths of the women were tragic—everyone in town agreed—but they were also for sale. The dead mothers brought warm bodies into town, bodies that wanted part of the story and were willing to pay. And everyone in the Swallows was good for it. Everyone had a story to sell, a fortune to read, a feeling or omen— a symbol witnessed that let them know the deaths were going to happen. They knew it was happening. They knew what was next. And Rose was not excluded, no matter how good. That was survival. Penance was in the act of survival too. It was in those nine hungry months of humbling that came each year in the Swallows. The nine months that took so many away with it, emptying out the apartment buildings and houses that lined Fullmouth's streets. Survival was hanging on, just a little longer. So, Rose did.

After she got Pearl to bed well after two a.m., Rose stayed awake. If she fell asleep, she would miss the morning rush. Still in the funeral dress she wore to the dumb supper to keep from getting too comfortable and falling asleep, she curled up in an overstuffed chair by the living room fireplace and read *Jane Eyre*. By the time Rose followed Jane into the red room, where the ghost of her uncle was haunting his kin, it was three a.m. Rose put the novel down and changed into coveralls and snow boots. She went out onto the front porch and paused to let the cold pass through her before she had to walk through it. The snow glittered in the moonlight, its soft curves perfect in their silent hovering along the pumpkin vines and pine trees. Rose breathed the cold in, setting it against the coffee that was starting to warm its way into her bloodstream, and finally, she got back to work. She spent the last hour of her short morning outside, shoveling the wet-heavy snow off the drive and digging her truck out of the makeshift snow caves. She shoveled until her hands were frozen, her palms forming blisters she could not feel. She shoveled nearly to the top of the hill on Rayburn Street, which she had to do if there was any hope of getting her old Chevy into the town proper. Rose felt the freeze on her face before she couldn't feel her face anymore. Icicles formed on her lashes before she couldn't see anymore. They ran down her cheeks before she knew they started as tears.

At four a.m., Rose was done with her morning chores. She separated the logs in the fireplace, snuffing them with ash. She splashed water on her face, put on her work dress, and carried Benny to the truck, still wrapped in the quilt from her bed. She held Pearl's hand, half asleep, and guided her to the passenger seat. It was time to take the children home. Time to put them to bed in their own rooms, where they could wake up when the sun was already high-set—a regal king far past his dawning—and make their way back into the steady routine of their lives. At least that is what Rose said to the stars as she climbed behind the wheel of the truck.

†

Pearl saw flashes of the silent drive home, viewing the transition from Rose's cabin to Henshaw's boarding house as miniature images through a telescope. She saw the stars go fuzzy— the waning moon a sloppy grin— as the night sky came in and out of her blinking view. The truck's thin-paned windows rattled in their frames over each bump. Pearl saw the door open through the sound of the lock unlatching, the hinges groaning with freeze. She saw

Henshaw's plaid slippers because her head hung so low with exhaustion. Pearl did not remember the truck jack-knifing when it slipped on the icy hill of Rayburn Street, or the curse and prayer Rose said after it happened. She did not remember Rose carrying Benny to his bed or tripping over a pair of boots in the hallway outside of her room. She did not remember the smell of coffee brewing, the smudgy juice cups on the table, the bottle of whiskey off the shelf. The telescope images of the transition of time were collected slides Pearl would put on a shelf in the far back of her mind, letting them gather dust in their simplicity. The silent transitions of her life had no bearing—not since she moved to the Swallows—not in the heart of her hauntings.

As Pearl sleepwalked to bed and found shelter in the cave of her blanket, she sunk immediately down the well of her dreams. Dropping slowly through the thickening blackness of her consciousness, her legs found ground, her knees bearing the gravity of a fall she could not feel. It was a sunny-green day. The light was strange, like when Dorothy opened the black and white door and walked into the technicolor dream of Oz. The colors were candied, too sugary sweet to ring true. Pearl was next to the jumping cliff at Silver Lake. The beach was short and sloped steeply as it approached the giant boulders and rock formations that jutted along the shore.

At points, the stones stretched far out into the water—farther than Pearl could see— their curves a crooked line of headstones. There were jagged glaciers bobbing across the lake, the sun melting their edges into daggers. Between the glaciers and lines of stones, thousands of swans floated atop the water— slowly— as if they were dreaming. Their long necks fallen to their sides. Their heads bobbing along the water like kites at the end of a string. Not one called to another. The sound and stillness of Silver Lake so crowded that it created a deep sense of unease in Pearl. She felt her stomach lurch, her skin shiver as it brought a thousand goosebumps to the surface. Something else was there. On the opposite shore, a small hut was tucked into a clearing beneath the trees. The hut had no windows. Its roof sloped deeply toward the only edge Pearl could see. The door was propped open. The chimney burned black smoke into the veil of trees. Pearl squinted into the small space of the hut's doorway, so far away. She could see movement, a swinging that blocked out the fire, back and forth, back and forth. A body in a rocking chair. There was nothing else on the beach. Pearl decided to head to the tree line, the hut, to see whoever it was that lived on the edge of Silver Lake's shore. As she started on her way, Pearl heard a shuffling on the water. Along the crooked line of footstones that traveled across the belly of the lake, there was a woman. Her long tan legs were bare beneath her plaid dress. Her hair was a halo of soft curls that seemed to move by their own breeze. It was Pearl's mother. Pearl called to her, but Diane did not turn. Instead, she watched the swans, their necks broken. The shuffling was the sound of her hand pulling pieces of bread from a sack. The tiny white loaves floated like snow along the surface of the lake, crowding the swans, the glaciers, the stones. Pearl called to her mother but could not hear her own voice. She screamed, the goosebumps vibrating along her throat and cheeks, but still. Nothing. Pearl ran back to the boulders, back to the path of headstones that crossed the lake. She ran, balancing on her toes. Diane came closer and closer into view. Her eyes were bruised, her throat like the swan's, sitting strangely on her shoulders, ringed in shades of red.

Diane turned to Pearl, finally. She smiled—grandly—and waved like a debutant. Pearl blinked. Diane was gone. In the doorway of the hut, a man came outside. He was bigger than the hut. He stooped to get through the doorway. Pearl could hear his heavy boots cracking the twigs beneath his weight. "Where's my mother?" She called. The man watched her, propped against a tree. He tossed stones into the lake, like bread. The stones made a heavy sound before they sunk beneath the lake's surface. Pearl slowly walked back to the beach, walked back to her bedroom, sand sticking to the cuffs of her jeans.

†

The late morning sunlight was vibrant and clear, its prismatic brightness catching the dust motes that silently floated through the space of Pearl's room. Over her bed hung a *Creature from the Black Lagoon* movie poster. The monster's fat-finned head peeked over the delicate woman in a white swimsuit and watched Pearl like a doting mother.

"Alright, alright, I'll get up," Pearl told the creature, her hair a nest of knots she sloppily pushed from her face. "Was it you at Silver Lake last night? Did you take my mom?"

She eyed the monster. His fat plastic lips hung open in a stunned, mouth-breathing response.

"Don't look at me like that. You know it makes sense," she said, "Blah, I don't want to wake up— please don't make me." Pearl rolled back into the cave of her blanket, seeing the sunlight commandeer her room through the loose weaves. She listened for the sounds of the morning news or spoons clanging on the kitchen table, bacon grease

popping in the skillet, or Benny's soft trill as he told some
story about staying at Rose's cabin. But she heard none of
those things. Rather, there was a shuffling. The sound of
cabinets being swung open and closed, a chair being
pushed in. A deep and muffled voice. Her mother's high-
pitched laugh.

"There she is," Pearl said to the creature as she pulled
herself out of bed and slouched to the door. "I'm sorry I
accused you, but you must get it all the time."

Pearl made her way into the hall, where the voices grew
louder. She heard her mother talking in a sing-song way,

the kind of voice she used when she was making
something magical happen, like Cinderella's fairy
godmother, spinning wonder out of nearly nothing.

"We won't need all that," a man said as Pearl passed
the framed photo of Henshaw's wife, her blonde bouffant
and kind eyes tilted toward the camera, her forehead
pressed against the glass.

"It's no trouble— and we'll be happy to have it," Diane
said as Pearl rounded the corner into the living room.

All of the shades were drawn, the framed photos of
Henshaw's family still asleep in their brass rectangles. The
only light on was the small bulb over the stove, which was
where Diane stood, holding a metal coffee thermos.

"Morning mom, why's it so dark in here?"

"Hey, Pearl. Sorry we woke you — I was trying to be
quiet. Benny is still asleep, but when he gets up, there is a
new box of cereal in the cupboard. I picked it up
yesterday."

"Where's Henshaw?"

"Oh, him— he left all in a huff this morning, mad about
something. I'm surprised he didn't wake you the way he

was carrying on. He said he was going fishing and wouldn't be back for a while."

"You know what he was pissed off about," a voice in the dark said.

Diane shook her curls and smiled.

Pearl looked around the murky space of the room to find the man with the low voice. He looked like a shadow on the wall. Dressed in all black, he stood by the front door, his large hand resting on the knob. He was taller than the doorframe, his bulk amplified by a winter coat and leather boots. His long hair veiled the sides of his face as he stared at Diane in the kitchen, filling the thermos with the last of the coffee and cream.

"What're you up to?" Pearl asked.

"Oh—" Diane looked over at the man by the door as she screwed the cap onto the thermos and stuffed it into her backpack. "We are going to hike Dark Canyon, around Rough Lock Falls and the Devil's Bathtub."

"We should probably get going," the man said to Diane.

"Can me and Benny come? I can get him ready real fast," Pearl pled. Saturday was Diane's day off—the weekends were always easier because that's when the high schoolers worked— and she usually packed Pearl and Benny into the Oldsmobile for some kind of secret outing— a movie in Spearfish or swimming at the lake, bowling, once to a bonfire with Eve, a flea market in Cheyenne, sometimes the mall in Casper where they'd eat ice cream and donuts and throw pennies into the fountain.

Diane looked at the mass by the door again. She gave him another sly smile, her cheekbones cutting the light from half her face. This was the painter from the diner, Pearl realized. This was the man Rose mentioned yesterday afternoon when Pearl went to her house, when Pearl had worse things to worry about. A dark sadness swept through Pearl's shoulders and chest, tightening the air in her lungs. This was where Diane had been since Thursday night. Since she put Pearl and Benny on Frank Turner's bus and everything bad started happening. Pearl remembered the faraway look on Diane's face when the bus drove away, the burn spot on her apron, how small she looked in her plaid dress.

"There's no room in Tom's Jeep. And you know my car hasn't been working right—it couldn't make the trip out there, not if there's ice on the road." Diane turned to the kitchen table and stacked the last of the sandwiches and fruit into her bag.

"It'll all melt off by noon," the painter said.

"But we haven't seen you in a while," Pearl complained.

Diane zipped up the backpack and put it on her shoulders. "I'll be back by dinner time. We can go out for pizza, or over to the diner. We'll spend the whole night together."

The painter sucked his teeth.

Diane giggled. "Well, most of it—and maybe Tom'll come too."

†

Pearl opened the shades when her mom and the painter walked out the door. The sunlight reflected off the melting snow, making the yard and pebble driveway look like a sandy beach, the blue sky high and clear behind it. The painter's Jeep was shiny as a black pearl, its newness making the whole view from the window seem like a magazine advertisement or movie poster. If only Diane was in a swimsuit instead of a parka, wearing the same red plastic wayfarers, her curly hair making its own sunshine around her face. The painter as the *Creature from the Black Lagoon,* Diane as the woman in white. Pearl watched her mother hitch her spidery legs into the bucket seat and close the door. She watched her mother lean into the painter and kiss his neck before nuzzling his chest. The painter kissed her forehead and turned the ignition, the Jeep's lights glaring at Pearl, a spotlight in reverse, highlighting her aloneness as she watched Diane leave.

When Benny woke up, Pearl clanged the breakfast spoons and brewed the coffee. She turned on cartoons and made everything as festive as she could, even though it was only Benny and her, alone on a Saturday morning, with no adventures set before them.

"Where's momma?"

"She had to leave for a little while, but she said we'd go out for pizza tonight when she gets back."

"Can we get pineapple pizza this time?"

"I'm sure mom'll order you a slice, but she wouldn't put the rest of us through that torture."

Benny smiled.

Sesame Street was on television in the living room. Pearl watched Elmo's arms and legs jolt from Benny's ears and neck, as the red monster danced out the alphabet song behind his back.

"I miss momma," Benny said, putting down his spoon.

"What do you want to do today?" Pearl poured two more heaping spoonfuls of sugar into her coffee and stirred it slowly. She'd been drinking coffee since she was eleven years old. Since Benny was born and her mother worked overnights and late nights, since it became Pearl's business to wake up every pale blue morning and get Benny ready for school.

"Where'd she go?" asked Benny.

Pearl sighed. "She went out to Dark Canyon."

"Then let's go there too."

"You know we can't— we don't have a way to get there. And even if we did get all the way out there, we'd never find her. You know how big Dark Canyon is."

Benny picked up his cereal bowl and slurped the dregs of chocolate milk, hiding his face from Pearl.

"Don't be upset, Bens. We'll do something fun. Don't we always have fun?"

Benny did not say anything as he set his bowl into the sink and went to the living room. Pearl followed behind, finding him on the sofa, hiding beneath his Scooby-Doo blanket.

"I miss mom too, Benny. I tried to get her to take us, but she said she couldn't. I told her we hadn't seen her in a while, and that's when she said we'd go out for pizza."

"Why's it always just us?" Benny's voice was muffled from beneath his blanket.

"Oh, Bens. I don't know. But if you weren't here—" Pearl altered her voice into one of an old ghoul. "— I'd be all alone— wandering the Earth— looking for Dr. Frankenstein."

Benny laughed and jumped out from beneath his blanket, imitating the Frankenstein monster's lurch across the living room. "Let's go—to—the library—and hunt—some ghosts!" Benny crooned back to Pearl.

✝

The Fullmouth Library was the greatest living monument of the Swallows. Constructed in 1920 by the private funding of the Rains family, the library's collection amassed to such enormity, that in the 1940s, when the Black Mountain gold had all but disappeared from the region and the town could no longer support a sizeable public building, the library was relocated from the original Custer Day schoolhouse and into the vacant opulence of the town hall building.

The town hall's original four stories of pale green mineral stone were mined from the Black Mountains and far too immense for the library's needs, so only the first two floors of the building were occupied. The two upper floors were left to the overall largesse of empty stories, the dark stairwells and labyrinthine halls echoing at the slightest footfall. Pastor Hall and the congregants of Righteous Dei Lutheran Church had worked for years to get the third and fourth floors opened as a community center for General Education and parenting classes, teen worship, and addiction recovery meetings, but to no avail. The town and church could not fund it, and the Rains family had never offered up their coffers.

Further, the Rains family had given their final answer on the subject of the community center by way of Pookie Rains, Bessie Rains' mother. When Pookie was near death and tucked comfortably into her crumbling mansion, before reciting the Last Rites, Pastor Hall entreated her to will a sizeable donation to Righteous Dei, which would then be used to open the third and fourth floors of the library. Pookie grimaced. "Wealthy families are used to closing up wings of their houses for a spell and leaving it to one of the future generations to air out the rooms and take the sheets off the furniture," she said. Then Pookie Rains closed her eyes and never opened them again. Bessie—seventy-years-old and only airing out the closed wings of the Rains' family mansion to home the orphaned children of Fullmouth— followed the same credence as her mother. Therefore, for almost fifty years, the vacant space of the library's upper rooms gave way to housing hundreds of local and historical ghosts. The cautionary tales of their sinful lives and gruesome deaths were invented and reinvented by a half-century of Fullmouth children.

Pearl and Benny had never seen any of the library's famous ghosts, but that did not stop the fun of the hunt, especially in October, when the library all but opened the upper floors into a haunted house of sorts. Armed with their stories, the children brought homemade maps and flashlights to explore the great wilds of dust and darkness. They searched for Denny Jo the biker, or Jackie Jean his mean and jealous girlfriend, who would scratch your eyes out if you found Denny, especially if he was with some pretty blonde girl named June or Julie. Also haunting the green stone rooms of the upper library were the old town butcher, Gerard, and his friend, Thomas, the mortician. They came to be living ghouls during the Great Depression when townspeople—both living and dead— were disappearing between the hospital and morgue. After upwards of twenty citizens had gone missing, Fullmouth was sure it was Gerard and Thomas. Armed with pitchforks and firesticks, they marched on the two criminals, either catching them or not catching them in the act of desecrating a grave. The ghost stories invented grew arms and legs each year—becoming both what they were and what they could be— but the moral was always the same for children in the Swallows since time in memoriam: don't trust the people you know or the strangers you don't know.

On the walk to the library, Benny told Pearl the ghost

story he had most recently heard during lunch at Custer Day.

"—And that's where I got the idea for the skeleton vampire. No one ever saw old Rooster Jones in the daytime. No one ever saw him eat — not any of the old people who still live here. They all say that the only time they saw Rooster Jones was after the sun went down, and he was always coming out of the graveyard gates."

"That big one by the school?"

"I think so. Weird thing is no one ever saw him go in. They think he was living in one of those little old houses they put in the cemetery. You know, where dead people live?"

"A mausoleum?" Pearl asked.

"I think so."

"Then what happened?"

"People started thinking he was a vampire, and he was all skin and bones too. His clothes were all old and dirty and way too big for him. He looked like a skeleton."

"A skeleton vampire."

Benny grinned. "Maybe he's hiding out in the library now."

"It's real dark up there—dark enough for a vampire," Pearl noted.

"And there's lots of rats to eat."

"And kids that wander up there looking for ghosts."

"Them too." Benny laughed and picked up a stick, trailing lines in the melting snow.

"You're not scared to go up there?"

"Not with you." Benny stopped walking and looked up at Pearl. His sprout of hair caught the fall colors of the tree behind him, the sunlight breaking through the branches.

He gave Pearl his biggest smile. There was a small gap from one of his baby incisors that had recently been turned over to the Tooth Fairy, making his canines look even sharper, just like their mother's teeth. "If you're there, all the ghosts'll run, and it'll be like Scooby-Doo. Those ghosts'll try to run so fast, they'll run in place, and that's when we'll catch them."

Pearl laughed the kind of laugh only Benny could make. "Let's get to it then, Bens," she said.

The pale green library was towering. When Pearl stood outside the line of glass doors at the entrance and looked up, she could only see the sky overhead—like standing at the bottom of a well— and none of the Black Mountains looming. Inside the front hall, where the checkout desk was located, a cobwebbed chandelier illuminated the granite floors beneath.

"No one has a ladder big enough," Benny whispered as they walked in.

"I bet there are ten spiders heading down here right now to scoop you up for their web," Pearl said.

"Shush," the librarian sounded from behind her book at the front desk.

Pearl rolled her eyes.

Benny brushed the invisible spiders away from his head. "Can we go to the kids' room first?"

The children's library took up the entire east wing of the building and opened onto a courtyard playground that snaked along an iron fence and framed the back of the library. It was a safe space – a play place without a gate, one that could only be accessed under the intense scrutiny of the librarians: women who Bessie Rains had handpicked on her travels to Eastern Europe over the last twenty years.

Five women, all white haired with stern faces, long chins, and thin lips. They were crones as feared in the Swallows as Bessie Rains, for they were all one in the same. Their authority interchangeable. Not one of the sister librarians would hesitate to call the Sheriff to have some ruffian removed from the building and cited for disorderly conduct. And almost immediately, the reprobate would find his or her name added to an extensive "No Trespass" list kept at the front desk, most recent mugshot included. However, the black and white photos were only for the benefit of the night watchman, as the librarians knew by sight all the faces of those who could not enter the Emerald City that Bessie Rains had built.

The children's wing of the library was a world unto itself. The polished floors were muffled by thick green rugs, woven with prints of castles and mythical villages, maidens with milk pails and white horses—magical worlds narrated by Mother Goose and the Brothers Grimm. The walls were layered in shiny wallpaper like a thousand crushed jewels, glittering in different tones as the light shifted throughout the day. There was a great Oak tree constructed in the center of the room. The wide trunk was a reading nook that was stuffed with pillows and reached far up into a canopy of ladders and limbs. The animal hollows were windows, and tiny white lights hung through the branches and leaves, like fireflies in the summer. On the wall opposite the window was a substantial fireplace, the stones engraved and set in chronological order to illustrate the story of Hansel and Gretel. A part of the myth's narrative was carved into the mantel: *Be comforted, dear little sister, and sleep in peace, God will not forsake us.*

The children's library was nearly deserted, save one girl reading a book at a table near the fireplace. Her dark hair was neatly parted and fell into thick plaits, reaching far below the chair back. Pearl could see the thin gold chain circling the girl's neck, the small cross at its clasp, as she approached. The girl was leaning over a heavy book, the pages gold-edged and so substantial they laid open on their own.

"Hi—"

The girl jumped, banging her leg on the underside of the table.

"I'm sorry, Ruby. I didn't mean to scare you."

"Oh, it's alright." Ruby rubbed her knee and looked up at Pearl. "My grandma says I shouldn't be so jumpy all the time. She says I'm always acting like a kitten in a bathtub, whatever that means."

Pearl laughed softly, so as not to draw attention from the sentries of librarians. "I get that way too, especially lately. I feel like I'm always looking over my shoulder."

Ruby frowned. "I heard about that."

Pearl sat down in the strict-backed chair across from Ruby. "What'd you hear?"

Ruby pulled the sleeves of her red sweater into her hands and put her elbows on the table— hands hiding her mouth— and shook her head. Pearl knew Ruby could not say the names of the two boys.

"You heard about John-Boy and Derry then?"

Ruby nodded.

"Yeah," Pearl exhaled and leaned back into the uncomfortable chair. "It's getting pretty bad, I guess. I don't know. I don't even know why it's happening. It seems like the whole town knows that those two are after me, but no one is doing anything about it."

"I know that." Ruby moved one of her fists from her face and banged it against the table, the crack so loud Pearl saw Benny's shoulders tense from across the room. "It seemed like I heard warnings for weeks— wherever I went, even in church. They put me on the prayer list like I was already a gone cause. Acting like I could do something about those two on my own. But I couldn't." Ruby pulled at the gold chain on her neck until she could clutch the small cross in her fist. "The Lord only gave me the strength to deal with it, not to stop it. I didn't have a chance."

"Your name has come up almost every time someone in town warns me about John-Boy and Derry, but no one will tell me what happened. They just say, 'Be careful— you know what happened to Ruby Teller.'"

"Like I'm a ghost or something. As soon as it was out that those two were after me, everything changed. Everyone treated me different, looked at me different. I was born here, you know. But they were too. The town chose them over me. Everybody was too scared of them, and probably Frank too, to help me out."

"Like that Shirley Jackson story we read in Lippincott's class."

"The Lottery?'" Ruby grinned, her two front teeth slightly gapped and bent in, like two dancers bowing to one another. "I shouldn't think that's funny, but it's true. I've been trying to wrap my head around it this whole time, and that's probably the best answer I've heard. I was an easy sacrifice for the town. Fullmouth gave me up and then moved on, pretending nothing happened."

"I'm so sick of that—everyone pretending nothing's happening."

"Me too. My grandma says I'm too small for my own good. She isn't lying. I was an easy target. To tell you the truth, I'm a little surprised they've been bothering you."

"Why's that?"

"I don't really know how to say it. You're just strong, like you know what's happening and you know how to handle it, and you're one of the fastest runners in P.E. And you always know the answers to Lippincott's questions."

"I sure don't feel that way. Everything feels like it's changing—just like you said." It wasn't just John-Boy and Derry. Pearl thought about the ghost mothers and Rose, the orphans and her mom, how all her connections to the world seemed to be either frantically growing or frantically disintegrating. "Do you think John-Boy and Derry have anything to do with what is happening to the women in this town?"

"The suicides?" Ruby asked.

"Yeah, but what if they're not suicides?"

Ruby shut her book and leaned her elbows on its cover. "It wouldn't surprise me if those boys—or even Frank—got wrapped up in something with those women. Everyone knew they liked to party and have a good time. My grandma says they were always like that, since they were kids. She says she'll tell me some story about Cindy Stewart and Molly Boutell when I'm older, but I'm sure it's just about sex and drugs, and probably Frank Turner." Ruby clutched her cross in her palm again. "But I think they probably made a suicide pact."

"Why?"

Ruby looked out the window, still holding her golden cross. "Sometimes it gets too hard out here, like it'd be better just to lay down and let go. I thought about that after what happened to me—and all that, that was about power. Those two have something over me now—they got power. If they drove those women to suicide, or if they were a part of their decision, it wouldn't surprise me. But I don't think they're killers. They like having that power and watching it working on others."

"How long were they after you before it happened?"

Ruby shivered. "I don't know if that's the worst part— sometimes I think it is. It's probably the part that makes me the most angry. It went on for weeks. It seemed like they were everywhere I went. I could hear John-Boy's creepy whistling when I was at the park or headed into church. It got to be where I was hearing it, even when it wasn't there. I'd be in the shower, hearing him. In my room. I got to be so scared. I was never alone— not once all those weeks— not even the night they found me."

"You felt like they were stalking you?"

"Hunting me."

"I heard that whistle last night when we went to Big Bear. John-Boy was in the park. The thing is, I'm mostly always alone. If I'm not with Benny, it's just me."

Ruby turned around to look at Benny. He was sitting cross-legged in the mouth of the tree trunk, surrounded by Batman and Scooby-Doo Early-Reader books. She turned back to Pearl. "Benny can't help you. It won't make any difference to those two if he is there or not."

"I know it. They came on us walking home from school the other day."

"You got out of it?"

"It was Benny that did it. He made Derry laugh and we ran— slammed right into Bessie Rains."

"John-Boy's probably mad about that."

142

"I can't imagine it'd make things any worse." Pearl shifted her body in the chair and watched Benny. "I'd rather Benny not be there."

"You can't really help when it happens—you can just count on the fact that they're coming for you."

Pearl nodded. The light in the library had shifted, slamming harshly against the rugs and bookshelves, washing out Benny's face, his mouth and eyes. The sunlight was so bright it absolved all color from anything it reached and only left something painful to look at in its wake.

✝

Pearl and Benny spent the rest of the afternoon wandering the cavernous third floor of the library, tracking their paths through the shoe prints they left in the dust.

"It's not as dark as I thought it'd be," Benny whispered, the flashlight bouncing in his hand.

"Me neither. I thought it'd be like wandering into a cave toward the center of the Earth," replied Pearl.

"And bats maybe."

"Roaches."

"Human-sized spiders."

"I bet the ones downstairs are bigger than the ones up here," Pearl remarked.

"If the ghosts are here, it's too bright to see them."

"Your vampire-skeleton costume will be scarier than this."

Benny kicked at the dust. "This isn't scary at all."

"What do you want to do, Bens?"

"Let's go home and wait for momma."

✝

The gold Oldsmobile was in the driveway, and it did not mean anything. Pearl tried to tell Benny as much

143

before he got too excited, but he still ran through the unlit house, looking for Diane in each room, hoping she was watching a soap opera and folding laundry, painting her face or her nails— anything to pass the time while she waited for Pearl and Benny to get back home. Benny always imagined Diane like that: always on the other side of the door, just waiting for him to open it. Willing her to be there. And Benny was sure his will would make it so, like his mother was a light show, all spectacle and brightness. A technicolor starshine in a black sky that gave life and meaning to everything else. But opening door after door in Henshaw's house, it was apparent that Benny's vision of Diane was not true. At least not this time. Pearl and Benny walked through each silent room, and by the time they reached Pearl's bedroom at the back of the house, stuffed only with stale air behind her closed door, they were nearly convinced they were the only two people who still lived there. Finally, from her bedroom window, Pearl saw Henshaw in the backyard. He was standing at his workbench, using a curved knife to carve into the speckled skin of a large trout. When he separated the gory entrails from their shiny suit, he tossed them into a bucket by his boots and carefully packed the dissected fish into ice. Over and over, Pearl watched Henshaw complete his method for carving trout, and on the fourth stab and separation, she decided it was time to go to the backyard.

"Hi, Mr. Henshaw," Pearl called as she closed the splintered backdoor.

Henshaw turned away from his knife and his fish and eyed the two children. He sighed heavily and turned back to his work. Over his shoulder, he said, "Have you been alone all day?"

Benny's eyes were glass, the thick panes of tears only held back by the dam of his thick eyelashes. He reached for Pearl's hand.

"We spent the day at the library," she said.

"You left the kitchen a mess."

"I put me and Benny's dishes in the dishwasher before we left," Pearl answered.

"Then your mother left the kitchen a mess."

"I don't know anything about that."

"Isn't today her day off?"

Pearl kicked a stone stuck in the dirt at her feet. It landed near the chicken coop, by the wire door where all the hens were crowded, restless with hunger. It was suppertime. Pearl's stomach growled, and she remembered that she forgot about lunch. She had forgotten to feed Benny. Her cheeks blushed with the failure of forgetting the most necessary of things. "She's always off on Saturday," Pearl said, her voice cracking.

"And you stayed with Rose the night before last?"

Pearl nodded, but Henshaw could not see her.

"And then you came home early this morning because Rose had to open the diner, and your mother left you alone again, this whole day?"

Pearl nodded again. She knew it was not a question meant for answering, and she knew Henshaw was witness to her small family life. He saw how it constantly disassembled, how the separations between Diane and her children were often too long, how Pearl mostly took care of Benny. Just that morning, before Diane left with the painter, she told Pearl that Henshaw was angry and stormed out of his own home. Henshaw was never mean to Pearl or Benny, but Pearl felt like she had just shown up at a stranger's house, just the same. Still holding Benny's hand, Pearl took a few steps toward the side gate that led back to the front yard, back on Mystic Avenue, just in case she and Benny needed an escape. Dusk was still an hour or so off, and if they had to, Pearl could get Benny to The Gaslight before nightfall. Rose would feed them, and it'd be warm at the diner.

As Pearl's mind wandered along the outer edges of a fallout plan, she watched Henshaw cut into another trout and dump the knotted intestines into a bucket. He set his knife down, wiped his hands on a blood-stained rag, and turned around to look at the two children, his eyes taking a second to track them near the gate. Their faces were drawn, their eyes wide with worry. "Did you eat today?"

"Benny had cereal for breakfast," Pearl said, "but we haven't been home since then."

"We were supposed to meet momma to go out for pizza," Benny whimpered. "I was gonna get pineapple on mine."

"When was this?" Henshaw asked.

"When she was leaving this morning, she said she'd be home for dinner, and we'd all go out for pizza."

"You saw her this morning?"

Pearl nodded.

Henshaw threw his rag at the worktable, but it missed the weathered boards and fell into the gut-bucket. "You spoke with her?"

Pearl nodded again.

"Was that man still with her?"

Benny looked up at Pearl, his cheeks tear-glazed. Pearl did not tell him about the man who left with Diane. "Yes," she said.

"And she still left with him?" Henshaw's voice boomed. The chickens clucked loudly in response, scratching frantically at the dirt.

Pearl watched the coop fill up with dust, the hens' ragged wings and small heads interchangeable in all that sound. She did not want to answer any more questions about Diane. Pearl did not want to talk about how her mother was, how she sometimes did this. How in the last town, Diane's best friend— Eve— was the one who took care of Pearl and Benny when Diane disappeared into the hillbilly bars on the edge of town, or when she disappeared on the weekends with a new boyfriend. Eve took care of them for a long time until she wouldn't do it anymore. Then Eve left, so Diane packed up the Oldsmobile and headed to Fullmouth. Now it was Rose and Henshaw who took Eve's place, but mostly it was Pearl. And this was the first time Pearl had to talk about it. Eve was witness to Diane's coming and going. Her leaving or staying. But Eve never pressed Pearl about it. Henshaw searched Pearl's face, his eyes narrow as a buzzard. He knew Diane packed up everything for a new start, but he did not know she did it in the middle of the night after one man and then another stopped coming by, stopped having breakfast in his shorts and boots, drinking black coffee at the kitchen table. Stopped forking scrambled eggs into his bearded face while Benny watched cartoons, and Pearl watched Benny, avoiding the man's gaze.

"Alright," Henshaw declared. "I'm sorry—I just, I don't understand it. You two are good kids, smart and good to each other, God help you. And you do your best, Pearl, but you can't do it all. Now, don't cry, Benny. I'm sorry I scared you. Your mother will be home soon, and it'll all be worked out." Henshaw shook his head. "Now, let me get cleaned up and we'll go inside and cook up some supper." Henshaw held up the ice bucket. "A fish fry," he said as Pearl and Benny frowned at the ground. "Can you two feed the chickens while I finish up here?"

Pearl nodded. Benny followed her to the chicken coop and the garbage can that stood next to it. Inside there was a milk jug cut into a scoop. "You want to be the one distracting the chickens, or do you want to be the one feeding them?" Pearl asked Benny.

"I'm probably better at distracting," Benny answered. He looked up at Pearl and grinned, his face puzzle-pieced together by tear tracks. "I'll just go in there and bark like a dog, chase them in a circle for a little bit while you surprise them with the food."

"Sounds good." Pearl leaned into the garbage can and filled the scoop. "You okay?"

"Yeah," Benny said, "Momma always comes back." And with that, Benny turned to the coop and waited for Pearl to open the door.

†

Pearl waited up for Diane. After dinner, she washed the dishes and ran a bath for Benny. She played blocks in his room, building kingdoms with gauntlets and moats, a medieval land for a dinosaur king and his dragon enemies. After the kingdom had lost most of its battalion to enemy fire-breathing, Pearl read Benny stories. Most every one of Benny's books was about adventure and danger, about obstacles overcome within twenty pages, ripened by boldly colored, black-framed illustrations of heroes and monsters. And when she'd read through all of these and Benny had yet to fall asleep, Pearl told her own stories, plucking from her mind's eye the heroes and monster both she and Benny knew. Pearl set her scenes in places they'd often been together, telling funny little narratives of easy problems and big fun that made Benny laugh until he curled onto his side— his eyelids a sluggish purple— and fell asleep. Pearl turned on his moon lamp and rain box. The color and sound softened the darkness when she closed his bedroom door.

At nine o'clock, Diane was still not home. Pearl wanted to worry, wanted to think Diane was in trouble, that she and the painter were lost in Dark Canyon, that he misjudged the sturdiness of a rock ledge, or maybe she got mad and decided to walk home the fifteen or so miles it would take to get back to Fullmouth. But Pearl knew better. She could picture Diane in a barroom, the air stale-smoked, the walls wood-paneled. She saw the light of the fluorescent red beer signs, the reflection of the liquor bottles in the bar back mirror, all lighting Diane's red-lipped, wide-grinning face. Through the frames of Diane's red wayfarers, Pearl saw the low tin roof and pool tables. Diane took off her coat and sweater and slinked to the jukebox in a camisole and tight jeans. She danced with a beer in her hand while the painter watched, while other men looked over their date's shoulders and watched her too. Diane loved that feeling of power, the queen bee with all the honey— and Pearl could feel it—the energy of all those eyes, all that hunger. The feeling made Pearl furious. She tried to yell into her mother's ear, to form a feeling of guilt, but Diane just kept laughing and dancing, chain-smoking cigarettes for dinner as the clock ticked closer to closing time. So, Pearl pulled her mind away from Diane's. She constructed a wall of sound as she sat with Henshaw in the living room and watched the old black and white shows of his childhood, waiting for her mother to return home.

At two a.m.— hours after Henshaw had gone to bed— white headlights rushed into the darkened living room. Pearl heard the Jeep doors slam, the sloppy footfalls and laughter as Diane and the painter ambled to the front porch. She heard her mother whisper, "Shh," and laugh as the keys rattled against the door, scratching at the wood before finding the lock. Pearl sat alone, waiting. And when Diane and the painter fell into the living room, their arms and legs reaching out of a single body of curves and sighs, Pearl kept her eyes on the coffee table. She heard the kissing and shuffling of coats as she stared at the headline of the *Black Mountain Daily News*: SUICIDE CRISIS in bold black lettering, thick and resounding as a line of marble tombstones. Boots thunked against the back of the couch, the rattle of a belt buckle, the slip of leather pulled from straps. Diane's muffled giggle. Pearl glared at the newspaper. Beneath the headline, a row of photos, printed like trading cards. Cindy Stewart, Molly Boutell, Kaia Goodwin, Maggie Teller, and Karen Kelly. In the dark living room, their black and white faces looked haunted. Their smiles hung like hooks. Their eyes drooped. The dead mothers watched Pearl, watching them. They watched Pearl keep her eyes off her own mother, who had all but forgotten about her daughter. Diane was pressed against the back of the couch, on the side opposite Pearl. The kissing was faster, fevered. The laughter had stopped. The painter loomed over Pearl, his face digging into Diane's, his hair covering them both like a veil. At the end of the row of dead mothers, next to the photo of Karen Kelly, there was a black box. Inside the black box was a white question mark. The question mark glowed in the dark room. It lifted off the page and set itself upright on the coffee table. The painter lifted Diane from the back of the couch and carried her into the black cave of the hallway. Diane sighed as she floated out of the room. The whole thing felt like a dream. The kind where you want to say something, but no sound comes out. The kind where you want to be seen, but you're not. Diane came home, finally. She came home with no thoughts in her mind beyond the only one she'd been sustaining for days: the painter. Pearl thought of Benny and all the lies she had to tell him. She thought of Henshaw and all the things she hoped he would not say. In some ways, Diane was already a ghost. She was never there but always talked about. She affected Pearl and Benny, but not in any way beyond cereal in the cupboard and her car in the driveway. She haunted Pearl and Benny with their waiting, with future dates unfulfilled. Or was Pearl the ghost? Diane and the painter were just there, and neither of them saw her. Her mother could not feel her presence. Pearl moved through life, carrying responsibilities like chains around her shoulders, bearing the weight of some sin she was not sure of. The question mark floated above the newspaper, above the faces of the five dead mothers. Pearl put on her boots, tightening the laces before knotting them. She put on her gloves, thoughtfully pulling each one over the wrists of her sweater. She put on her winter hat and her coat. She took her time with the buttons, still waiting for Diane to come out of her bedroom. For Diane to see her, to say something. To hug her and guide her to the kitchen table. To pull the hat from her head and tell her not to be mad. To toast some Pop Tarts and brew some coffee, to say she was sorry. To talk like she used to: a Virginia Slim in the hand propped against her chin, her golden eyes on Pearl. But the house was still, a stone at the bottom of a lake. Pearl put her hands to her face, pressed her palms into her cheeks, her fingers into her eyes, until she saw trails of darkness shifting beneath her lids. When she pulled her hands away, the stillness was heavier. More permanent. Pearl unlocked the front door and silently closed it behind her.

✝

The night was brighter than the house, though not by the waning moon's papery light. The thin air of Autumn shuffled the red and orange leaves in the trees, the collective movement like torch flames alighting the sidewalk. Pearl heard car doors slam and a Honky-tonk song blaring from the bar a few blocks over. A small woman walked her dog on the opposite sidewalk, the chain rattling as the dog tugged her toward a neighbor's mailbox post. The shades were pulled on all the windows, but the panes still glowed from lamps inside. Most of the porch lights were on, the fluorescent light eye-piercing and impossible to look at. Mystic Avenue was patterned with stalactites of shadows, all reaching toward the sidewalk, replicating the needles of the Black Mountains beyond.

Pearl knew the whistle would come before she heard it. She knew it was waiting—just outside the front door— even before she left the house. The wind was stronger, like crushed glass, and through its sharpened barrage, Pearl felt John-Boy's song pass through her before she caught a single note. As suddenly as the wind came on, it was gone. Only the whistling dirge remained. Pearl stopped in the street and looked around. The woman with the dog had disappeared. All the shades were still drawn. Long shadows shifted with the quivering movement of leaves. Near Bancroft Street, John-Boy walked through the darkness, his jackboots beating the street as he approached Pearl. He had a cigarette suspended from the side of his mouth; the ember bright against his cheek. The glow more sinister than the relief a warm fire could bring. Pearl kept her eyes on John-Boy, watched him drag his feet, and between the melodies of John-Boy's song, she listened for Derry on the border.

The cords and strings of her muscles tensed, sinewy and strong. Her hands were balled into gloved fists, small stones ready to throw, rigid with the want of something to do. She was certain Derry wasn't there. He would be out of the shadows by now, circling John-Boy's periphery, giving him the bulk and mass of a cratered and inelegant planet. But below John-Boy's whistling, Pearl heard another sound. A sigh and a shuffle, a whispered *hello* from beneath a dark patch of trees clustered near the street. Like sheets on a clothesline, the dead mothers gathered. Their gauzy robes and curly hair flickered in the dim moonlight.

Pearl smiled at the dead mothers. She smiled with the sureness that John-Boy was alone. His thin shoulders hunched into the cold; his leather jacket too ill-fitted to his frame. John-Boy grinned behind his cigarette, the red embers dying against his missing teeth, black cavities for his tongue to lick. Cavities that extended the hollow sound of his whistling. John-Boy was marked by a black fog, one that trailed behind him, permeating the air with the acrid smell of sulfur and decomposition. His face and hair were smeared with grease, shiny in the midnight darkness, an x upon his forehead. Pearl could see it all. John-Boy's was the kind of vicious that made the Swallows into a sinking hole, a grubby palm trapped by the skeletal fingers of the Black Mountains—a fist closing in, crushing the town, and especially the girls within it. Pearl was done with John-Boy's malevolence, done with the easy violence he carried as a constant threat. She felt the goosebumps along her skin blink open. The blinking widened as each eye rolled from the black comfort of bone and skin and turned to the outside world. The million eyes gathered like regiments, uniform and staunch, forward-facing to the enemy. Pearl felt the blinking like a shudder, like a smile, like the best joke was on its way and she was the wolf in wait. Her body was hinged—a bear trap of tight strings, vibrating with cutthroat intensity. She felt the static move along her spine. From her eyes to her ankles, it trailed in sprinting circles, each breath a mallet against an anvil, the weight flying up the meter and smashing into the bell of her mind, over and over.

"Pearly-Pearl," John-Boy called in a sing-song voice. "Looking for me? I'm looking for you."

Pearl sneered. Her lips pulled back nearly to her eyelids, the skin bunching by her ears. Her teeth were sharp mirrors, reflecting the waning moon, the line of dead mothers along the street, the million eyes upon her skin.

"Some girls look straight ugly when they smile, and you're definitely one of them. Good thing I don't like to make girls smile." John-Boy's knees buckled into a strange step, a sideways waltz in the street. He threw his hands out to keep from falling.

The dead mothers laughed. They stood in a row beneath the trees, in the dark egress outside of any porch light's reach.

"I'm a better lover with a little whiskey." John-Boy's

laugh was high-pitched and shrill.

Pearl heard the call of Cindy Stewart's nightbird echo down the avenue. The air was static, all the oxygen siphoned off by currents of electricity permeating from Pearl's body. She closed her eyes and raised her palms toward John-Boy. He was still laughing, still trying to get up from the street. Pearl felt the thin air's dramatic shift in temperature, felt the sweat rolling down her cheek. White light and white heating expanded the immediate atmosphere. Rolling thunder like a speed train barreled down from Bear Mountain, gaining power, an iron mass bearing down on John-Boy. His laughter became confused, higher pitched. He could not get up. His hands stuck in street tar, the world melting around him. The orange and red leaves were fires, high reaching. The sound was deafening. When lightning finally struck, it cratered to the earth between John-Boy and Pearl. Pearl stood in the white light as John-Boy bled from his ears and nose, the corners of his eyes. When it was over and only the thin air remained, John-Boy found his footing. A sob cut through his throat. He wiped the blood from his eyes with the back of his hand.

"You won't torment another girl in this town," Pearl hollered, her ears ringing.

The train of thunder disappeared, gathering in a cloud of ash, bearing its way down the street and up Iron Mountain, on to haunt more primordial things. The leaves ceased their trembling. They lost their firelight and became limp and curled, crudely handed things. Cindy Stewart's crow called, a gurgled and choked sound. Pearl heard the scratch of its taloned feet as it left the branches of trees— the black magic of dead queens gathered beneath its wings— and flew back to the Black Mountains, back to more primordial things. Pearl watched John-Boy rise to his feet, his ankles at odd angles in the jackboots. He dragged his feet more slowly. He used a grease rag the color of a school eraser to wipe away the rusty blood on his neck and cheeks. Pearl's heart slowed its beat. She returned her hands to her pockets and kicked at the pebbles along the street. She watched John-Boy turn the corner before she went to the dead mothers. They looked like a receiving line of debutants in their white gowns and rose crowns, the sincerity in their faces as they clapped for Pearl and shouted congratulations from beneath the shadows of trees.

CHAPTER NINE

When the Man Comes to Town

Pearl walked home with the dead mothers. In the late hours, the honky-tonk music had stopped playing from the bar down the street. Twangy guitars and pianos were replaced by the sharp and encompassing chirp of cricket wings. Porch lights and lamp lights clicked off one by one, each house falling into the sleepy grey shadows of recent darkness. With the curtains of artificial light extinguished, the stars came closer and took their places like fireflies between the bare branches of trees.

"This is the kind of night when everybody wants to sleep but nobody can," Molly said. "If the moon were brighter— full or nearly so— this is the kind of night I would've driven out to Silver Lake for a swim because I knew I wasn't going to bed."

"Or we'd all go to Rose's house. Stay up all night playing cards, then make a big breakfast at 3 a.m." Kaia sighed.

"And hike up Bear Mountain with that giant picnic basket. Eat pancakes and watch the sunrise." Maggie leaned on Kaia's shoulder.

"I miss that," Cindy said.

The moon was a thin grin, sheltered by the bright crowd of stars. Pearl imagined the Cheshire Cat taking form behind that grinning moon. Hundreds of teeth widened his mouth. The yellow stars clustered into yellow eyes. Tree branches bent into a wreath of horned ears; the brittle leaves his claws. *Anything can happen now*, Pearl thought.

Anything at all.

"What was all that back there?" Pearl finally asked.

Cindy pulled a cigarette from the folds of her gown and put it to her lips. "You really want us to go first?"

Pearl nodded.

"Well, we heard you call. When we got to your house, the living room was dark, and you were walking out the door," Cindy said.

"I didn't call."

"You thought about us," Maggie answered.

"It must've been your photos in the newspaper. All of your pictures were printed in a row on the front page of the *Black Mountain Daily.* At the end of the row, there was a big question mark."

"Who's next? Like an assembly line." Molly scoffed.

"Anyway," Cindy took a drag off the unlit cigarette and crossed her arms. "We followed you. It didn't look like you were just out for a walk, either. It looked like you knew exactly where you were going."

"You were 'late, late for a very important date'," Molly sang.

"If anyone else could actually see us, we must've looked really spooky—all of us trailing right behind you in these get-ups." Maggie pulled at her dress, adjusting the lacey sleeves.

"Like in those old Scooby-Doo episodes—all the bad guys dressed in sheets and floating around on roller skates." Maggie grinned.

"My little brother loves that show," said Pearl.

"Were you looking for John-Boy?" Karen asked.

"I guess so. I knew he'd be around. Wherever I've gone the last few days, if I listened for it, I could hear him whistling." Pearl pulled the collar of her coat up around her ears and exhaled to watch her breath's spirited escape and disappearance. The night had gone on too long. The gravity of the moon and inky sky, the restless trees and empty streets leaned their sleepy weight onto Pearl. She bore it slowly, her steps heavy.

"So, you left your house—" Cindy started.

"In the middle of the night," Karen interrupted.

"In the middle of the night, to go find some boy—"

"A monster who has a reputation for raping girls in this town," Kaia declared.

"And do what?" Cindy pulled the cigarette from her mouth and flicked the invisible ash.

The stars were cut glass suspended in the cold night air. Pearl sighed. "I wanted to stop him. To stop all of this. I was so angry, and so much is happening that I can't do anything about." Pearl gestured to the row of dead mothers walking down the street, to the town, the mountains. "I knew I could at least do something about John-Boy."

Kaia whistled. "You did something alright."

"Practically stabbed him through the eyeballs with a lightning bolt." Molly laughed.

"Which was a shock, after seeing all those teeth you suddenly grew. I thought you'd rip right into him," said Maggie.

"You mean, you didn't make any of that happen?" Pearl asked.

Cindy smirked and shook her head. "We can't even turn a doorknob, let alone light a cigarette. That was all you, Pearl. You're the one talking to ghosts and calling down thunderstorms."

✝

Pearl's home was as she left it. The painter's jeep was in the driveway, parked behind her mother's Oldsmobile. Across the yard, snow melted into the crabgrass, frozen miniature ponds in spots, muddy bogs in others. Empty flowerpots lined the front of the house. The shades were drawn; the front door locked. Every part and every person in the house was hunkered down into sleep, curled up and dreaming against the early hours of Sunday morning.

Pearl left her wet boots on the porch and walked through the living room in her socks. She heard Henshaw snoring on the other side of his bedroom door as she passed his wife's photograph in the hall. Pearl did not know his wife's name, but she would know her face anywhere. Her blonde curls pressed against the glass. Her face turned toward Henshaw's night sounds, smiling into the dark. Pearl waved goodnight to Henshaw's wife as she pulled off her gloves and opened her bedroom door. Her bedroom was the same as it had been that afternoon when she and Benny had searched for Diane and finally found Henshaw in the yard. The plum shades were dark shadows, the moon too dim to climb through the sheer folds of fabric. Pearl's bookbag was slack beneath her desk, the math book a bleached tongue, dry with disuse. Her chair was covered in comic books and dirty laundry, her alarm clock buried beneath the stack. She took off her dirty clothes—caked with dust and ash—and put on an old baseball jersey. She climbed into bed, too tired to brush her teeth, to take a shower. She stared at her yellow walls, sure they had further fallen in, the crumbling rocks of a cave, sinking closer and closer the more earthquakes that came. The day felt like it lasted the entire span of the Dark Age—dim and rocky, crags and lava, monsters emerging from volcanoes and mountain lakes, from thorny deserts and mildewed forests. Monsters lived in every land yet to be explored. And nothing had been explored, ever, not back then, not before fire and the imitation shadows it made. There were thick animal skins, fearsome night sounds in the light of day, the curved bones of rib cages baking in the dry sun. Tall, chalk-skinned trees, their leaves and branches too high to climb, too out of reach to see anything.

Pearl wandered into the desolate landscape of her dreams. The horse was dappled grey but lame. His face and hips were narrow, the harness and saddle too big. The horse's spine sagged beneath the weight. The sun was sickly-bright, carving out the shadows of the rocks. Pearl climbed down from the horse, her boots briefly snuffing out the shimmering silver of mica scattered like breadcrumbs along the path to Wonderland Cave. She pulled his reins toward the small pond near the cave's mouth, tying the leather straps to a painted sign, the red arrow still wet. Pearl heard laughter echo from the darkness of the cave and settle into the blinding sun. She covered her eyes with her palm and peered into the cave's mouth, watching the shapes of thin men—their backs bent and beards skimming the dirt—reflected in firelight shadows on the cave walls. The lame horse neighed behind her, kicking his feet against the ground. The horse shook his head. His yellow teeth wincing, and a trembling cascaded nose to tail. The horse could not be saved. Pearl untied the leather reins and left him at the mouth of Wonderland Cave.

Hundreds of field mice skittered across the trail, their fat bodies not moving fast enough, breaking into fire lilies as Pearl came closer. The trail was cluttered with bodies moving and not, with blossoms pulpy and not. Pearl walked slowly to avoid stepping on the mouse-blossoms, but someone was following her. The sun was bright but not hot, and hardly any wind blew the distance between Wonderland Cave and Jewel Cave, hardly any at all. Behind Pearl, she heard the sound of boots dragging a body and legs, a man too tired to keep moving, to keep climbing the path to the mountain's peak. Peal could hear the man breathing. Sometimes she could hear him inhale sharply, cough. She thought it was probably one of the bent-spined men from the cave, tripping on his beard, but she could not see him. The field mice and fire lilies turned into a field of bluebells, a bridge over a stream, now hundreds of monarch butterflies, their orange wings floating over the water and perched at the mouths of the flowers. It was here that the man began to whistle. His coughing broke into a high-pitched laugh. The dragging of his boots turned into a deliberate, quick step, and he started whistling John-Boy's song. All at once, the goosebumps on Pearl's skin emerged. She thought to hide in the field, beneath the heavy petal heads like blue velvet, and wait for the man to pass. But she could not enter there. There were too many butterflies. Their painted wings too fragile, too easily destroyed if Pearl brushed against them, if she tried to hide beneath them. And there were no trees to climb. Not there. Pearl walked faster. The field began to disappear behind her and was replaced by rock faces that reached into the sky, the needles like praying hands surrounded by rosary beads. The field mice and fire lilies— the butterflies and bluebells— were gone. In their place were infinite rocks, a path littered with pale blue eggshells like breadcrumbs—like the shimmering mica outside Wonderland Cave— fallen from the black forest firs that bent into the path and blocked out the sun as Pearl climbed. There was nowhere else to go. The man laughed again. This time it was a deeper laugh— a full one that bellowed against rock faces, vibrating the stones. The man's step was hollower, more like the narrow sound of horse hooves overgrown, long fingernails gripping into the rocks, climbing the mountain with ease. The man's song had changed too. The slow whistle transformed into a hum. It was a nursery rhyme Pearl recognized but didn't know. She kept climbing. There was nowhere else to go.

The trees became thicker, their spiky tendrils leaned into the lane, making it narrower. The pale blue eggshells were replaced by small bones, curved and dark, bones that glistened in the darkness, bones that grew in size the higher Pearl climbed. Soon there were skulls lining the dark path. Pearl walked through rib bones. The man with the hooves laughed again. He was closer. Pearl turned around, but it was too dark to see anything. Only the new bones glistened. She could hear his light breath, could feel his smile, his eyes on her shoulders and her long hair. There was nothing else to see. On the other side of the fir trees, Pearl knew there were great cliffs. What else could there be? She was almost breaking through to the summit. Ahead of her, she could see the blinding brightness, the light at the end of the tunnel, more terrifying than the cave of trees. But there was nowhere else to go. Pearl was at the end of the line, only the peak was before her. The trees were replaced by sunshine, the blue sky so low, pressing into the valleys and rock faces below. The bones were replaced by nothing. The path was worn smooth as a sea pearl. When Pearl turned back to the cave of trees, she watched the horned man appear. He was holding a book. The pages wet and bloated looking, the skin of the cover water-logged and too swollen to close.

"Pearly-Pearl," the horned man purred. His hooves clacked against the smooth stones as he approached Pearl, her back to the peak edge. "You're finally here." His eyes were missing their pupils. They were a yellowed white, the color of a rotting egg. The horned man reached out for Pearl's hand, the book of skin—red ink wet and dripping onto the smooth stones— rested against his hip.

†

Shelby woke up in the backseat of her mother's Buick. She was wrapped in the old flannel-lined, moth-eaten sleeping bag her mother always took on camping trips. Shelby plucked herself from the sleepy haze of a dreamworld and worked to pull at the threads of true memory: the hunter green roll wound to the top of her mother's hiking pack, tied with leather cord and bouncing up and down as she followed her along Lost Cabin Trail, singing Patsy Cline songs as they hiked to the peak. Knee high wool socks the color of trees— brown hiking boots so well worn, the toes curled up.

It was always warm when they went camping. They would swim in the White River, slip along the flumes, polished smooth by centuries of water traveling the span of the Black Mountains. In the summer, the light was yellow through green leaves—the speckled sound of the breeze. The air sweet. It was bluebells and afternoon thunderstorms. Afternoons when Shelby could hear the thunder rolling through the range, like a stampede. It was a double rainbow over a butterfly field—fire lilies and field mice, all the paths shimmering with silver rock and fool's gold. Shelby had never gone camping at night— she'd never set out to break ground or set up a tent, gather wood for a fire. All those things were done in the sunshine. Night camping was firelight and a hot plate. Potatoes wrapped in foil and baked beneath the fire. It was smores and ghost stories, shadow puppets on tent canvas.

And though it was dark in the backseat of the Buick, and the windows were frozen over with ice— preventing Shelby from seeing anything— she knew where she was. She was at the trailhead to Black Elk Peak - the tallest mountain East of the Rockies, at least that's what her mother always said. Shelby could hear the night owls and crickets. A cuckoo bird singing into the black forest firs. She could hear the White River rapids—the song they only sang at the trailhead, just past Wonderland Cave. Shelby knew where she was, even if she could only hear it. She'd never been camping anywhere else.

Shelby waited in the backseat for a while. She bit the skin around her fingernails and picked at her lips. She chewed the insides of her mouth and sucked on her hair. She slapped her legs when they fell asleep and when it got too cold—too cold for even the sleeping bag to keep out the numb burn of freeze. Shelby listened for the sound of her mother's boots breaking the snow. She listened for the ice scraper on the windshield. Shelby had no idea what time it was. The Buick was black-cold, a frozen igloo. She tried to fall asleep and wait for her mother to return, but every time she closed her eyes, dark shadows moved behind her eyelids, like frantically beating bat wings. What was happening? Her eyelashes were caked with ice. They were too heavy to blink. She wiped her eyes on the sleeping bag. Her cheeks were so cold they burned. Shelby tried to remember the hours before, when she was at home sleeping beneath the quilt her Grandma Bee made for her fourteenth birthday, the spinning pinwheels cut from Shelby's childhood dresses. Her mother had not spoken when she woke Shelby from her dreams and wrapped her in a coat and hat. And Shelby was sure the sleeping bag was not there when she buckled into the backseat. Did it mean something? The Buick's cabin was still black but lightening by degrees. Shelby could see the light green mittens on her hands— the glittery thread woven into them. She also saw a flashlight on the front seat. What was Shelby supposed to do? Did her mother want her to wait there and sleep, or carry supplies and follow? Shelby took inventory: hat, mittens, parka, boots, sleeping bag, and a flashlight. Her mind worked through these offerings. She tried to put them in an order that would logically point to an answer, but she kept returning to the fact that her mother had never done such a thing.

Shelby reached for the flashlight. Her bones were stiff from the long exposure to cold. She clicked on the lamp, testing its brightness. She caught her face in the rearview mirror. Her nose and cheeks were red, her lips chapped. She'd never seen her face like that. She didn't know it. She watched the light green glitter-gloved hand touch her cheek in the mirror, but she could not feel it. Something was wrong. And it would only get worse the longer Shelby stayed in the backseat of the Buick. She could foretell the future on her face: the grim mask horror movie lit by the flashlight.

It was time to leave. Time to find her mother. Shelby threw her shoulder into the car door, but the hinges and frame were frozen shut. She tried to roll down the window, but the ice was too thick on the panes. She laid across the backseat, the sleeping bag bunched behind her head, and kicked the door as hard as she could, working to break the ice loose from the seals. When she finally got the door open, a gust of wind from Wonderland Cave pushed against the car and slammed the door shut.

Shelby swore she heard laughing. The low whispers of men around a fire. She held still and listened. She only heard the owls and a cuckoo bird. The squeaking break of the black forest firs shifting in the wind. She slowly pushed the door open again. No one was there. The mouth of Wonderland Cave was dark, the pond frozen over. The glitter path of silver stone and fool's gold painted over with white. Only the red arrow pointing to the cave was visible— a shock of contrast to the neon-white world. Shelby tucked her sweatpants into her boots. She was not wearing socks and could already feel her toes curling against the freeze. She pulled her hat low over her brow and zipped her parka, tucking her gloves into the sleeves. Then Shelby wrapped herself in the sleeping bag— hiding most of her chapped face in the flannel folds— clicked on the flashlight and climbed out of the Buick.

The Buick must have been there for a while, unless there was a sudden blizzard she had slept through. Shelby did not know which hypothesis would lead to a worse outcome. The ice was nearly an inch thick on the glass, and the tires were buried in three inches of snow. There were no footpaths to follow. Either her mother was never there— and Shelby had woken up, her face misplaced, in a land that had no past or future. Or, her mother had been gone so long, the snow had filled in her footfalls, disappearing her path like it was written in invisible ink. Shelby walked to the dark pit of Wonderland Cave. The muted whisperings of hiding men rode the wind from the darkness. Shelby imagined bank robbers, escaped prisoners, or mental patients hiding out — finding refuge in the dark world of the Black Mountain caves. They would not be the first to find refuge there. Shelby swallowed her fear.

"Mom?" She called. Her voice echoed the one word into a hundred folds. Shelby called, even though she knew her mother was terrified of caves. Between her mom's bad sense of direction and the fear that a compass could not possibly work the closer it was taken toward the center of the Earth, Shelby's mom did not trust herself not to get lost, even if the tour path was well lit or marked with glow-in-the-dark paint. Shelby heard the wind laugh again. She saw the dark shadows shift like bats. She could not tell if the sounds she heard were an amalgamation of the wind, the men, and the fluttering of batwings. Or if it was something else altogether. Something she could not identify. Shelby shivered. There was no way her mother would break ground in Wonderland Cave. Shelby would have to climb to the summit. It was the only place her mother would go.

Shelby left the mountain hollow and walked past the sunken space where a small pond was frozen beneath layers of ice and snow. She imagined the minuscule animals who lived buried beneath in glacial darkness, their small bodies bared to the elements, slowly moving to stay alive. Shelby started to sing. She'd once read that distance runners sang to keep their pace, that if they could sing and run, they were okay. They were going to make it to the end. She sang, "I Fall to Pieces"— the easiest Patsy Cline standard to remember— as she navigated the trail between Wonderland Cave and Jewel Cave. The path was generally easy to negotiate, but the trail markers were defaced by snow and the path itself was thick with drifts. Every step broke through new snow and sounded like bones shattering, a pain that buried her leg nearly to her hips. It was like climbing a ladder four steps at a time, then falling three. Shelby hoped the men of the laughing wind had pulled these drifts together at the bottom of the mountain— putting the punchline before the joke—and that the snow would somehow be less deep the higher she climbed. That the laughs were those of friendly jester spirits— the old nature gods her mother liked to tell stories about— left to a modern world with nearly nothing to do. She hoped it was not men in hiding. Men of warm blood and free will. Men of violence and past histories that had resigned them to days and nights in the frozen mountains. Men whose lives had set them down right there with Shelby, right behind her, climbing a nearly impassable slope.

Shelby crossed the curved spine of the wooden bridge, the snow sinking between the planks, giving it the look of vertebrae. A sleeping dinosaur of the Ice Age. Shelby knew the pond— usually cluttered with long-winged monarch butterflies— was frozen beneath the bridge, beneath the snow that nearly reached the lower arcs. She paused to listen. The Patsy Cline music of her mind had changed. Her lone voice in the icy shelters of the immediate world had grown in breadth and fullness, had ripened into melodies. When she stopped singing, she could hear the music carry on. At first, she thought it was just the fatigue, just the fear of her situation, the bone-deep cold that was altering the patterns of her mind. But then, between the whistled melody, she heard a cough. She heard a hack and spit before the song picked up its pace again. Shelby turned in a circle but saw no one. Dusky light had splintered the vast darkness of the nightscape, but the air was still fuzzy and grey, foggy and vaporous. Shelby could not see anyone. But the song continued, and it was close.

She moved faster, pulling her knees higher to her breastplate with each step, not allowing her leg to fully find ground before hiking the next one up into a continued climb. Shelby was in the meadow—the easiest part of the Lost Cabin Trail's passage— and though she could not see the trail any longer, she could see the rock faces in front of her. The jagged shadows were looming towers, shadows more felt than seen. Shelby always thought the mountains along the meadow looked like points on a chart, connected, steadily climbing upward, easy to proximate. But in the grey fog, they looked like old men with crowns, the long beards of grey gathered around their mouths, the length trailing into the meadow. They demanded reverence. And with the whistling still behind her, gaining ground, Shelby could not concede. She could not call out, could not call for her mother, so she kept climbing closer toward the dark mouth of the mountain.

When she reached the narrow point of the passage, when the trail was hemmed in by ancient black forest firs, their depth and reach too far to find their points— too tangled to follow each limb to its end— the snow was not as deep. At least not on the forest floor. The heavy cold was tangled in the branches, suspended precariously above the trail, the weight keeping the trees from shifting. The knotted arms and spindles creaking from the weight of the bundles they carried. Shelby made fast work of the dark trail. The whistling had stopped, but now she could hear breathing, hear footsteps. It was too dark in the tunnel of firs to see. Too dangerous to stay too long, to hide between the dark bodies of trees. She could not see anything except the light at the end of the tree-lined hollow, the light that said she was near the peak. Near where her mother would inevitably be. Shelby ran as fast as she could. She could not feel her feet. Her legs burned. Snow caked and hardened onto the legs of her sweatpants.

When she finally broke out of the tunnel and into all that light, she felt relief of finally reaching the end. Finally knowing the point of the experiment. The laughing and the whistling—the cough and breathing and footsteps—were gone. It was one of her mother's ancient spirits or old gods chasing her up the mountain, forcing her forth, into the reckless courage it would take to climb to the peak with nothing to carry. Nothing to ease the suffering of climate and altitude. A forced step toward an inevitable truth. There was nothing else to hear, nothing else to wait for. Her mother's boots were on the rock ledge. Her forest green socks were stuffed into the boots, the tongue gagging on all that cotton. There were two prints in the snow: both round-heeled and deep, both slipping from the ledge of the peak. Shelby knew that when she finally looked over the ledge, who she would most likely see.

CHAPTER TEN

The Pretenders

Long after his hour of morning chores and toil, Henshaw's rooster pecked at the flowers painted on the frame of Pearl's bed. His rough claws scratched at Pearl's legs beneath the quilt until she woke and startled his sudden flight to the desk. There, he stared at her. Square-headed, the red fan atop his skull, a giant mohawk, his waddle's bright red folds menacing in their constant movement. His red eyes and narrow beak were well hidden within the fleshy helmet. Pearl could not see the rooster's eyes, but she felt them tracking her. The rooster was larger than most. Head to tail, he took up all of Pearl's desk. He kicked off a stack of comic books, pecked the pencils, their soft pink parts exposed to his sharp beak. The rooster was regal in his anger. His thick neck was the color of meringue. His collar was laced in a lion's mane, and his chest to tail feathers spangled in iridescent shades of blue and green, even in the gloom of Pearl's room.

"Why are you here?" Pearl rasped, sleep still in her throat.

The rooster chortled. His long claws clicked against the wood of Pearl's desk. He pecked at the glass of the only framed photo in the room: Diane just out of delivery, clutching tiny Pearl to her chest. Diane's smile so large it was terrifying— sharp teeth and ecstasy. A smile so big it hid her eyes and flattened her nose. The rooster pecked at Diane's cheek, at her bare shoulder.

Pearl sighed. She heard the clatter of spoons on the

kitchen table, the melodies of Benny's voice and her mother's laugh. The monotone bleat of morning news.

"It's time to go," she said to the rooster.

The rooster nodded, his waddle shaking. He kicked at a stack of magazines.

Pearl climbed out of bed the side opposite the desk. She opened the curtains and blinds, the cold sunlight flattening the bedroom's color and warmth. The window stuck, but she finally pried it open. The frigid morning wind funneled into her bedroom, catching the sheer curtains, and filling their bodies with floating ghost shapes that eventually flattened when they reached the ceiling. Pearl pushed the window screen into the yard, giving the rooster plenty of room to leave.

"I won't tell Henshaw about this, but I expect you'll be gone when I get back," she said. Pearl plucked a damp sweater from the rug in front of her dresser and left the bedroom, not once looking back to see what the rooster would do.

Cindy Stewart was waiting in the hall. Her back was arched against the bathroom doorway, her spidery legs extended to the opposite wall. The white gown was shorter on her than the other mothers. Her freckled shins always peeked out. They were girlish legs—tan and strong, buzzing with energy. They were not the legs of a ghost. But the momentary brightness of Pearl's bedroom window flooded the hallway, illuminating Cindy in a spotlight. She cast no shadow. She did not squint. Cindy sluggishly pulled herself up from the wall, the permanent accessory of the unlit cigarette dangling from her thin lips.

"You look like I feel," Cindy said. "I was going to warn you before you went in there," she tilted her chin toward the living room and kitchen, "but seeing you like this, I don't think you should go in there at all."

Pearl knew how bad she looked. She could feel the oiliness of her hair and forehead, feel the layer of grim on her skin. But her stomach growled louder than Cindy's gravelly voice. Pearl could smell the coffee brewing, hear the gurgle of water making its way through the caffeine beans and into the urn. She'd barely eaten at Henshaw's fish fry, and a lot had happened since then. She needed food and coffee before anything else.

Pearl shrugged and walked past Cindy, right into a room full of bodies: household familiars and ghost mothers, living strangers and ghost strangers. Pearl paused in the doorway. The living room and kitchen had transformed into a waiting room, the sour air siphoned off by the smell of breakfast. There were not enough places to sit.

"I tried to warn you," Cindy said as she brushed past Pearl and took a spot against the front door, her back curved away from the brass knob.

"Good morning, Pearl." Her mother was standing beside the table, smiling, a skillet of eggs in her hand. Yesterday's makeup was smudged and smoky around her eyes, gathering into the small creases at her temples. The painter anchored Diane into place with a meaty arm around her hip, his elbow suffocating the bow of her frilly apron. Here was the painter at the breakfast table: green khaki sweater stretched out around the collar; hair pulled back with a rubber band. Dirty jeans and bare feet. Legs straight, his hairy toes flat against the linoleum beneath Benny's chair. His mug more cream than coffee. The sugar bowl unlidded at his elbow. A dirty spoon on the table.

Pearl took in the parts of the scene as she flattened her body between Benny's chair and the wall, making her way to the cabinet of coffee mugs and the loaf of cinnamon raisin bread beside the toaster.

Pearl nodded to her mother as Henshaw leaned toward the television, adjusting the volume. The conversations of the living and the conversations of the dead halted simultaneously as the breaking-news graphics and overwrought jingle spurted from the television screen.

"Good morning and welcome to KOTA TV News, Sunday Edition." Chip Gordon shuffled a pile of papers on the news desk and tapped them vigorously before continuing. No longer was he Chip Gordon, rodeo cowboy, born in the back of a pickup truck. The emotional baggage Pearl witnessed him heave onto his viewership just Friday night — the strange grimace of his painted face beneath the studio lights— had been packed away. The rodeo cowboy was bad for ratings. South Dakotans did not want their man at the news desk to be one of their own. They wanted their anchor to part the clouds and drop a pin into place. They wanted Chip Gordon, Talking Head, to send someone free to toil in the muck—anyone but himself. There was a kind of hope in the separation between news and news desk, between people and narrator. And accordingly, the Chip Gordon of the Stepford Wife brigade was back. His brown hair neatly waved back from his face. His jawline crisp and straight, so large it made his mouth look like a mistake, like a small blip on the screen of his face.

Pearl filled her coffee mug and took the sugar bowl to the living room, finding space on the rug between the television and the coffee table. She moved Henshaw's

Bible to the stack of newspapers and began spooning sugar into her mug as Chip Gordon finished his vanity pause and a large graphic of pine trees wrapped in police tape— "Fullmouth Suicide Epidemic" bannered across the top— took its place in a close-up shot beside Chip Gordon's pancaked face.

"The town of Fullmouth has been coping with a suicide epidemic since early August, and doctors say that it does not show signs of stopping. Socio-economic status, isolation, seasonal depression, and more encompassing mental health issues are all factors, but doctors say that what the town of Fullmouth is facing is better labeled as a 'suicide contagion', meaning that exposure to suicidal behavior can increase suicidal tendencies. And unfortunately, it looks like the doctors are right." Chip Gordon tapped his papers against the desk. His mouth was a grim line, governing his role as messenger. "Early this morning, the body of a young woman was found in the Black Mountain region, near the summit of Black Elk Peak, about twenty-five miles North of the town of Fullmouth." The camera flashed away from Chip Gordon's face, and a map of South Dakota appeared on the screen. The graphic moved quickly, funneling through the state to the county, the county to the mountain range, the range to the mountain, and finally, the graphic dropped a pin on the exact coordinates of Black Elk Peak. There, the red pin burst into a small screenshot of Theresa O'Malley, microphone in hand. Within the miniature frame that balanced precariously on the peak's graphic, Theresa O'Malley stood thigh-deep in snow, puffed up in a white parka that looked like a hazmat suit. Chip Gordon's voice boomed over the map and over the snow globe scene of Theresa O'Malley in the small frame. He was Chip Gordon, Wizard of Oz. Pearl rolled her eyes.

"Though the name of the deceased has not yet been released, the Sheriff has confirmed that she was a resident of Fullmouth and still has family living in the region."

Pearl looked around the room. On the couch, sitting next to Kaia was another mother. She sat pin-straight, hands gripping her knees, her shoulders peeled back, ready to take flight. Her olive skin was freckled with small galaxies of beauty marks. The constellations followed along her neck and collarbone. Her eyes were small and hooded as she hunted the faces on the television screen. The lines and points of grace that articulated the woman's features were antagonized by her expression. The woman was all fury. The bones of her face were poison darts, sharp and angled. Somehow, she'd removed the rose crown. Her long black hair needled at the white lace hem of the dead-mother uniform, making her look more like a vengeful spirit and less like a debutant on holiday.

"No foul play is suspected at this time, though it has not been ruled out. We now go to Theresa O'Malley, who is at the crime scene with Deputy Sheriff Stone. Good morning, Theresa." The graphic zoomed along the grid of the Black Mountains until Theresa O'Malley was perfectly centered in the frame.

"This is bullshit," the spirit on the couch said.

"You look like death, Pearl. You need a shower. And wash that hair." Diane announced in the transition between the newsroom and the muck. She had taken off her frilly apron and was wearing her old high school track shorts. She and the painter had moved toward the hallway, toward the row of bedrooms at the back of the house.

"That man needs to start paying some rent if he's gonna be here all the time," Henshaw grunted then slurped on his coffee.

"Whatever," Diane muttered as she left the living room, holding the painter's hand and pulling him down the hall.

"I wish he'd leave," Benny mumbled from the kitchen table.

"It's different seeing it all play out from this angle. I feel kinda bad about what I did to Charlie whenever Carl came back around," Cindy said.

"Oh God, Carl was such a loser." Molly laughed.

"Shh!" Kaia turned to Cindy and Molly, her eyes wide and head tilting to the vengeful spirit on the couch. "Give her a break."

"Thank you, Chip. On this frozen shelf of the Black Mountain region, at the top of one of the tallest mountains in the country, police are fighting against time and deteriorating weather conditions. A possible crime scene that spans over seven miles—from the trailhead where the decedent's car was found, all the way up to the peak, where her remains are in the process of being recovered— police are working to gather every shred of evidence they can find." Theresa O'Malley's thin lips wrapped around a grandiose frown, made possible by the orange lipliner and matching lipstick she used to amplify the size of her mouth, hiking the peaks to just beneath her nostrils, the corners drawn onto her lower cheeks. The effect was clownish, sadistic in its comedic amplification.

The vengeful spirit sucked her teeth. Her legs began to bounce up and down feverishly, rocking the coffee table.

"What in the world—" Henshaw's voice wandered as he attempted to still the trembling oak. He ran his hand across its surface and down the nearest corner leg, trying to figure out what was upsetting its balance.

Pearl put the sugar bowl on the rug and held her coffee mug in her hands. She leaned closer to the television as the Deputy came into frame.

"With me is Deputy Franny Stone of the Fullmouth Sheriff's Department. Good morning, Deputy Stone," Theresa O'Malley squawked as she thrust the microphone beneath the Deputy's khaki hat.

"Good morning." Deputy Stone nodded, her blunt brown bob as curt and serious as her voice.

"Can you please tell us around what time you received word that a body had been found at Black Elk Peak?"

"Well, I am not at liberty to relate the specifics, as this is an ongoing investigation, but I can tell you that a Park Ranger was in the process of conducting his standard trail reviews— making sure the trails throughout the park are still passable or if they needed to be closed up for the season— when he came across a witness, located about two miles from the peak. The witness showed him where the body of the woman was located."

"Shelby—" the vengeful spirit whispered.

"However, the witness was in bad shape. She had been out in the elements for a while, though for how long, we do not yet know. With the assistance of a state-issued snowmobile, the Ranger was able to get her medical attention quickly. It was pure luck that a Ranger was on these trails today, this early in the morning," Deputy Stone continued.

"The hand of God," Henshaw said.

"Is the witness related to the deceased, perhaps her child?" Theresa O'Malley asked, her head tilted to the side like a confused puppy.

"I cannot release that information at this time." The Deputy tilted her head down, hiding her eyes from the camera as she attempted to exit the interview.

"Shelby—" the vengeful spirit cried.

"Is Shelby your little girl?" Kaia asked, reaching for the spirit's hand.

The spirit tore her hand from Kaia's reach. "Shelby is fifteen. She is strong and brave. She went looking for me. She was too late."

"Poor girl."

"What she must've seen." Maggie shook her head.

Molly sighed. "That's the first time that's happened."

"Deirdre—" Karen choked.

"I know, darlin'." Kaia pulled Karen into a hug.

"Poor Deirdre saw blood and the state of your place, but she didn't see you," Cindy chimed.

"That's a big difference," Molly said.

"God help her," Henshaw mumbled.

Theresa O'Malley caught the deputy's coat sleeve and pulled her back into frame. "One final question, Deputy," she said. "What do you believe brought the deceased from her home, all the way up to Black Elk Peak—possibly with her child— in the middle of the night?"

The Deputy shook her head sharply and kept her face to the ground, only the crown of her hat and blunt bob visible to the camera's blinding eye. "I cannot comment at this time," she spit into the microphone and stalked out of view.

The camera voyaged for an ill-advised close up on Theresa O'Malley's face. Her purple eyeshadow and thick mascara had braved the elements of wind and snow but found itself caked on the apples of her cheeks and smeared into the lines of her forehead. Her eyebrows melted into the creases of her eyelids. But still, the orange clown-mouth rang out bravely, its plastic presence most reliable and fixed. "Thank you, Deputy Stone, and thank you to all the law enforcement officers who have worked tirelessly this early Sunday morning—a day God made for us to rest and regroup, to be with family and friends. But an officer's work is never done, is it? Especially in the small town of Fullmouth, where a suicide epidemic is plaguing the citizens, and the officers are working tirelessly to keep up with the demands of the deceased."

"Now that's in poor taste," Henshaw remarked.

Theresa O'Malley bowed her head for a breath, then looked directly at the camera, her face a strangely painted death mask. "This has been Theresa O'Malley for KOTA TV News, Sunday Edition."

Henshaw turned off the news and hiked himself out of his chair, grabbing his Bible on his way to the kitchen. "What're you kids doing today?"

"You have to go to Bessie's house to see the kids. *Now.*" Cindy pushed herself off the front door and stood over Pearl, her freckled chin a forest for the trees. "Get cleaned up and head over there *this morning*. You've got to. The kids must know something, especially Deirdre and Shelby. Things have only gotten worse with each death."

"Closer—" Maggie interrupted.

"And you can tell just by looking at her—" Cindy jutted her sharp chin toward the vengeful spirit "— there is no way she killed herself. Not a chance."

†

The eight street-facing windows of Bessie Rain's

whitewashed mansion were all black-eyed and vacant. The porch and its roof dramatically bowed in the center, giving the house a grimacing mouth, one that had separated from the house and was nearly sick of itself. The eight windows were like eight spider eyes, so black who knew when they were blinking? The tin roof rusted ages ago. Melting snow hunkered into the eves, beneath the shadows of the largest peaks, and eventually fell into the yard thick as battery acid and the same color too. The only beautiful part about the crumbling mansion was the front yard. Framed in black iron fencing of ornamented flowering vines molded in a fiery kiln, even in the dry and frozen months, the flowers burst open in bloom against the season's imposing conditions. Within the blooming iron rails was a tree line of ancient black pines that stood on each side of the house, tall and lean like sentries. Their pin heads and trim bodies grown uniform by age and decoration. Between the tree-soldiers and the grimacing porch was a small courtyard made of clay bricks. Patterned like the sun, each row orbited an ancient fountain that was a Rains' family pride, as the fountain and its artisan beauty was what kept the eye away from the decomposition of the family plot. At least for a time. The fountain itself was nearly as tall as the house. Hand-carved from black marble, the three tiers rose from the base in ornate design. Runes significant and mysterious to all but the Rains' family were carved in repeated patterns on every curve of the tiers. And at the fountain's base were four horses, their strong legs reaching for the ground, their hooves searching for traction.

Most of their bodies invisible, hidden within the earth, as if they were sinking in quicksand. The horses' nostrils flared, their eyes wide, teeth bared. And on each of the horses' backs was an image of stark contrast. Each saddle held a man, and each man was unique in his mission. These were the Four Horsemen of the Apocalypse. Death was a scull draped in robes, a scythe at this side. Famine was gaunt, hair thin, his shoulders hunched over a spine too long for his body. War carried a sword, his face square and angry. And Conquest was regaled in crown and robe, the clasp on his chest a row of carved stones cut like diamonds.

There were always birds in the fountain at Bessie Rains' house. Even in the frozen months, when the wind was bitter-blown and almost everyone had flown south, birds perched along the edges of each concentric bowl, their feet clasping at the runes, their eyes on Bessie Rains' porch and the screen door that endlessly knocked a ghostly *hello.*

The birds watched as Pearl banged her fist against Bessie Rains' door. Five mangy crows, oily and frost-mottled, far smaller than Cindy Stewart's familiar. And where was Cindy? Pearl stomped the cold from her boots and looked around. No one was there. She thought the mothers had wanted to follow her, to find their children warm in their beds, their clothes folded nicely in cupboards, their small plates stacked on a shelf in the kitchen. There is a world of comfort in things. The meager presence of small objects, worn but well loved.

Pearl noticed a few carved jack-o-lanterns on the sills of the two windows framing the door. She knocked again— louder this time. She rocked back and forth in her boots. The jack-o-lanterns faces were lopsided. Teeth were missing or noses, one eye was bigger than the other. One had eight eyes like Bessie Rain's house, and a strange grimace to match. Pearl could see the purple marker

outline of the drawn faces the children had made before
the carving began. She imagined the kids around a table
covered in newspaper, scooping the guts from the pumpkin
bodies. Maybe flinging the stringy insides at one another.
Maybe laughing. Where were the dead mothers? Pearl
closed her eyes and thought about their faces in the
newspaper lineup; she thought about the women in her
house this morning, whispering and watching the news. She
thought about the vengeful spirit, her vulture eyes. When
Pearl opened her eyes, still no one was there. She knocked
again, heavier and in a static beat that could not be
mistaken for anything else.

"Cindy, are you all coming or what?" Pearl called.

A crow squawked behind her and kicked at a fountain
rune. But it was not Cindy's crow. Pearl remembered the
story her mother had told her about Bessie. It was last
Thursday, right after school. Right at the start of everything.
Bessie couldn't get some bird to leave. Diane said it was a
pigeon trying to peck through the screen and get into the
house. Bessie was scared and got one of the kids to chase
it off with a broom. Diane thought it was funny. Maybe it
was then. Pearl shivered and stomped her boots on the
porch again. She eyed the line of crows and thought about
the birds in Rose's grimoire. The crows as sin. Their
messages of destruction and death. What was happening?
Where were the dead mothers?

The door swung open. Dust crowded into the sunlight—
escaping the shadowy dark— and immediately transcended
into the wind. A girl Pearl had never seen before opened
the door. She was tall and long-limbed, with glittery green
gloves on her hands. Her dark hair hung loose, matching
the length of her thin arms. She was wearing sweatpants

and thick socks, a Doors t-shirt that was ripped at the collar. Around her neck hung a necklace of glass beads, and at its end was a pair of vintage cat-eye glasses covered in pink sequins and glitter.

"These were my Grandma Bee's," the girl said, unfolding the eyeglasses and putting them on her face. Her small brown eyes were instantly magnified. "They're blinding, but eventually, I'll see something."

Pearl smiled. "I'm Pearl. I just came by to say 'hi' to some of the kids from Custer Day. I've never seen you there, but I'm pretty new to town."

"Oh no, my mom would rather die than send me to a school with that namesake." The girl's eyes started to water, and she swept her gloves against her hollow cheeks. "This just keeps happening," she said, gesturing to her tears. "In my mind, I won't be crying at all, but my body just can't hold it together." She laughed. "There's an old set of encyclopedias in the library, but I haven't found out what this phenomenon is called. Not yet, anyway. I hope it doesn't mean I'm going crazy."

"I doubt it—not with all the weird stuff happening in the Swallows lately."

"My mom hated that name too."

"Well—"

The girl rocked back and forth on her heels. "Well—I'm Shelby." She paused and brushed the tears from her cheeks again. "My mom homeschooled me since I was little, so I'm probably really weird—I *know* I'm unsocialized— but I don't know how weird, not yet, anyway. I won't really know until I start going to Custer Day and observe how all the other kids interact with each other, which'll probably happen this week. What grade are you in?"

"Ninth."

"Eighth," Shelby responded, pointing to herself.

"We'll have the same lunch— the same P.E. too. And a couple of the kids who live here are eighth and ninth graders. That'll make it easier." Pearl did not tell Shelby that the children who lived with Bessie Rains—the children of the dead mothers— had been kept away from their classrooms all year for fear that their presence would upset the standard student body, who had enough problems to worry about, according to Vice Principal Richards.

Shelby smiled and took a step back from the door. "Well, you can come in. Most of the kids are at church with Ms. Bessie, though. Only Emma and Genie are upstairs."

Pearl crossed the threshold into the dark foyer. The walls were oak and stained nearly black, the veins and knots like waves on a stormy sea. There was a small table next to the door, surrounded by many pairs of boots, all in neat rows. At least half were brightly colored. Kid colors. Pearl closed her eyes and breathed deeply. Five parts to sink the air into her belly and find the dead mothers. Five parts to pull them up— to dredge their spirits to the surface— and into Bessie Rains' foyer. She gave an extra two beats. Enough time for her lungs to fully exhaust their tensions, enough time to feel the air shift in the room, to possibly hear the rustle of white gowns, to hear Cindy Stewart's crow caw.

At last, Pearl opened her eyes. Only Shelby was there. She was still wearing the green gloves and squinting behind her grandmother's sequined glasses.

"Are you okay?" Shelby asked.

"It's just so dark."

Shelby nodded. "It's spooky."

"I don't think I'd ever go anywhere alone in this house. I'd probably tie my brother to my hip— he'd get so sick of me."

"If he saw this place, I don't think he'd want it any other way."

The heavy slam of an object falling to the ground from a great height flared from the back of the house and made the two girls jump.

"Sheesh," Pearl whispered. "Is someone else home?"

Shelby tilted her head to examine the unlit hall behind the staircase. She shook her head softly and closed her eyes. Her lashes looked like great sea fans behind the magnifying lenses. "I don't think so. Emma and Genie are upstairs, last door on the left. I guess I'll come up with you, though. I don't really feel like talking, but I don't want to be by myself either."

"I don't blame you."

"You can put your coat there." Shelby pointed to the banister, draped from top to bottom in children's outerwear. Scarves were braided through the balusters. Gloves waved from the spindles. "But you may want to keep it on, just in case. If I were you, I'd leave before Ms. Bessie gets back. She seems pretty strict about who is allowed to come around here. She made me stay home this morning because she didn't want anyone asking me questions."

"Are you going to be living here?" Pearl asked as her boots sunk into the thick rug that slunk along the curved staircase.

"God, I hope not," Shelby answered. "But I don't think

I have anywhere else to go."

The darkness on the second floor shifted and flickered— a candle's light curling into the shadows and pushing the muted shades back and forth— even though there were no candles or lanterns lit.

"There aren't even bulbs in the lamps," Shelby whispered. "We couldn't turn a light on if we tried."

Pearl nodded, afraid of what the darkness would hear.

The far corners of the hall were composed of infinite obscurity—a galaxy beyond Pearl's sightline. She imagined the hall framed by trees; bulky spider webs reared at each branch's end. Walking the hall felt like déjà vu. It was Pearl's dream of climbing Black Elk Peak, of being chased within the tunnel of black fir trees, all the way toward the mountain top and into an ominous light that was impossible to escape. In Bessie Rains' house, it was not bones along a mountain tree path. It was eyes. It was the silent wet blink of the walls scanning from left to right and back again. Pearl shuddered and pulled her coat around her. It was colder upstairs than it was on the porch.

"I haven't really talked to anyone yet." Shelby paused in front of the door at the end of the hall. "Just you and the shadows."

Pearl could hear muffled voices on the other side of the door. The yellow light of lamp shades reached from the room, its thin arms stretching into the hallway from beneath the carved maple. "These are the same symbols as the ones on the fountain outside," Pearl said and held her hand close to the sigils but did not dare to touch them. "Are they in all the doors?"

"I don't—"

"Who's out there?" a small voice called from the

bedroom.

"Don't just stand out there and scare us if you don't mean to," said another.

Shelby frowned and turned the knob. "Well, you have to unlock it first," she replied. "And we didn't mean to scare you. You have a visitor—"

"A visitor!" the two girls shrieked, and a loud tumbling came barreling toward the locked door.

"Maybe to take us away!" a small girl said as she threw open the bedroom door. She was wearing a sweatshirt over striped footed pajamas, the feet coated in cobwebs and dust. Her long red hair was neatly tied into twin braids and wrapped like a crown atop her head. When she saw Shelby and Pearl standing in the shadows, the smile on her face sank into a tight frown, but she quickly recovered. "Hello," she said formally. "I sure hope you're not new here, for your sake," she said, her green eyes on Pearl.

The elfin girl looked just like her mother, Pearl thought. Too bad Maggie was not around to see her. "Hi, I'm Pearl."

"I've seen you at Custer Day. You're always hanging around that little kid with the funny hair."

"That's my brother, Benny," Pearl mumbled then cleared her throat. In that dark mansion on the other side of town, it felt like it'd been forever since she had seen her little brother. "I just— we just moved to town this summer, and some of the things that are happening here—I just, I had this feeling that I should come over and talk to you and make sure things are okay around here."

"And what'll you do if they're not?" a voice from the bedroom asked. The other girl was sitting on the bed, her legs crossed and a book in her lap. She was wrapped in blankets, her hair neatly braided and rolled into a crown, just like the elfin girl's. A comb and a brush were stacked on a bedside table. Soggy cardboard boxes—bloated with clothes and books—were neatly arranged at the foot of the bed.

Pearl felt heavy. This was Emma and Genie—Maggie and Kaia's daughters. She could see their mothers in the shapes of their eyes, the way they held their heads, the lilt of their voices. In the small space of the bedroom, Pearl could tell they were doing the best they could, just like their mothers were, trapped together in some separate loop of the universe. Pearl closed her eyes to keep from tearing up. She was tired, but worse than that, it was the moment she realized that time destroyed everything. It was impossible to hold together— impossible to bring the mothers back to this plane, back to their lonely and fractured children. Pearl missed Benny. She missed her mom.

"I had a bad feeling," she said.

"It's fine— I'm Emma, and this is Genie," the elfin girl pulled Pearl and Shelby into the bedroom and closed the door. She locked it before returning to a corner of the room that was draped in blankets. "And your feeling isn't too far off."

"I'll say." Genie whistled. "You show up the only time Bessie has ever left us alone. That's really something, actually. If she knew you were here, she'd brick up all the windows and doors, and none of us would ever escape."

"It's that bad?" Pearl asked, unzipping her coat.

Emma nodded. "It's worse than that."

"I wish Charlie were here," Genie lamented. "He's the oldest. And he's been here the longest, so he is probably the best person to talk to. But Bessie knows that, so she never lets him alone. Never. She's about to make him and Connor move into that closet right off the kitchen because that's where she always is."

Connor and Charlie, Maggie and Cindy's sons, Pearl remembered.

"She said somebody's got to live in that pantry because more kids are coming." Emma wrapped a thin flannel blanket around her shoulders. "Bring that comb over here so I can do your hair."

"Miss Bessie said that?" Shelby asked as she plucked the comb from the brush bristles. She sat cross-legged in front of Emma, her back curled so Emma could reach the top of her head.

Pearl pulled off her hat and gloves and stuffed them into her pockets. She looked around the sparse room. There was only one small window, the glass mildewed, its sickly green light creeping along the walls, reaching for Genie's neat braids and slim neck as she bent over a book. There was a small cat lamp on the bedside table that cheered the room, though— that and the small yellow rug set on the wood floor between the two brass-framed beds.

"Yeah, she said they're the oldest, so they'll be the first to go," explained Genie.

Emma frowned and stopped combing Shelby's hair. "Connor wouldn't leave me here alone."

"Bessie wouldn't let him take you."

"Do you think she'll kick them out?" asked Shelby.

"No, but they want to leave, and she knows it. She wouldn't stop them," Genie added.

Pearl sighed and sat on the small bed across from Genie, the creak of the springs punctuating the pause in conversation. The green light from the window highlighted the pages of the book in Genie's lap. The raised image was of a mermaid breaking through the surface of a wicked sea, octopus tentacles wrapped around her waist and fins, aching to pull her back into the suffocating darkness.

"She says they're already too old and too rotten," Emma said as she resumed her work, taking the comb to a matted knot near Shelby's scalp.

"She doesn't treat the girls and the boys the same— not really."

"None of its good."

"No—"

Genie sighed and closed the book, smothering the mermaid between its thick pages. "I wish they were here, though. They could tell you the most."

"They're not scared of her, not like the rest of us, especially the little ones. Most of us try to pretend she's not as scary as we think she is, so the little kids don't cry. But sometimes they cry anyway because—" Emma tumbled on. "She's awful."

"The house being so cold and dark doesn't help," Pearl noted, her eyes wandering around the dark room.

"Bessie keeps it like that on purpose. It's easier for her to creep around the house and spy on us," Emma said as she hacked at the knot above Shelby's grimacing face.

"Charlie thinks there are secret tunnels all over the house that connect the rooms. He thinks they're passageways without stairs that kind of snake around the house, so Bessie can go wherever she wants," Genie divulged. "About a month ago, Bessie found one of Charlie's maps. She sat all of us down at the dinner table to question us and wouldn't let us eat until someone told her what was going on. Finally, around midnight, after we'd been sitting there for near eight hours—not allowed to go to sleep or go to the bathroom or anything— Connor said he had been sneaking around the house, looking for secret passageways. But Bessie found the map in Charlie's things, so she knew he wasn't telling the full truth. She was so mad, she locked them both in the attic."

"She walked all the way up there?" Shelby swallowed her voice as her head jerked back by the force of Emma's hand at another knot.

"She did," Emma answered. "And she locked every single door in the house—except for the two bedrooms we live in—on her way up."

"It took her forever, and Charlie and Connor were up there for three days without anything to eat." Genie set the book of fairytales next to the cat lamp and picked up the brush. The leather volume was a collection of Grimm's stories, the gold-embossed letters and filagree design pressed into the soft skin.

"Her arthritis got really bad after she climbed all those stairs too, and she said she couldn't climb back up there."

"For three days?" Pearl's voice was sharp.

Emma shook her head. "She wouldn't give any of us the keys either, she was so paranoid about us stealing them."

"Did they have water?" asked Shelby.

"That's the thing," Genie answered, plucking the matted hair from the brush bristles and rolling the mess of strands between her palms. "She made them carry up a pot and three jugs of water. She knew they'd be up there for a while."

"Since then, we haven't seen her upstairs. She spends most of her time in the kitchen."

"Which is why she's making Charlie and Connor move into the pantry."

"Someone still comes upstairs, though. The night Charlie and Connor were locked in the attic, Deirdre said she woke up to a man standing over her bed. He had on a black hat like Abraham Lincoln's that hid most of his face, and he was so tall and dark, he was mostly a silhouette. He had long hair that was the same color as his black suit. His eyes were hard and red— like rubies, she said— and his nose was long and thin, like a beak. She knew he was a bad man. She could feel it. She tried to scream but couldn't, and she couldn't move at all. He stared at her, his boney fingers and sharp yellow fingernails just hovering over her body. He was there for a while, she said, and then he just disappeared." Genie set the ball of hair beside the cat lamp. "When he was gone, she could move again. She climbed out of bed to find Charlie or Connor because they kind of take care of us, but she remembered they were locked in the attic. She said her face was covered in tears— like she'd been crying for a while— but she couldn't feel it while the man was there." She pulled her sweatshirt around her fists and trembled.

"That's kind of what keeps happening to me," Shelby murmured.

"Deirdre drew a picture of the bad man, but Bessie took that one too. And fast. Bessie told us kids that Deirdre was just hysterical. That some girls were prone to hysterics and that her momma was probably the same way. She said we should just ignore her until she straightens up."

Pearl felt her eyes and cheeks go red, her fingers knot into fists. The million eyes along her spine and neck, her arms and mouth, blinked open. She thought about Maggie on Frank Turner's bus, surrounded by grocery bags, bartering with the Devil to keep Pearl from harm. "Did anyone recognize the man from Deirdre's drawing? Was it someone from town?"

Emma and Genie shook their heads.

"After that, Deirdre didn't sleep for a week." Emma drew the comb down the center of Shelby's scalp and sectioned the hair into two parts.

"And she doesn't really talk anymore."

"She's supposed to sleep in here with us, but she doesn't. We don't know where she goes. And we lock the door, so we know she doesn't come in while we're sleeping."

"You lock her out?" Pearl chided, her balled fists in the pockets of her coat.

Genie frowned. "We don't want to, but we have to."

"We tried to teach her a secret knock, just in case she ever wanted to come in, but she didn't care."

"She doesn't look good either," Genie said as Pearl's shoulders stiffened.

"I think she pulls her hair out."

"She definitely does."

"It's a wonder Bessie drags her out of the house at all," Shelby noted.

"She's afraid Deirdre will run away, I think," Emma said.

"And it looks good for Bessie—that she's taking care of this messed up kid."

"I still don't really understand why you lock her out," Pearl hissed.

"We don't have a choice."

"She disappears. We try to look for her every night, but

then something starts up the stairs. Something big. The steps are so loud it feels like the whole house could fall down around the sound. Then it gets upstairs, and it's like a giant monster is walking down the dark hallway, scratching his fingernails along the wallpaper and doors. It moves so slow— all the way down the hall— until it gets to our door. It's so quiet then. Like the monster is holding its breath. Right when I think I'm so scared I can't take it and I'm gonna scream, the footsteps start up again and it goes back to the stairs."

"It isn't the boys?" Shelby asked, her head pulling to the left while Emma braided.

"There's no way they could make a sound like that."

"And it happened while they were locked up in the attic too."

Pearl stood up and took her hands from her pockets. She paced the small space between the beds. "Has anyone else heard it?"

"Everyone has. Every day it feels like something is at the edge of what we can see." Genie wrapped her arms around her knees and slowly rocked back and forth. "I turn my head, and it's gone. We all feel that way." The bed creaked with each small shift of her weight— hollow and tinny growls from beneath the bed.

"So, you lock the door and try to stay together—except Deirdre," Pearl mumbled, her voice trailing off into the dark corners of the room.

"I think she hides from the bad man," Emma said.

"You weren't scared to stay here alone today while all the other kids went to church?"

"Nothing ever happens when Bessie is out of the house," replied Genie

197

"The monsters are hers—the bad man and the giant."

"Sometimes we can hear her downstairs at the kitchen table, talking to someone. With none of the lights on, we can sit on the stairs and listen to her. I don't think she knows we're there, but we can hear her. Whenever she talks to the bad man, she stirs a spoon inside of a teacup, scraping the edges. And she talks low, lower than the sound of the spoon in the cup, so we can't hear what she says. We can hear his voice too. It's low, like the bottom notes on a piano." Genie continued, "A few times we've gone all the way downstairs, made it all the way to the kitchen door. We heard snatches of their conversation, back and forth. But each time we've opened the door, it's only been Bessie there, stirring her tea, laughing at us. We know the bad man is still in the room, but we just can't see him."

Pearl halted her step and turned to Genie, her boots dragging the rug out of place. "So, no one else but Deirdre has seen him?"

"No," Emma replied as she wrapped a band around Shelby's braid. "Every night, I think we should unlock the door and keep it open, wait for the giant or the bad man to come, but I get too scared. I'd rather just fall asleep and forget where I am for a while."

Shelby sighed. "Poor Deirdre."

"Have you tried to tell anyone else about this?"

Emma made a face. "No one would ever believe us. They think Bessie is a saint and that we're all messed up kids with messed up parents."

"She's the richest person in Fullmouth—her family founded the town," Genie added. "And no one else wants to take care of us. It's easier to believe she's a saint."

"If we said anything, it'd only get worse for us. At least

now, we have each other."

"Can you think of any way we could prove any of this?" Pearl asked.

"Bessie has a big old book in the kitchen that she's always reading from. Sometimes she walks in circles around the house, carrying it under her arm, talking to herself."

"She keeps that book hidden, though."

"Probably in the secret tunnels, with the bad man and the giant."

"I bet that book is somewhere in the kitchen. She doesn't let anyone in there unless she's in there." Genie stopped rocking and uncurled her body.

"And she keeps the cupboards locked," said Shelby.

Emma wrapped Shelby's braids into a crown and admired her work. "It's getting late," she said. "Bessie is going to be home soon. And right when she walks through the door, she'll know something isn't right."

"Right." Pearl zipped her coat and looked around the room. The three girls appeared smaller now, their shoulders rigid and mouths tense. They looked like their mothers: matching braided crowns, eyes grey smudged, cheeks hollow. They appeared huddled together against a great wind, the dark house rocking to pieces around them. "I'm going to the kitchen to look around. If I can't find that book, maybe I can find Charlie and Deirdre's drawings. Maybe there's something else."

"We can come with you," Emma gathered the flannel blanket around her shoulders and stood up.

"No, you stay here. If Miss Bessie comes home while I'm downstairs, I'll just make something up about the backdoor being unlocked." Pearl rested her hand on the doorknob, listening for anything on the other side, hiding within the infinite gloom of the hallway. The goosebumps along her spine trembled in their sockets. She could not hear a thing, but she felt the tension of an arrow taunt within a bow, the sharp edges focused on the heart of the door. She gripped the knob tighter and closed her eyes, trying again to call the mothers. She inhaled in five parts, each breath a stone down the well, and exhaled in equal measure, working to shake the mothers awake and call them to the living tomb of Bessie Rain's house.

†

The kitchen was just as Pearl had imagined, just as Genie's story had woven together. There was a regency door that freely swung between the hallway and kitchen, but a bolt lock was fixed flush to a low point on the kitchen wall, allowing Bessie Rains to lock the room against the rest of the house. The kitchen table was black oak and carved, covered in cheesecloth and teacups, small spoons and herb dishes stacked in the center. The window was large and overlooked the black pines that outlined the stone wall framing the backyard of the house. Mold crept through the gaps of the window's double panes and fermented the tiles, the faucet, and sink basin. The cupboards looked pulpy— the color of soggy bread sporing into radiant shades of green and black— within the cold darkness of the kitchen. But despite the damp rot of the wood, each cupboard door's mouth was bolted shut. Pearl pulled at each locked door, but not one rattled on its hinge. The pantry door was swung open and pinned to the wall by an antique anvil. Pearl walked into the small space. The shelves were bare: two towels laid across the racks, a pillow at the end of each. The same bloated cardboard suitcases that squat at the foot of both Genie and Emma's beds were also in the pantry, lined up against the wall. A football helmet and a deck of cards rested on top of the nearest box. Pearl shuddered. Her anger had become both bow and arrow. It had become the dark force of the house, her million eyes searching the hidden passageways, hunting the bad man and the giant. She knew it was all smoke and mirrors. What Bessie was hiding was in plain sight, just like Genie said— *it was right at the edge of what she could see.* The locks on the cupboards were Chinese finger traps. They were x-ray specks and magic coins. The locks were vocal distractions that openly told the story of something else, but it was not where the book was hidden.

Pearl walked slowly around the room, tapping the heel of her boot against each board. She was running out of time. A grandfather clock in another cavernous room unknown to Pearl struck ten beats. Ms. Bessie was too old to stoop to the floorboards. She was too old to reach up into a bolted cupboard. Pearl knocked along the oak-planked walls, the veins and knots now grimacing faces, screaming mouths commanding Pearl leave. Finally, she found the hollow. The oak panel was cleverly hinged, an entire board—only eight inches wide—that swung open, floor to ceiling. Pearl did not have enough time to take everything, but she found Bessie Rain's book. It was one she had seen before. It was the Devil's book, the one from her dream.

When she held it in her hands, felt the cover of skin, the bloated pages, water-logged and swollen from centuries of use, she was back on the mountain peak. She could hear the Devil's cloven feet clicking against the smooth stone faces, the book on his hip as he moaned Pearl's name. She unlatched the cover, ran her fingers across the red-written notes, the lines inconsistent. Bloody blots in places, thin and nearly transparent in others. Folded into the crease of the book were two crisp white pages, bright and welcoming against the dingy half-life of the rest. It was Charlie's map and Deirdre's drawing of the bad man, just as Genie had described. Behind the children's pages, written on the ancient sheets of the Devil's book, were the names of the dead mothers, all in a row, just like their tombstones, just like the circadian cover story of the *Black Mountain Daily News*:

Cindy Stewart— August 1, 1998
Molly Boutell— August 22, 1998
Kaia Goodwin— September 19, 1998
Maggie Teller— October 3, 1998
Karen Kelly— October 27, 1998
Suzanne Dubray—October 29, 1998

Pearl ran her finger down the page, the million goosebumps quaking with the tension of foresight. When she reached the final name on the list, a name written in red that was still bright in its newness—a name on the list without a final date— it was one she knew well. Pearl's hand stopped. She traced the letters slowly, taking them into her body, pulling them into her blood. She traced the name in parts, pulling it into her breath, dragging it into her belly, into the protected cage of her ribs. She did not exhale the name. She swallowed it, she pulled it into the muck. She hid it inside of a darkness that was stronger than the drudgery of Bessie Rain's monstrous house. She closed the book softly and zipped it into her coat. She closed the secret door. The million goosebumps blinked and shuddered, they turned outwards, watching the sightlines from Pearl's shoulders, her forehead, and throat. Pearl walked out the door backwards; she locked it behind her. She covered her footprints to the tree line and walked between the stone wall and the black oaks. Every time the name tried to come back up, to find its way into her throat, making her choke, she swallowed it back down.

Diane Adler—

She stuffed it with air and sunk it into her belly, between her rib cage and hip bones. The air was important. The blood was important.

CHAPTER ELEVEN

Devil's Grim

Edging between the tree line and the fence, Pearl felt the book wrap its dead arms around her waist, its cold skin pressing against her rip cage, searching the dark and crowded spaces between her heart and stomach. Her heart beat the cold hands back, her lungs purpled against the book's body weight— the feeling of stone after stone set against Pearl's chest, making it harder to breathe. Her boots to the snow, the near run, was the sound of cut glass on that early Sunday morning. There was no one in the streets. No one she could see, anyway. She felt the thousand goosebumps along her skin blink slowly. The eyes wide and focused, they reflected the savage fury Pearl buried in her chest, right along with her mother's name. She needed to get somewhere safe.

Pearl tucked her ponytail beneath the collar of her coat and pulled the down-stuffed hood as far over her face as she could. The book held on. Pearl swore she could feel its heart beginning to beat, or a hand knocking at the skinned cover of its face. She decided to keep to Brighton Avenue—the long road that ran behind Bessie Rain's house and toward Bear Mountain and Rose's small corner of the town. The late morning sky was low. It was too cold for the clouds to burn off. Instead, they crowded together to keep warm. Each shape was distinct in the overall fog. The long thin ones skirted the edges of the robust and massive ones, their bodies muscled and overbearing. And at the top were

205

the small cartoonish clouds, their presence a high laugh in the otherwise grey world. Without any true shape, the fog curled low along the street. It wrapped itself between the porch rails and scratched at the front doors of each silent home that Pearl passed. She walked faster as she felt the book's heartbeat— the book's knocking— grow stronger. She looked at the bold face of Bear Mountain, her eyes straight forward— the million goosebumps slowly blinking, still shifting around as they surveyed the street—but the clouds hid nearly everything. She could not go to Rose's house. She could not bring such an evil thing across Rose's threshold, could not open it within the warm space of her cabin, letting whatever was knocking— whatever dark heart was beginning to beat— free to roam and make a home within Rose's cabin. It was the wrong thing to do. No matter how much Pearl needed Rose right then, she could not take the book to her, just like she could not take the book home. Its heartbeat and knocking grew nearly constant. The same pattern over and over as the book's dead arms tightened around Pearl's waist. She heard its muffled laugh— *little pig, little pig let me in*, the book called.

Pearl felt the savage fury she'd buried in her belly laugh a little too. She smiled. Pearl pictured the green space of the graveyard within her. She saw the headstones of all the things she had lost already. But her fury was different. The headstone was still shiny and new—a fresh retreat. Pearl felt her fury press against the door of its casket. She saw the coffin latches snap, the buried lock broken. Her fury had its own arms. They were long and strong, wrapped in striped clothes. The skin of her fury was green-veined and slick as it ripped at the graveyard dirt. The long fingers broke the surface—a rebirth of animus. Pearl ignored the book's knocking, the book's heartbeat, its dead arms tightening around her waist. Her fury was Frankenstein's monster, pieced together by everything else dead that surrounded it. It was born of this graveyard, born of everything left behind. Her fury sat on its headstone. It flicked a match against its thick-soled shoe. It smoked a cigarette and waited.

Pearl knew where to take the book.

A block ahead of Rayburn Street—the last western road before the Swallows became the great mountainous beyond— Pearl turned south on Prospect. Bordering the town's edge, she walked the five blocks quickly, keeping her eyes on the ground. Despite the season and the melting snow, Prospect Street on Sunday morning was always well-polished and well-heeled. Pearl mumbled the formal responses of *good morning* and *peace be with you* to each pair of shoes that passed. She hoped that none of the legs she came across were thick-veined and slow, that none of the Bible-burdened hands would halt their spiritual ponderings, clear their throats, and whisper a raspy *hello*. Mostly, Pearl prayed that Bessie Rains had not decided to take the long way home.

The morning sun was well hidden behind the steeple of Righteous Dei Lutheran. A wan illumination, its thin arms reached out from the church's stone peaks and arcs—a sickly cross— making it no farther than the sidewalk at Pearl's feet. The rest of the town was swallowed up by dense, low-formed storm clouds and the shrouded doom they carried. As Pearl said her final *hellos* to the final churchgoers crossing the street, she felt the book turn into a snake. She felt its arms grow longer— more muscled— as they wrapped around her torso again and again, pressing tighter. Pearl climbed the stone steps of the church, passing the street bulletin that rotated Martin Luther's teachings. In the dim light, the church bulletin's glass was fogged against the cloth letterboard.

"God does not need your good works, but your neighbor does," the board declared. The snake hissed. Pearl felt the flick of its forked tongue at her neck as it constricted. The wind grew stronger, stripping the hood of her coat from her face. Pearl held the railing rigidly. It was getting more difficult to breathe. The snake's heart thumped against her belly. Its knocking skipped along after her own. She focused on each rung of the stairs, on walking into the wind, on the pair of oak church doors that loomed before her. The doors were well-lacquered beams secured together with iron hinges and nails. Pearl waited for the gust to pass, waited for the space of still air to come so she could open those heavy doors. She imagined the doors of Dracula's castle. They would have the same dark planks, the same black hinges. The book hissed again. Pearl felt scales against her skin as it curled closer. She felt lightheaded. A man in a dark blue suit appeared from inside the church. The wind plucked his thin hair up from his mottled scalp. He clutched his Bible and leaned into the gale. He was not wearing a coat. The man held the door for Pearl and then disappeared into the approaching squall.

From inside the narthex, Pearl could hear the strange tune the wind played on the bell in the old tower. She heard the creaking groan of the ropes straining to hold the bell in place, the heavy vibrations of the melody. The bell sang from great heights. It trembled. It was a guillotine, miles above Pearl's head. The wind rattled against the rows of high windows, fingers gripping the panes like the strings of instruments. The book whistled along with the bell's strange tune. Its forked tongue retracted back into the book's flat face. The muscled scales withdrew into the book's belly; its skin returned to porous leather. Pearl searched the walls for a light switch, then thought better of it. The rows of high-set windows gave enough light to reveal the shiny surface of river rocks polished and mortared into the floor. The chairs that lined the oak-paneled walls were filled with shadow shapes of men taking off their hats, checking their jacket pockets, and crossing and uncrossing their legs impatiently as women bounced small children on their knees or pulled at the seams of their stockings. Pearl blinked and they were gone. The book laughed and went back to its knocking. Pearl quickly took off her gloves and hat and crammed them into her pockets. She unzipped her coat and hung it on a peg along the wall, next to the brightly colored activity bags the women's league made to keep the children quiet and occupied during church services. Pearl tried to take a deep breath— to call the dead mothers to the church— but she couldn't. The book had made it impossible.

The ancient doors that separated the narthex from the nave smothered all sound of the world outside. The silence was immediate— a body holding its breath. The nave was darker than the narthex, and when the doors swung closed— severing the high windows of the narthex from the vast tomb of the nave— Pearl felt her heart beat harder, challenging the book for space and sound. *Little pig, little pig let me in*, the book rasped again. Its giggling unnerved Pearl. Her boots sank into the thick red carpets that formed the aisles between the rows and rows of pews.

When Pearl was a little girl, she used to go to church

with her best friend. She did not remember the girl's name or the town she lived in. Pearl remembered the pale-yellow dress she always wore. She remembered that through the whole of Sunday service, she stared at its lace edge and ribbon, keeping her eyes from the altar and the crucifix of a suffering Jesus. His presence in the church was overwhelming and distant. And whenever Pearl saw the Holy Cross, she felt like she was looking far back into the past, witnessing something she did not want to see. She felt the sand in the wind, the burning sun. She heard the hammer, the vultures circling the sky. It was too much for her to see then, too much to feel that she did not understand. And when the service was over, and all the worshippers gathered into the community room for cake and coffee, Pearl could never bring herself to go too. She felt weird about drinking that sticky red juice and eating Entenmann's pastries when Jesus was right there, on the other side of the door, hanging on the cross.

So, Pearl began to disappear. She hid in the infant cry room or the sacristy until the nave was cleared. When everyone was gone, milling about on the other side of the wall, too occupied with desserts to wonder about her, she spent the Fellowship hour crawling beneath the pews. On her belly, she went all the way to the front row and lay beneath the smooth wooden bench. She knew Jesus was right above her head, His face turned toward her but not seeing her. She knew the crown of thorns was there, that someone had painted the blood by hand. She imagined who would have done that. If they cried when they put the brush to His face. After a while of laying beneath the pew, she felt like she was in the belly of a ship. She imagined she was in a bunk beneath the sea, the power of the sea waves above her and below, rocking her to sleep. Pearl and her mother did not live in that town for very long. And then Benny was born, so there was more responsibility—for her— at home. She had not thought about the church and her pale-yellow dress, of falling asleep under the Holy Cross and how it made her feel since she had left that unremembered town. Not until that moment.

Pearl closed her eyes. She could feel the book's heartbeat against her chest, its frightening melody knocking heavily against her rib cage. *Little pig, little pig, let me in,* the book whispered again. She imagined the filmy skin of each page, warped and damp, sewn into the leather boards with hair— blonde and dark, the ends curling between each page like a finger holding its place.

With her head bowed, Pearl walked the aisle to its end. She drew her right hand across her forehead to her chest and each shoulder. Then she walked past the high brass candle holders, the flames snuffed and cold. *Please help me,* she chanted as she made her way behind the altar and to the side door that led to the sacristy. It was the only place to hide the book, the only place to set it at Jesus' feet.

✝

Pearl pushed her way into The Gaslight, her boots tracking mud onto the yellow terrazzo floors. For six blocks, she leaned into the late morning storm's pummeling devotion of wind and hail, her face tucked beneath the hood of her coat and fists tight in its pockets. Cold wind rushed through the spaces between her bones, shivering her skeleton like a wind chime. The persistent chattering of her teeth marred the bell's greeting and confounded the doo-wop shimmer of Ronnie Spector's song, which was radiant in the near-vacant spaces of The

Gaslight's interior. Save for the dancing skeletons and voodoo skulls, Victorian ghosts, Macbeth's three witches, the Bride of Frankenstein, and every other ghoulish painting that marred the windows in flaking paint, there was no one at The Gaslight except Rose and Benny. They sat side-by-side at the counter, leaning over a picture book, surrounded by Benny's crayons and his Batman figurines, his Scooby-Doo bookbag on a hook by his knee.

"What happened?" Rose bellowed as Benny spun around in his chair, an empty milkshake glass at his elbow.

"I—"

Rose's low heels clicked across the muddy floor, and she immediately pulled Pearl into a tight hug. Though Pearl's ears were numb, and her cheeks burned in the thawing warmth of the diner, Rose set her face against Pearl's and whispered into her ear. "Your momma brought Benny round here hours ago, just pulled up to the door and unbuckled him from the front seat—just dropped him off on the doorstep like an orphan. I don't know where she went. She just told Benny to come on in here until she got back—didn't say anything to me, didn't even come in. Then she went off somewhere with that painter. Benny was pretty torn up about it when he came in. I don't know what happened at the house this morning."

Pearl nodded and looked at Benny. His hair was full of static, cowlick fanned like peacock feathers. His eyes were glassy marbles, crystal balls streaked in tears. Pearl bit the inside of her cheeks to keep her own tears away. She swallowed them deeply, flooding her fury and the graveyard where it slept, drowning her mother's name, deep within her belly.

Then a throat cleared from an unseen place. In the

hidden booth painted in the golden tomb of the dead mothers, a small white-haired couple sat side-by-side. They were shrunken behind the table's standard height. The man's arthritic fingers slid coins into stacks next to the sugar jar. The woman leaned against him so she could see the full height of the five women decadently painted in the booth's mural. Her face pressed firmly against the viewfinder of a Kodak disposable camera, she snapped photos of the dead mothers, painted in roses and robes, lying languidly across one another. The first flash made Pearl jump. Rose sucked her teeth and stomped her heel against the terrazzo floor.

"Hang up your coat, Sugar, and go on over there with Benny. We were just chatting about what we're gonna cook up for brunch." Rose winked at Benny and then reached across the counter, pulling two menus and cutlery from their rightful baskets. "I'll be right back."

Benny gave Pearl a small smile as he swiveled back and forth on his stool. His red sweater was fraying at the neck, and the legs of his jeans were so short they stopped at his calves, revealing a pair of dinosaur socks. "You look like the Wolfman— your muscles have gotten so big your clothes don't fit anymore."

"On Friday, Ms. Freyling moved a big kid desk into the classroom for me because I can't fit in the kindergarten desks anymore, and she said she was sick of telling me to be still. It wasn't my fault my knees were always knocking it, making it like an earthquake, so my books would just fall right off. The other kids thought it was funny, but Ms. Freyling said I was a distraction."

"Are you the biggest kid in your class?" Pearl hung her soggy coat on a rack by the door. The wind still raged on the other side of the glass, bellowing between the cracks of the diner's windows, and dragging tumbleweeds and debris through The Gaslight's parking lot.

"Probably—I never really looked. I probably have the longest legs."

"Do any other kids have big kid desks?"

"Mrs. Freyling does— hers is giant."

"She's not a kid."

"Yeah."

"So, it's just you?"

"Probably."

Pearl watched Rose in the corner. A coffee urn cooled on the table as she talked to the wizened couple and wrote down their order. The white-haired woman had the sugar jar suspended above her coffee mug— the crystals pouring into the small porcelain cup— for a surprisingly long time.

"I think that old lady likes sugar as much as you do, Bens."

Benny turned toward the back of the diner. The white-haired woman was still absently pouring the sugar, her eyes locked on Rose. As one hand poured the sugar, the other stirred it around the cup. "I can't believe it all fits in there."

"A bottomless cup."

"It's really pouring all over her feet—a giant pile under the table."

Just then, Rose tore the ticket from the pad and picked up the coffee urn. As soon as she turned her back from the table and made a silly face at Benny and Pearl— her eyes wide and tongue to one side— the white-haired woman set down the sugar jar and slowly blinked.

"Standard weirdos, come all the way from Cheyenne to find out what's wrong with us out here that makes all the mothers die. They asked me if the water is okay to drink. Isn't that something? They think maybe our water's gone bad and we're all losing our minds over it."

Pearl cringed. She felt the hollow knocking of the book, as if it were still there, wrapping its arms around her. She felt her stomach turn, the queasy tears captured in buckets by her fury and stacked into the corners. "But you wanted the peepers to come to town, right?"

Rose set the menus back in the stack behind the counter and got to work on the white-haired couple's order. She pulled a crate of blueberries and a bowl of her famous pancake batter from the small refrigerator under the counter. "You all want chocolate chip with Halloween sprinkles, or do you want blueberry pecan?"

"Chocolate chip."

"Blueberry."

Rose laughed. "I could have guessed it."

"I'm making all four of you some eggs too, 'cause those two need some brain food," she pointed her spatula at the corner booth, "and you two need some protein. And you're having some banana slices— especially you Benny. You're getting too big for your own good."

Benny smiled and spun on his stool.

Rose heated the skillet and set two bowls in front of her, dividing some of the batter between them and mixing in the different ingredients for the orders. In the smaller one, she added chocolate chips and sprinkles. In the other, she added blueberries and pecans. When she had the batter prepared, she turned back to Pearl. "And as for wanting the peepers to visit, you know how much things change around here and how fast. It's noon on a Sunday morning— usually one of my busiest mornings of the week— and those two are the only paying customers I've got. Now, it could just be the terrible weather—" Rose paused, watching the hail slap against the windows. Great gashes of paint were hacked away from the murals with each icy bullet that hit. "But it's probably more than that. I think I'd be happy if this storm just stripped all those paintings from the windows, especially that one." She tilted her head toward the booth where the white-haired couple sat. "I'm realizing I can't influence anything that happens around here—not really—and because things are changing so fast, it's probably better to stay out of it."

"None of that's true. I mean, you can't just let people believe what they want to because they think it's easier or something. I mean—" Pearl paused and looked at the golden mural of the dead mothers. The painting held all the gravity and truth that the women held as ghosts, just this morning, in her living room. "Those women are your friends— you did all this for them. And now they're my friends too, and they need our help. I have to talk to you, Rose. That's why I walked all the way over here."

Rose nodded solemnly. "I figured, seeing you rushing in here like the storm itself. And by the look on your face, I can tell it's nothing that is gonna make today any easier. After I finish cooking this up, you and I will go to one of those back booths for a talk."

While Rose turned her back to the counter and sang along to the Doo-Wop and Soul groups that cascaded from the small speakers suspended along the ceilings throughout the diner, Pearl sat with Benny. She smelled the strawberry shampoo in his hair, and noticed the peanut butter crusted along his knuckles from scraping the sides of the jar for his breakfast. The purple veins that etched the backs of

Benny's hands looked closer to the surface than they'd ever been. His skin looked thinner, more translucent. The purple moons around his eyes more predominant. It felt like forever since Pearl had really looked at her little brother, and what she saw shocked her. Did Benny have any idea what was happening? Had he heard her and Rose talking Friday night when they slept over at Rose's cabin? Did he see the dumb supper, or all the dead mothers in the living room that morning? Pearl had been so concerned with all the new troubles—all the new pitfalls of the immediate world she had been walking through—she forgot her number one trouble. The one who had changed everything from the beginning. She would never tell Benny—not in a million years— but he was her best friend. He was more family than anyone. Pearl had to figure all this out, and soon. She had to save her mother. And not just for her own sake or her mother's sake, not for the dead mothers or for the ones who could come after, but for Benny. Because ever since her mom had met that painter, Pearl felt like she was the only one looking out for Benny. Rose and Henshaw helped, and maybe they did more good than Pearl did. But mostly, it seemed like Benny was taking care of himself. And he was doing his best, but his best was terrible. He was too young. Pearl was probably too young too, but that did not matter to her. While Rose cooked and sang along to the radio, while the white-haired couple counted their change and took flashing photos of the mothers' golden mural, Pearl played tic-tac-toe with Benny and tried to forget everything else but him.

The hot plates did not take too long to make. While Rose served the old couple in the dead mothers' booth, Pearl cut up Benny's pancakes.

"You get the food, and I'll get the coffee," Rose said when she made her way back over to the counter. She filled two cups and pulled a small pitcher of milk from the refrigerator. Pearl grabbed the two platters of pancakes and fruit and headed to the booth farthest from the white-haired couple.

"Eat up those pancakes, Benny. We won't be too long, now," Rose called over her shoulder as she rounded the counter and followed Pearl to the booth painted with Macbeth's three witches, their cauldron bubbling with seeing eyes and spiders. Rose sat down heavily in the booth and put her feet up on the bench beside Pearl's leg. "I saw in the morning paper that a new mother was found late last night. I can't think it's anyone I know because no one called to tell me. Have you heard from any of them? Have you met her?" Rose asked as she poured milk into her coffee.

"I guess so. They were at the house this morning. We all watched the news report, and the new mother was there on the couch, glaring at the T.V. She hardly spoke, but it was apparent she was furious. The rage bubbled right out of her. I think all the mothers believe they were murdered, and they just need evidence to prove it. Something concrete enough to make them remember. And Cindy is dead sure there is no way the new one committed suicide— not with all that anger saying something different. So, this morning, she sent me over to Bessie Rains' house to talk to their kids."

"Did you go?" Rose sipped her coffee, her painted eyes the color of fall leaves.

Pearl nodded. "I was there for a while. Most of the kids were gone with Miss Bessie to church, but I talked to three of them. One was the new girl—she had just gotten there this morning. Her name is Shelby. And Maggie and Kaia's daughters were there too. They faked being sick so they didn't have to go to church. The things they said were terrible. Bessie has been abusing the kids—especially the boys—and they are all scared of her. They try to keep their doors locked at night, but it doesn't help. She has some real bad men over to the house. One is real big. They call him the giant, but the other one is like the Devil himself. No one but Deirdre has seen the Devil Man, and he hurt her pretty bad. She tried to say something, but Bessie put a stop to it. Now Deirdre just hides in the house, skittering around like a mouse, trying to keep away from the Devil Man. She can't keep away from Ms. Bessie, though. Emma and Genie said that Ms. Bessie is kind of obsessed with Deirdre—won't let Deirdre out of her sight."

Rose's eyes went glassy behind the coffee cup. "Do they know who these men are?"

"No, never seen them before. They think they're monsters."

"I'm sure they are."

"And Bessie locked the boys in the attic with no food or water for days. She locked them up the same night the Devil Man went after Deirdre. Since then, Miss Bessie moved Charlie and Connor into the kitchen cupboard so she can keep an eye on them. But she also told Emma and Genie that more kids'll be moving into the house— and this was just before Shelby showed up this morning."

"Like she knew there would be more deaths?"

Pearl nodded. She took a sip of her water and continued. "They said that Bessie carries this big old book everywhere and she talks to herself a lot—chants things—

and that sometimes, when she's alone in the kitchen, they can hear her having a conversation with the Devil Man. They can hear the man's voice, but they've never seen him. Whenever they've snuck downstairs to see, he disappears right when they open the door. Bessie laughs at them, but the kids are terrified. At night when they're in bed, they hear the Devil Man and the giant upstairs. They hear the giant coming down the hallways, banging on the walls. They hear the Devil Man's footsteps right next to their beds, watching them. But they don't see them."

Rose put down her coffee mug. "And you believe them?"

"I do. I think Miss Bessie conjured them. Cindy wanted proof, so after I talked to the girls, I snuck downstairs into the kitchen. I figured that's where Miss Bessie hid her book because that's the only room she's always in. And I found it."

"Well, I'll be."

"It gets worse, though."

"Go on then."

"The book is evil. You can feel it. Just holding it, you can feel the evil trying to get inside you. I could only look inside it quick because it was getting so late, but I saw a page that had each of the dead mother's names listed—in order—along with the day each of them died. Shelby's mom—Shelby is the new girl at Ms. Bessie's house—was in there. Her name is Suzanne Dubray. They'll say it on the news tonight. And after her name—" Pearl's voice broke. "—was my mom's name."

Rose's beautiful eyes widened. "Was there a date by your momma's name yet?"

Pearl shook her head.

"Did she say anything this morning about where she was going? Do you know anything about that painter she's with?"

"No, but I thought of that too. He could be the giant or the Devil Man. Both descriptions sound like him."

"He's new to town, so no one knows him. And he's the only one who has really seen Diane in the last three days."

"Yeah—"

What do you know about him?"

"Not much. He has a black jeep, and he takes mom out all the time. It seems like she's been drinking a lot lately. He's been spending the night at our house, and Henshaw is mad at mom about it. Benny doesn't like him."

Rose sat back heavily against the booth bench and sighed. "His name is Tom Boudreaux. The morning he painted up the windows, he was at the diner even before I got here. He followed me in and sat at the bar while I fixed a pot of coffee. He seemed alright, a little moody, a little like I didn't want to turn my back to him. He kept bunching up his fists like his hands hurt. When he finally went outside to get to painting, I felt relieved. I had no idea Diane would fall in with a man like that."

"That's not much to go on."

"No, but at least we have a name and the make of his vehicle. God help your momma that we're having a conversation like this."

"There's more."

"Lay it on me."

"I took the book and hid it. I've been trying to get ahold of the dead mothers since I was on Bessie's doorstep, but they haven't come."

"That's strange."

"It's never happened before."

"Well, that's all of it?"

Pearl nodded and took another sip of her water. Her stomach growled but watching the curved scoops of butter melt slowly into a deep crevice of pancake made her nauseous. She nibbled at an apple slice and pulled her coffee toward her.

"So, Bessie Rains is abusing the kids, has two men working with her, and collectively, they are killing the town's single mothers—and maybe more than that, they are murdering mothers with no relations—and taking their children. The kids are terrified of Bessie and the men, you stole Bessie Rains' book, which may have all you need to prove she planned all this out, and beyond that, the dead mothers have disappeared."

"That's everything."

"Alright." Rose pulled her plate of pancakes toward her and moved the butter to the side of the plate. "Where's the book?"

"Righteous Dei."

Rose let out a laugh so hearty and true that it momentarily muted The Marvelettes pleading with the postman. "Oh, Sugar, you are a wonder. You need to eat up because we have things to do. And don't you worry about your momma. She's tough like you— she's always had to be— and your worrying won't help anyway."

Pearl kept her eyes on the Formica tabletop as she pulled her plate toward her. "What are we going to do?"

"After you eat and these two fuddy-duddies leave, I am going to close up the diner long enough to drive you and Benny home. You're going to wait for your momma and see if Henshaw knows anything about the painter, and you're going to try to get in touch with the other mothers. Then you and Benny are going to go to church with Henshaw, and I'll meet you there. We are going to get that book and figure all this out."

"You're not going to want it in your house, Rose."

"I figured as much. We'll wait till everyone leaves the church and do our work there. You and I talked about the evil in Fullmouth the last time we called to the mothers, and I have a feeling Bessie's book is going to have all the poison we need to prove that's true. Her family started this town, so it makes sense that they'd be at the origin of all its dark parts too."

†

Rose left the heat on in the truck, and the Oldies station on the radio mumbled along just above a whisper. "I'll be right back, you two keep a lookout, see that I don't get blown up into a tornado or something else," she said as she unbuckled her seatbelt and adjusted the thick scarf knotted around her face and hair. When she climbed out of the truck, the groaning of the door's rusty hinges was subdued by the squall. Rose quickly ran across the yard, avoiding the empty flowerpots and car parts haphazardly scattered throughout. Pearl and Benny watched her trip only once, her patent leather kitten heel caught in a divot. Wrapped in a giant overcoat that muted her features and kept her work dress and nylons protected, Rose looked like a giant beetle scampering to the front door of Henshaw's house. Before she knocked on the door, Rose unwrapped the scarf from her face and hair and wound it loosely around her neck.

Pearl used the arm of her sweater to clear the condensation forming on the truck's window. The gold

Oldsmobile was not in the driveway, but Pearl still hoped her mom would be the one to answer the door. Maybe the Oldsmobile had broken down somewhere like Big Bear Grocery, the spark plugs always going bad when the weather turned. Maybe Diane got a ride home, and she was just on the other side of the door, watching her soaps. Maybe there was a grocery sack full of bananas, a bright orange carving pumpkin, Count Chocula, and those little ghost face cookies sitting on the counter in the kitchen, waiting for Pearl and Benny to arrive. When Rose knocked, the door opened with a force that did not belong to Diane. Right then, Pearl knew her mother was not home. That she had not been there all morning—not since Pearl had left for Miss Bessie's. Not since Diane and the painter dumped Benny at The Gaslight.

Tall and long-faced, boots on his feet and a thick flannel buttoned to the collar, Henshaw rocked back and forth on his heels as Rose spoke. He nodded a few times and looked to the truck. Rose smiled and squeezed his arm, thanking him and waving before she wrapped the scarf around her head and ran back into the weather. Henshaw ducked into the house momentarily, then reappeared with a rain slicker over his flannel and a wide-brimmed cowboy hat on his head. He followed Rose to the truck. As she climbed into the driver's seat, Henshaw opened the passenger door. He took his hat off and put it on Pearl's head. As Henshaw nodded goodbye to Rose, he asked Benny if he was ready to go, then picked him up. In three lumbering steps, Henshaw and Benny were back on the front porch. Pearl moved much slower behind them. Already tired from the morning, she felt well-adjusted to the ferocity of pummeling weather. Navigating the yard full of flowerpots and car parts, Pearl was sure she looked just as much a giant insect as Rose did, scampering through the yard.

"Pretty bad out there," Henshaw said as he locked the front door behind Pearl.

Benny yawned. The purple circles around his eyes had grown, the dark shadows smudged across his forehead and cheeks. He leaned against the wall to pull off his sneakers, then headed to the couch where his Scooby-Doo blanket was still curled into a ball from its morning use.

"You look dog tired, young man."

"The weather always takes it out of him," Pearl said. "Come on, Benny. Let's get you some warm clothes and you can take a nap for a little while."

Benny followed Pearl down the hall and into his own room, which was about the size of a large cupboard. When Pearl's small family first moved in, Henshaw said that he and his wife built the room by taking down the wall between the hallway closet and the bathroom one. He said his wife used the space to work on her quilting projects. The room had no windows, but it was a cheery yellow, and Pearl had hung a hundred glow-in-the-dark stars within the tiny space, which always gleamed in the sunless room. Benny's bed was on stilts, and under it, in a neat row, was his dresser, bookshelf, and toy chest. The room was a shoe box, but it was the first bedroom Benny ever had to himself, and he said it was like living in a tree trunk.

Pearl pulled a pair of sweatpants and a Batman pajama shirt from Benny's dresser and sent him to the bathroom to change while she moved all the stuffed animals against the wall of his bed and laid the Scooby-Doo blanket across the mattress. When Benny returned, Pearl had already turned off the lamp, and the hundred glowing stars welcomed him into their dream world.

"Nice place you got here," Pearl whispered as she tucked Benny into bed. She left his door cracked when she closed it behind her.

Pearl found Henshaw at the kitchen table, a toasted turkey sandwich and pickle wedge on a small plate in front of him. Under the plate was the morning paper, ink smudged and corners curled from the thorough reading it received earlier that morning. Pearl poured herself a glass of water from the faucet and leaned against the counter. She took a deep breath—appraising its depth—before she spoke.

"I feel like I haven't really seen my mom since last Thursday. It's probably not that long—not really—but it seems like it has been forever. Have you seen her?"

Henshaw set down his sandwich and wiped his mouth with a napkin. "No, not too much since then either. Thursday afternoon, I took her to get a car battery and helped her install it. Then after that." Henshaw cleared his throat, "only late at night or early in the morning."

"And sometimes not even then."

"Not Thursday night, but she's been here every night since then."

"But with that man."

"Tom."

"Tom."

Henshaw picked up his coffee mug and took a long sip. The black coffee ring left on the newspaper circled a Sioux Falls Bloomingdale's advertisement.

"What happened this morning?"

Henshaw returned the mug to the same newspaper ring

and picked up his sandwich. "Your mom and Tom were trying to leave. I was headed out to church, and you were already off somewhere. I don't know if you didn't tell your mom that you were leaving, or if she didn't hear you say it."

"She wouldn't come out of her room. I told her through the door."

Henshaw frowned, then continued. "Well, she got mad when she couldn't find you. She stormed through the house yelling your name, and when she realized you weren't here, she stormed through the house cursing. Tom just stood at the door, jingling his keys and tapping his foot like he couldn't wait another minute." Henshaw took a bite from his sandwich. "Your mom had enough by then. She threw Benny in the car and tore off in this weather, those old tires peeling out in the driveway. I locked up and went to church. I don't think Benny had even brushed his teeth or changed his clothes."

Pearl frowned. "She dumped him off with Rose."

"Rose told me. Your mom didn't say anything about bringing Benny over to the diner, neither."

"Do you know where she went?"

Henshaw shook his head. "She wouldn't say. They both just looked impatient as hell to get out of here— excuse my language."

"And you don't know when she'll be back?"

"No, but I would guess she'll be home by tonight. She's been here every night since Thursday."

Pearl nodded. "Yeah," she mumbled and dumped her water into the sink.

†

The room was full of ghosts. Their dresses looked less

227

like lace and more like gauze, denser than spider webs but close to the same design. Their rose crowns were crumbling. The leaves were curled and blanketed in downy mildew; the roses were scrawny, and what petals were left had gone translucent brown. Cindy Stewart sat at the desk, her back straight and bony, her long fingernails more like claws now, yellow and curving as they tapped slowly against the surface of Pearl's desk. Cindy's hair and nails were longer than the last time Pearl had seen her— *was it just this morning?* —and her cheekbones had sunken farther into dangerous angles. She smiled at Pearl. She was missing a tooth. Her skin was pale blue. Pearl could not bring herself to look at the other women in the room—not yet—but she could feel their fading presence. The window was still open from her morning with the rooster in her room. Grey wind pushed pearl strings of rain into her bedroom. The purple curtains were heavy with rainwater, unable to move. The sheer fabric was denser than Cindy Stewart's body, her long legs crossed neatly at the ankles.

Pearl let her eyes become cloudy, let her fury kick over all those buckets of tears. Her shoulders curled as she put her hands to her face. Everything was changing again. "Where have you been?" Pearl gasped through her hands. Her shoulders heaved under the weight of her sobbing.

"Something's happened," Cindy whispered, her voice more cracked than the last time Pearl heard it.

"It's like we're being poisoned." Kaia Goodwin sat on the floor in the small space between Pearl's bed and night table. Her long black hair was muted and stringy, the part so wide the small animal shape of her skull had become her most predominant feature. "It's like what I'd see on those late-night murder mysteries I used to watch."

"*Arsenic and Old Lace*," said a whisper from beneath the bed.

"*Madam Bovary*." Maggie Teller laid flat on the bed next to Suzanne Dubray, her gaunt hands across her heart.

"I'm glad you think this is so funny." Molly Boutell sat cross-legged on the floor, staring into the mirror that hung on Pearl's closet door. She pulled at her thin skin, which looked to Pearl like dried glue. So fragile it was opaque in some spots, threatening to tear open in others, particularly in the small hollows between her jaw bones.

"We're already dead," said the woman beneath the bed.

"We were never supposed to be here." Suzanne Dubray's voice was a venomous hiss that cut through Pearl's weeping. Her wrath immediately altered the gravity of Pearl's heart. Her rage bolted up the pearly gates, put away the violin, and forced Pearl back into the present.

Pearl moved her hands from her face and walked over to her bed where Suzanne was laying. Suzanne Dubray's rage had hardened her skin. It had crusted her eyes lids. She looked like an angel of revenge that would grace a tombstone for eternity, staring down into the earth, fist raised toward the heavens.

"I met Shelby this morning," Pearl offered.

Suzanne opened her eyes slowly, the stone dust falling to her cheeks.

"We need to help her—we need to help all of them before you all just lay down and die."

"We're already dead," the voice under the bed said again.

Molly rolled her eyes at the mirror.

"Karen," mouthed Kaia.

229

Pearl nodded. She put her hand on the bedpost and stood over Suzanne Dubray. "Miss Bessie is abusing them. She has it out for Charlie and Connor because she wants to run them out of the house."

"Connor wouldn't leave Emma," Maggie declared about her son and daughter.

"No, he wouldn't either," Kaia replied.

"Charlie has been mapping the house—that's what really got a target on his back. Him and Connor were hunting out all the secret passageways. When Miss Bessie found the map, she threw them in the attic for days without food or water. The kids tried to get them out, but Miss Bessie wouldn't climb the stairs—she can't really—which is why the passageways are so important."

Cindy scoffed. "Charlie won't leave if there's still something to prove," she said about her son, the oldest of the orphans at Bessie Rains' house.

"No, he wouldn't either."

"There are two men living in the house, and the kids think the men are living in the passageways. One is a giant who comes around when they go to bed, banging on the doors and trying to get into the rooms. The kids lock the doors at night— they try to put furniture in front of the doors to block them up— but they really don't have much in their rooms. The other man is worse, though. He's the one with all the power, more power than Miss Bessie. I think he's the one in charge. The kids call him the Devil Man, and he's the one who comes into their rooms at night. The night Miss Bessie threw Charlie and Connor into the attic, something real bad happened. Charlie and Connor are the ones that protect the kids—"

"Of course they are. They've always been in charge of

those kids."

"With the boys out of the way, the Devil Man was free to go in and out of the rooms without confrontation—the rest of the kids were already afraid of Miss Bessie. She has a grimoire, and she called that man to her. Probably the giant too. The Devil Man runs the show, though—I saw him in a dream last night. He was carrying Miss Bessie's book and trying to get me to sign it. It seems like Miss Bessie's only job is to collect kids. She isn't even trying to hide it anymore. Before Shelby showed up, Miss Bessie started moving the kids around the house—she told them that more kids would be moving in."

"What a bitch," Molly whispered at the mirror.

Kaia sat up on the bed. "So, it's her, then."

"She's the one—or them—they're the ones who murdered us," Molly said to the mirror.

"To take our kids," came Karen Kelly's voice from beneath the bed.

"Because Miss Bessie would know we have no relations," Maggie whispered.

Cindy Stewart pulled a cigarette from the sleeve of her dress and set it between her pale lips. "That old croon knows everything about everyone."

"Looks like it," Pearl said. "Anyway, I don't think the Devil Man or the giant are from this world. They're like you, but not. I don't think they were ever human."

"Like demons?" asked Molly in the mirror.

"That's a stretch," replied the voice under the bed.

"I'd believe anything at this point," rasped Cindy.

"I stole Miss Bessie's black book. There's a lot of spells in there. Your names are there too—right next to the days you died—all written in blood."

"Blood?" Kaia gasped.

"I kept calling you all to come, but you never showed up."

"We couldn't find you," Cindy said.

"We tried. We were locked in the dark for a while, then the door opened, and we came out like this," Molly growled, still poking at her face.

Kaia sighed. "It was a miracle we got back here."

"You stole her grimoire?" Karen asked.

Pearl nodded. "My mom's name is next on the list."

"That makes sense," Suzanne said matter-of-factly.

"So that's why you can see us, huh," Molly wondered.

"Maybe."

"It's more than that," said Kaia.

"Tonight, I am meeting Rose at the church—that's where I took Bessie's book—and we are going to try to stop all of this. I don't know how yet, but I think Rose does."

"Call those men back to hell," said the voice from beneath the bed.

"That sounds about right."

A skeleton of lightning danced on the other side of Pearl's bedroom window. The amber light of the lamp blinked off and on three times, then came back with a static start. Cindy Stewart pulled the cigarette from her lips. She finally stopped drumming her nails against Pearl's desk. The sounds had become hypnotic. It was so familiar— like an old jingle on the radio in another room— that it was only really noticed when it ended. She slowly stood up. Her long spine sloped like a question mark from her hips as she walked across the room. Cindy's sandals made no sound as she trudged into the puddle beneath the window. Leaning across the frame and into the wind's grey squall,

Cindy Stewart raised her arm and whistled twice. In moments, the wind was torn away from the room in a rush of black shadows. Cindy smiled and turned from the window. On her arm perched her familiar. The large crow's feathers were still a daunting oil slick, but a white mask had formed around his eyes. He had returned from the Black Mountains, back from more primordial wanderings. "We'll go with you," Cindy pronounced as she touched her head to the crow's crown.

CHAPTER TWELVE

The Great Destroyer

The crow's talons clung to the rail of Henshaw's truck when it rounded the corner of Mystic Avenue onto Prospect Street. The dead mothers gathered in the bed of the truck, their sandals and skirts bunched together, their opaque bodies swaying with each shift and jolt of the road. The storm had stopped its whining moans and pummeling hail. The wind climbed upwards into the high points of the atmosphere, winding the clouds into a carousel of shadows. The powerful airstream forced the clouds into such a frenetic spin, clumps of their bodies flung to the earth under the weighty gravity of movement. The sleet from the spinning clouds was ceaseless, its density dragging the slush straight to the earth, without the grace of a gale to ease the fall.

"Turn around, Benny. Your seatbelt won't work if you don't sit right." Henshaw wiped the windshield with a red mechanic's rag.

Benny's knobby knees dug into the seat and his arms rested on the bench as he stared out the back window. "Where'd that crow come from?"

"Crow?"

Pearl turned. Cindy's crow was right next to the window, its large body blocking the driver's side view.

"No crow—" Henshaw said, looking into the rear-view mirror. "Come on, your shoes are getting grime all over my seats." Henshaw slapped the mechanic's rag lightly at Benny's shoe.

Benny shrugged and turned around in his seat. "He has a mask. He looks like a bandit."

"Maybe he's going to rob the church," Pearl said.

The sleet was too heavy for the windshield wipers, so Henshaw had to pull over in front of the Black Buffalo Saloon to scoop the icy rain from the crevice between the hood and windshield. As Henshaw set to his work, Pearl watched the saloon door. From the street, she could only see red lights blinking against the wood-paneled walls. She saw what could have been the leg of a bar stool, a work boot, the ember of a cigarette. But the door was a blaring black hole, hiding faces and conversation beneath the sound of steel guitars and fiddles. Pearl heard one voice though, bellowing out to Henshaw relentlessly, calling his name over and again, like a threat or remembrance. Henshaw kept his head down— his bare hands clearing the ice— and finished his work quickly.

Pearl turned her back to the passenger door for the rest of the ride to Righteous Dei Lutheran. She watched the windshield wipers and the ghost mothers sway back and forth, in the same steady rhythm.

"You two are mighty quiet," Henshaw said a block from the church. He was silent for a moment as he wiped the windshield again. The grey light of dusk was setting in, combining with the sleet and condensation on the windshield. The Swallows looked like it had gone static through the glass of the Bronco's windows. "Reflective— that's what Pastor Hall calls it. When Maxine first died, I was real reflective too. Thinking on change is the best way to deal with it, and it opens up your mind to the Word. He helped see me through some tough times."

"I'm thinking about that crow back there," Benny said.

In the grey light of the cab, he wore his best green sweater and brown corduroys. His coat was tight against his body, the sleeves too short. He wore Pearl's black gloves, which were long enough on his thin arms to tuck his sweater into. She'd combed his hair before they left the house, but Pearl knew that as soon as Benny took off his hat in the narthex, his hair would set itself back into a fan of vibrant feathers.

Henshaw parked the Bronco as close to the front door as he could. He reminded Pearl to push the truck's door handle in when she closed the latch so it would lock, then he quickly carried Benny up the church steps. The dead mothers progressed slowly, but Pearl waited for them to assemble on the sidewalk before she left the truck's cabin. They climbed the stairs together, the women arm and arm, leaning on one another for support.

The strange procession calmly followed in line behind Henshaw. Pearl kept her head down, for fear she would see Miss Bessie, as they walked to the front row of pews. Henshaw always sat in the front row, his back to the rest of the town and his eyes on Jesus, never swaying. Benny sat next to Henshaw; their coats stacked between them. Pearl sat between Benny and Cindy Stewart; her crow pecked the thick carpet at her feet. The women on the pew were nearly translucent, their shapes fading in and out within the catacombs of candlelight. Their thin frames and full dresses lined the pew in the order of their chronologies. After Cindy Stewart sat Molly Boutell, Kaia Goodwin, Maggie Teller, Karen Kelly, and Suzanne Dubray. Pearl imagined her mother at the end of the line, brighter than the rest, her rose crown still new, not yet touched by the poison of existing between two worlds.

Before Pearl could think too long about her mother,

the heavy notes of the pipe organ began, and with it, the sound of shifting bodies as everyone was called to stand. Benny had the hymnal in his hands. He'd turned to number two-hundred-sixty-two, and "A Mighty Fortress is Our God" was printed in a neat scroll across the header of the music page. The notes were difficult for the worshippers to meet, the melody carrying the words into strange angles, but they worked through the hymn from memory, from the decades they had stood in the same places. Their family lines had gathered in the same pews as each generation grew up, as some passed into the next world, leaving the children of previous years to still stand and sing. They followed the onerous hymn out of love. The sound was not beautiful, but the song was. Pearl felt the weight of the pipe organ's notes in her chest as she listened to the congregation. She mouthed the words to herself like a prayer. Every one of the dead mothers was standing as well. Each gripped the ornately carved rail before her, bone fingers holding tight the rose and thorn engravings. Pearl could hear Cindy next to her, singing softly as her crow tested the strength of its wings at her feet.

"The peace of the Lord be with you all," Pastor Hall called to the congregation when the pipe organ hit its final, resounding notes.

"And also with you," replied the assembled communicants.

"Please, share the peace."

In response, a number of the parishioners milled about the nave, walking between the pews to greet one another and shake hands. Henshaw turned around and nodded to those who nodded to him, but he never left the two children. He never left the row of dead mothers, each woman suspended in place, leaning on one another or holding hands, passing the peace between them. Not one parishioner walked through the line of ghost women to meet Pearl and Benny, who appeared so small next to Henshaw. Pearl saw Rose in the back of the nave, speaking to Hubert Broderick, who was curled over his splintered cane. The cancer that kept him on the church's prayer list for the last two years had recently spread from the lymph node in his hip to his stomach and liver. He grimaced as Rose spoke softly and patted his hand in an act of consolation.

As everyone returned to their family plots within the church pews, Pastor Hall bowed before the crucifix then took his place at the pulpit. "Please, stay standing and let us pray like our Father taught us."

Pearl could hear the silent gathering of breath behind her. She mimicked the postures of the dead mothers, head bowed, eyes closed. The light from the altar candles flickered through the women's bellies as the parishioners began to speak. "Our Father, who art in heaven, hallowed be Thy name. Thy kingdom come, Thy will be done, on earth as it is in heaven; give us this day our daily bread, and forgive us our trespasses as we forgive those who trespass against us; and lead us not into temptation, but deliver us from evil. For Thine is the kingdom and the power and the glory forever and ever. Amen." The Lord's Prayer rang like a bell throughout the caverns of the church. At its end, the sleet returned to the density of hail, beating irregular time against the tin roof. The amber bulbs of the streetlights that highlighted the stained-glass windows sputtered twice and blinked out. Candle flames grew full-bellied under an invisible weight and were nearly snuffed to smoke. Pearl could hear the Devil's book cackle on the other side of the wall, where she'd buried it beneath the folds of choir robes in the sacristy. The goosebumps along Pearl's arms and neck blinked open, their swollen faces staring at the image of Jesus on the crucifix before them.

"Please be seated," Pastor Hall bellowed from the pulpit's sovereign protection. The sound of shifting bodies was muffled by the thick carpets and deepening candlelight.

"Even on this dark evening that our Lord God has set before us, I see a few new faces, though most of the faces I see belong to those who have been away from the flock for a while. I see many who the storm has returned home, and I am glad to see you. On a night like this—when the weather makes it difficult to travel to the house of the Lord, and we've lit as many candles as we could find to make sure we can keep at our worship, even as the lights go out—well, brothers and sisters, it is nights like this that are truly special to me. It is nights like this that we do not gather out of obligation. We are all here out of love. We are all here out of need. Our flock has gathered together on this stormy night— here, within the Lord's house— to feel His protection and to lay our burdens down. That's right brothers and sisters, we are here to lay our burdens down. What we are going through as individuals and as a community is a condition that only He can solve. It is a burden that only He can carry for us. Now, we try. We all try to shoulder our burdens alone. We take on one, then another. We talk to our children, and we carry their burdens too. We take on the burdens of our aging parents, of our relations who are struggling. We have the burdens of our homes, our jobs, our disappointments, and losses.

And tonight, we come together—at the hour of our greatest struggle— to lay those burdens down at the feet of the Lord."

Pastor Hall took off his glasses and set them next to the Lutheran Biblical canon on the Communion table. He descended the three stairs from the altar and paced back and forth, the white collar of his uniform bright against the blooming blush climbing his neck and cheeks. He shook his head, then turned his back to the congregants and bowed deeply before the crucifix. Only then did he return to the pulpit.

"Please stand for our reading of the Gospel." Pastor Hall paused as the shuffling of Bible pages and bones began. "The Holy Gospel according to Matthew, chapter 11, verses 28-30."

"Glory to you, O Lord," the worshipers called.

"'Come to me, all who are weary and burdened, and I will give you rest. Take my yoke upon you and learn from me, for I am gentle and humble in heart, and you will find rest for your souls. For my yoke is easy and my burden is light.' This is the Gospel of the Lord."

"Praise to you, O Christ," chanted the congregants.

Pastor Hall set his hands behind his back and paced back and forth between the pulpit and lectern. From the front row, Pearl could see his leather oxfords sinking into the dense carpet, black leather against the blood-red fibers.

"We all know this verse—both the new faces and old ones—we have all used it, at one time or another, as a touchstone through tough times. And right now, with the loss of so many mothers in our community, our burden is heavy, and our hearts are not light. We worry about our own families, about the women of our struggling town. We worry about the children. But the Lord lights the way. He is our keeper. In these times, when we want to lock our doors and peer out the blinds at any knock that we hear, when we want to close our hearts and minds to those around us because we disagree, because we are upset, because we do not feel like we are being heard—well, brothers and sisters, that's the time we must turn to God. And not just from our living rooms. Not just in our bedrooms at night, where we pray in whispers, alone. This is the time we need to come together—like we have done this evening, on this brutally dark night—this is the time we need to raise our voices and pray to our Lord as one mind and one heart." Pastor Hall paused his pacing and looked out at the congregants, his small brown eyes scanning the dimly lit nave.

"Now, Matthew 11:28-30 has even more to tell us," he began again.

"Thanks be to God!" A voice exclaimed from the back corner.

"As cattle folk, we all know the burden of a yoke to an animal. We all know what that heavy weight latched across the backs of animals feels like. We know what it looks like— how heavy it is— and we all know that heavy yoke is only there to drag the tremendous burden that is just behind that animal's haunches. We know it is rough. The Lord knows it too. The Lord tells us that if we come to Him unburdened, if we come to Him weary and defeated, if we come to Him with our heavy load of worries, worries too heavy for any man to carry, we can lay them down. We can lay that burden down before the Lord, and He will give us rest. He tells us to take his yoke, to be 'gentle and humble in heart', to learn from Him, to follow in His teachings and His ways, and if we do it—if we can set aside all the negativity we focus on, all the burdens we let cloud our minds and hearts—well, brothers and sisters, if we humble ourselves at the feet of the Lord and let him be our guide, then our yoke will be easy, our burdens light. That's faith, brothers and sisters. That is the faith and love that Jesus gives to our hearts and souls, gives to the heavy burdens we carry. God gave his only son as an act of love for us. And now it is our work— especially in times so dark as these— it is our work to set aside our differences and come together as a community under the love and guidance of our Lord."

"Amen," a voice beside Pearl whispered.

Pastor Hall bowed his head. "Let us pray."

After a few moments, Pastor Hall slowly recited the names of the dead mothers. Pausing after each name, he gave grace to each woman on the pew. Then he listed the names of those she had to leave behind. "Cindy Stewart, loving mother of Charlie; Molly Boutell, loving mother of Jack; Kaia Goodwin, loving mother of Dakota and Genie; Maggie Teller, loving mother of Connor and Emma; Karen Kelly, loving mother of Deirdre; and Suzanne Dubray, loving mother of Shelby." He paused.

The evening news had come and gone. Tomorrow morning, the *Black Mountain Daily*'s lead story would include Suzanne Dubray's face in the long lineup of women who were sacrificed to the Swallows. Her name would be boldly printed below the photograph, like an accusation. From now on, her legacy as a woman and as a mother had ended. Any good she had done in her short life would only be recalled by her daughter, Shelby, and the rest would fade behind the abyss of an assumed suicide. On the grand stage of the Black Mountain range, Suzanne Dubray would be eternally fabled for the worst day of her life. Along with the other mothers, she would be permanently defined under the same banner of tragedy.

As each woman heard the names of her children, she curled into herself, the gauzy light of her edges dimming further.

"Please, Lord, bless them and keep them safe, both mother and child. Amen."

Benny held Pearl's hand. The women wept on the bench. The book cackled within the choir robes, mocking the dim procession of life playing out in the church. Pearl heard the clearing of throats and the shuffling of feet behind her. Nothing would ever be the same.

†

When the service was over, Benny collected the hymnals and stacked them on a small shelf by the door. He smiled at families as they passed and waved goodbye to the kids in his class. As the room emptied of warm bodies, leaving only the ghost mothers in the nave— wan and sickly, weak from their earthly wanderings— the thin air grew colder. The stained-glass windows framing the nave rattled softly. Each frame of the ornately cut and colored glass depicted pictorial scenes from Christ's youth, of Martin Luther, the dove, and Luther's Rose. These images lightly trembled as a biting wind found its way into the small pockets between the lead and glass. The wind wound its way into the church, a cold serpent hissing down the darkening aisles.

As voices faded into the deepening storm, Pearl could hear the Devil's book knocking from within the sacristy. Along with Benny collecting the hymnals, Pearl stayed behind with Henshaw to extinguish the candles and set everything in its place. She and Henshaw slowly walked the church, cupping their hands behind the long-burning flames. Each candle snuffed went cold quickly. The wax hardened and the shadows overwhelmed the edges where the golden light had shortly lived.

"I can't believe these are so tarnished," Henshaw said as he stacked the blackened candle holders into a box. "We used most of them last Sunday for Lucy Beckett's baptism, and they were high-polished then. The women's league makes sure the church's silver is always at its best. I've never seen silver tarnish so fast."

The book cackled. *I'll eat all your silver, and I'll eat your gold. I'll eat all your children, and I'll eat your souls.*

"Maybe it's just the change in weather." Pearl latched the lid of the candle box and stacked the small striking box of matches on top. "You light worship candles with these?"

Henshaw frowned. "Only when getting things done is more important than how we do them, which seems to be happening more and more lately." He heaved the box of candlesticks onto his shoulder. "We'll take these back through the side door, make sure not to approach the altar."

A white sheet was swept across the shrine, hiding the shapes of the body and blood of Christ beneath. In the shadows of the church, the Lord's table looked like a house not yet occupied, or one quickly left behind. There was an emptiness in the relative ease it took to hide away the parts of our unseen God. The book laughed. Pearl thought about her mom in the kitchen, the way her footsteps sounded against the floorboards of every house they'd ever lived in. How she'd lay in bed at night, listening to her mom walk around the house, comforted by the rhythmic sound, the pendulum swing that drew Pearl into dreams. She held the candle box tighter and followed Henshaw through the north transept, along an unlit hall on the gospel side of the church, and through the small door leading to the sacristy. Pearl listened for Rose in the dark corners of the room, but she could only hear the book's gurgled breathing and muffled knock from beneath the stacks of neatly folded choir robes.

Henshaw unhooked the latch on a glass cabinet and stacked the boxes of silver candle sticks neatly inside. Pearl passed him the box of white candles and studied the corners of the room. There was a curved window too high to reach, a harp and music stand, an upright piano, shelves of pamphlets, and free copies of Luther's Small Catechism. Rose was not there. The wind snaked into the small sacristy. The book purred in response. Pearl felt the air coil around her neck, the book vibrating against her shins. Henshaw finally closed the cabinet and returned a small skeleton key to his pocket. He looked at his watch, its neon-green glow hushed by the gloomy vestry. "Rose said she's going to help you with some homework?"

"Algebra," Pearl said, turning back toward Henshaw and the door out of the dark room. "Ms. Lippincott's been on my case about not finishing my assignments. Last week, she told mom I was hiding my worksheets in my desk. Rose is going to help me catch up."

Henshaw nodded. "Rose has got a head for math. She's done the books for the diner all these years. I was never too good at math either—my wife handled all that—and I'd be lying if I said I ever used Algebra after high school."

Pearl took a few steps toward the door that would return

her to the chapel. She saw a shadow bend into the room and then quickly move past.

Little pig, little pig, let me in, the book wheezed.

"And Benny's going too, I suppose."

Pearl nodded as she balled the sleeves of her sweater into her fists and crossed her arms. "I don't know what happened at the house this morning, but I feel bad about it anyway."

Henshaw sucked his teeth and scuffed his boot against the carpet but made no motion to leave. "There ain't nothing you could've changed about that, and you shouldn't worry about it now, anyway. What's done is done."

The book giggled. The sound of soft shoes tapping beat a rhythmic time within the dark room. *You better watch out! You better not cry!* The book sang loudly. *Because that old man is gonna huff, and he'll puff, and he'll blow the pearl right from that dark little clam.*

Pearl shivered. The million goosebumps along her neck and arms blinked in unison, the wet snap of their lids silencing the book. They were a million poison darts and a million land mines waiting to crack the Swallows apart. Pearl breathed deeply. The air opened the sky within her belly. Her ribs parted like tree branches, making way for the million eyes like stars. They turned inward. They blinked again and saw Pearl's fury, sitting on its headstone, green hands gnarled ugly and caked with grave dirt. Pearl imagined her mother in the front seat of the Oldsmobile, driving west in the sunlight, her knuckles white on the steering wheel, wearing her bathing suit the whole time because where they were headed, it was always summer.

"Thanks for everything, Henshaw," she said and

opened the door between the vestry and the nave.

Rose and the ghost mothers were gathered in the narthex. The women were in a circle, a pale green light visible only at the lace edges of their dresses, their fingertips and eye sockets, the twisting ends of their hair. The wind was an animal on the other side of the massive oak doors, repeatedly butting its head into the planks until they splintered. Each gust was a force of startling hostility. Benny alone ignored nearly everything around him. Much like when he was five years old, feeding the ducks potato chips at Silver Lake, in the church narthex, Benny drummed his fingers along the river rocks grouted into the floor, working with all his might to get the primordial crow's attention.

"I think it's about time we got to work," Rose whispered.

"Henshaw is still back there."

Rose nodded and tilted her head toward a door in the corner of the narthex. "We can see his truck pull out from in there, and not in a million years would he look in the cry room on his way out."

Rose pulled Benny up from the stone floor. She held him tightly, his brown corduroy rolled up to his shins. Rose pressed her finger against her tangerine-painted lips and signaled for Benny to keep quiet as she led the solemn and stately procession of Pearl, the ghost mothers, and the old crow, into the corner cry room.

When Henshaw finally left— his old Ford Bronco chugging oil as the heater warmed up, defrosting the ice on the windshield as he scraped the glass— the gale at the door finally halted its wailing violence, and the snaking wind had returned to the bands of Black Mountains far beyond the reaches of the church. A sharp blackness descended on Righteous Dei, siphoning all sound from the surroundings. Walking through the nave toward a crucifix she could no longer see, Pearl felt like she was inside the shell of an egg. She felt the domed roof, the fragile curve between two worlds, but it was too murky to fully see. The walls were too close and the caves near the roof too absolute in their architecture. Pearl held Benny's hand and tried to imagine that the sickly light of the ghost mothers could become warm, could return the candles to their places along the walls, could heat the church into a golden lantern. Benny hummed a song Pearl did not recognize, but as the ghost mothers walked hip to hip, their arms and necks leaning into one another like a bevy of swans, Rose plucked the verse from the shadows and sang the mournful lines into the decaying rafters.

"Sometimes, I feel like a motherless child, a long way from home. Sometimes, I feel like freedom is near, but it's so far away, it's so far away. Sometimes, I feel like a motherless child, and I wish I could fly a little bit closer to home. Sometimes, I feel like I'm almost gone, way up in the heavenly land. Sometimes, I feel like a motherless child a long way from home, but there's praying everywhere, then I'll find my home."

Rose held the notes deep in her belly, the weight of the words like ornaments strung next to each trawling step of the ghost mothers, bearing their weight to the ground, to the earth-bound melody, for as long as they could. The women were further out now, past the point of speech, their tongues swollen, too thick in their throats to swallow. Their ears were lined in pale green light, their eye sockets wide, their thin arms and debutant dresses like aging ballerinas, mirroring the tragedy of the words to their natural movements.

Benny concluded his humming melody at the cusp of the sacristy. The room gasped then held its breath as Benny and Pearl, Rose and the crow, and each of the six ghost mothers, entered. The door clicked shut behind them, the whoosh of a shadow leaving the space. From under the pile of robes the book growled. *Hello, little pigs.*

The mothers made their way toward the dusty assembly of instruments in the far corner of the room. They lined the music benches before the harp and piano.

"He should stay where we can see him," Pearl said, letting go of Benny's hand.

Rose looked around the dark room. "Come on over here," she said to Benny. "You can sit under the window, where the light is good." Rose pulled a pencil and notepad from her purse and set them on a small table under the window. "Now, write me a list of all the things you want to do for Halloween tomorrow. I'll talk to your momma, and we'll figure out what we can make happen."

"Can I play with the crow too?"

Rose looked around the shadowy room. Though she could not see Cindy Stewart's crow, she remembered its existence. "Maybe he'll follow you over here if you don't try to get him to. Animals can tell when you're trying to catch them, and there's nothing they hate worse."

Benny nodded sagely and headed toward the small table beneath the window, where the wind was loudest, his back turned to the book.

With Benny and the dead mothers drawn into the internal worlds of future dreams and future landscapes, Pearl and Rose approached the basket of choir robes, tucked into a corner between a garment rack of religious vestments and the locked silver closet. The book whistled the same melodic dirge that John-Boy always whistled when the hunt was near. Pearl unburied the book cautiously, using her fingernails to graze the oily skin of the book's face. She set the grimoire on the rug, and both she and Rose leaned into the book's reach.

Here you are lovies, the book cackled.

"Can you hear it?" Pearl whispered.

Rose looked at Pearl, her eyebrows bent into a question mark.

"Can you hear the book talking?"

Rose shook her head. "Has it been talking this whole time?"

"Talking and whistling—talking to us. It's been waiting for us."

"You better let me be the one to touch it then. If you can hear it, that may mean more than we know."

Pearl sat back on her heels. "Be careful— it'll sink its teeth into you if you let it."

Rose nodded and opened the Rains' ancient grimoire. The book moaned when its face pressed against the rug. The pages were yellowed, the parchment thin as tissue paper. Rose turned the pages quickly. A Rains' family tree, a chronology, recipes, and tinctures for headaches, for fertility. Potions to prolong pregnancy, incantations to bring Rains' children to bear. Then pages and pages where the family tree tapered off—early childhood sickness, deformities, stillborn births. A few kids made it through to their teenage years, marriages, more fertility potions. One birth, then another, all ending in tragedy. Then just one Rains left. Just Bessie Rains, the lowest hanging fruit on the family tree. She was the final dot on the timeline.

The handwriting changed often. The potions became more desperate, stranger. The spell book went to work on calling for help, on reaching into other worlds and pulling through dark creatures of power. There were incantations to Pan and the reed flute he played to seduce children from their sleeping beds and into dark and unknown forests. The Rains called to Moloch, to Chemosh, to Dagon and Belial, to Beelzebub, and to Satan. Their power had grown. The spells for money disappeared just as the family line dwindled. The Rains had wealth but no one to pass it to. The magic grew darker, calls for graveyard dirt, for human hands, for sacrificial chickens and lambs, for infant's blood, for eyes to see and shape the sight of monsters that could pass from the needle of their world and into the Swallows. Finally, in a thoughtful hand, the lists of dead mothers began. The careful studies of the children of the Swallows. A shopping catalog of age, of family lines, of health issues, and intelligence. A catalog compiled by the five librarians Bessie Rains had collected on her travels. Women who were most likely living in the Rains' mansion, in the secret corridors the orphans knew were there but could not find.

"Do you think it could just be them?" Rose, her violet-painted eyes wide in disbelief.

"I think they're probably part of it. They probably do live in the house. But the kids only know they saw the Devil Man and the giant."

From the catalog of children, those desired first were circled. Notes written in the margin about their schedules, where their mothers work. The times of day they often spent by themselves. Who could be paid—like Karen and Deirdre Kelly's neighbor, Wanda—to find out more. In the end, there was the list of women Pearl had previously seen. The list of women who had been found alone. The list of children who were plucked from their own worlds and forced into the family Bessie Rains was building at the sacrifice of all that could possibly be good.

"Go back to the part on the kids."

Rose slowly turned the pages, her finger hovering above the list until it stopped on the tidy cursive of *Benjamin Adler, seven years old*. *Pearl Adler* was written into the margin next to Benny's name—a side note, a consolation that came along with the prize. Benny's interests, the books he read at the library, what he ate at Rose's diner, all recorded. His grades in school, his family ties—only Pearl in the margin and his mother listed as *occupied*.

Rose closed the book and set it back into the choir basket. She covered it in the choir robes and made the sign of the cross before turning back to Pearl.

"This is going to take some powerful magic, nothing we are ready for tonight, but that is okay, Sugar. Tomorrow the veil is at its thinnest, and we have a better chance of calling those demons back to hell. We have a better chance of rendering Bessie Rains and all her monsters mute."

"Do you need me to do anything?"

"You've already done all this yourself. Tomorrow, you just need to keep Benny close. Hopefully, your momma gets home tonight."

Pearl looked over Rose's shoulder. Benny was still concentrating on his list, the ancient crow easing closer and closer to the table as the wind on the other side of the small sacristy widow rattled the panes of glass above Benny's head. On the music benches, the six ghost mothers were losing their edges of pale green light. The tired lines of their bodies merged into one form, the six heads nearly indistinct.

CHAPTER THIRTEEN

Frog Teeth, Bone Trees

Lightning cracked across the midnight sky, starless and godless, only the pale electric skeletons danced into oblivion above Pearl's head. Through the sheets of frozen rain, Pearl swore she could see her mother— miles away— sitting on the back of the Oldsmobile, her bare feet pressed into the dented bumper. Wrapped in Benny's Scooby-Doo blanket and smoking a cigarette to stay warm, Diane was there, scanning the sky, watching each bone of lightning pop into place as she waited for her children to return home. Pearl could see the image of her mother as if through a crystal ball. She could spin the vision through her fingers, clasp the cold orb between her palms, hold it inches from her eye, and search between the prisms of glass, finding her mother there. Her curly halo of hair, her golden eyes and long limbs, her shift dress and painted mouth, sharp teeth and nails. Pearl knew the pinprick of space that Diane occupied, she could see it all unfold before her, could nearly smell the slowly burning tobacco of Diane's cigarette. But despite the fleshed-out visions that came to Pearl so clearly, she could not get to her mother. From the best that Pearl could guess, she and Benny were lost along a high ridge trail, a skeletal spine that wound a lean and muddy path through the Black Mountains. The air was thinner than in the Swallows, the wind a harmless ghost, and even in the darkness, Pearl could feel the gravitational pull of the cavernous abyss on either side of the trail's tree line. She had no memory of what brought her and Benny into the mountains. Only the buckling of her legs and the ache in her shoulder from holding Benny's hand signaled they'd traveled long. She and Benny took the route slowly. The mud was slippery, and the path was the smallest vein on an endless lattice of trails. Pearl tried to follow the mountain ridge's decline, but she couldn't see too far into the shadowy world before her. The rain rolled through in gossamer sheets, silent and heavy, curling like smoke before colliding into the thick putty of mountain earth.

As Pearl and Benny rounded a dark ridge, moving from the muddy ledge and further into the black forest of bone trees, she held Benny's hand tighter. Skeletal and thin, the black rot of limbs creaked from the weight of spiderwebs shaped like teardrops. The teardrop spiderwebs were crystalized by the rain, the silk-like spun lace and hundreds of insect skeletons were piled at the bottom of each web. Pearl imagined each invertebrate wrapped in the soft warmth of eight never-ending legs, eight black eyes made small with ecstasy as spider teeth sank in and bled each body into a brown husk, a trophy turning to dust at the bottom of the supreme web. She imagined the spiders like panthers in the trees, silently stalking new prey, each leg mistaken for a vine, a branch, a limb. The rain fell differently among the bone trees. The mud gathered between the knobby roots or within the pits of tree trunks, making the trail bearable. Keeping her eyes on the upper limbs of the bone trees, looking for a twitch of a branch, eight blinking eyes, or the darting of a body too big, Pearl worked to remember how she and Benny came to be in the Black Mountains.

She remembered leaving the church. The silent drive home. The warmth of Rose's truck and "You've Lost that Lovin' Feelin'" on the radio. She remembered the rain freezing to the windshield, the black ice puddled in street corners. How the old Chevy chugged idly around the corner of Mystic Avenue, and Pearl's heart sunk. From two blocks up, Pearl could see Henshaw's boarding house and the one white fluorescent flood light— like a searchlight— tracking the darkness into the distance, and she knew her mother wasn't home. She knew her mother would never leave the light on. If Diane were there, she would be just as Pearl could see her: sitting in the dark on the back of the Oldsmobile, wrapped in Benny's blanket and smoking cigarette after cigarette, watching the stars and waiting for her children to return home. Pearl shook her head. Diane would never turn on a light. She was the light. Her chin always tilted skyward and never to the earth at her feet. As Rose's truck pulled into Henshaw's driveway and Pearl saw the front curtain move, she imagined her mother was a kite. Diane was never a rolling stone, not like Henshaw said right before Pearl took Benny off to bed. She remembered that. Benny's pajamas, the rain machine. Pearl and Benny were the stones, caked in mud, slowly making their way across the mountain. They were the stones that tethered Diane to the Earth. They kept her looking at the stars and not existing among them. Pearl felt the goosebumps blink open along her spine and held Benny's hand tighter. She shook loose the image of her mother in the stars, buried the vision of her mother in the front yard, and focused on the creaking branches above her, so close she had to duck beneath them. The bone trees groaned in the darkness, the sound of agony, the sound of weight walking along the branches, the soft tap of bare feet, legs like pendulums, legs like Diane's—long and thin. One reached out from the brambles of vine and limb to stroke Pearl's hair, to tug her ponytail softly before returning to the creaking shadows of the bone trees. Pearl could feel the eight black eyes on her back, her shoulders, as hot blood made endless laps between her heart and brain. Her ears rang from the pressure of being a hunted animal with no direction home.

As the bone trees began to thin, the sky pitched open like the black-mossy stones of a well, endless in height and density, barely keeping the earth from filling in the space overhead. The moon became a menacing thing— the reverse of a pinhole, a seeing eye peering through another dimension, one that was brighter, one full of a white light that shattered every dark corner, every shadow creeping into sight. The moon was a stage light into another world, one where her mother was performing in a black box theatre, the hinges on the stage doors creaking as they settled into place, creaking as her mother tapped her heel against a stone, tapped her cigarette ash into a net of stars. Pearl resented the moon's face, its watchful eye. She resented the golden blink of her mother flitting past the pinhole like a canary, her red mouth like a welcome sign. As Diane began to dance, the gold swivel of her sequined hips caught the deeper melodies of an unknown timpani and tightly wound strings. She snapped her fingers slowly, spun her hands like honeybees around her body. As she began to pluck her earrings from her ears and wink at the world from her black box theatre, a ghost wind pulled the clouds across the velvety curtain of sky, hiding Diane and the moon, and all the stars like candlelight at cocktail tables. When the sky finally cleared, only the hard face of the moon remained— a granite tombstone, polished to a shine— marking the place where Diane once stood.

†

Pearl woke in anguish. Her long hair knotted into her sweater and eyes bleary with sleep, she looked around the small space of her dusty yellow room. Lumps of laundry grew on the rug. Books and magazines— dog-eared or sprawled open on their bellies at different points of being read— were piled atop the wooden desk and bedside table. Pearl took in each object slowly. She waited for her sight to focus. *The Creature from the Black Lagoon* movie poster, the half-open closet door, the photograph of her mother on the day Pearl was born. Every face and door looked different— pinched and angry, hunched and tense, preparing for the moment to scream and pounce. Every book looked posed. Even the laundry appeared to be purposefully stacked into a heap, made to resemble the heaps left behind in Pearl's other home—the real one— the one in another dimension, the one that existed before the murders and the ghost mothers, before Miss Bessie, the Devil Man and giant, before the orphans and the painter.

"Is she here?" Pearl asked the Creature, his eyes flat and leering, his fat mouth slack. "Is anyone here?"

Pearl lay in bed and listened through the walls. She could not hear the morning news or the sound of spoons clanging against the breakfast table. She could not hear Benny's sing-song trill or her mother's high-pitched laugh. The house held its breath, at once grey and empty—the shades drawn. Pearl imagined the house as a skeletal husk, just like the insect bodies piled within the bone tree spider webs of her nightmare. The house was bled dry and empty, drained of color and light. There was no sound or smell.

Pearl imagined that her home had transcended into the shadow world; it hung on the mountain trail, suspended by a string of silk, creaking among the bone trees in a ghost wind.

But then, from beneath her bed, Pearl heard a sleepy sigh. She pulled her arms free from her quilt and peered over the edge of the mattress. New and bright in the morning's blue light, Benny was there, curled on his side beneath his Scooby-Doo blanket. Pearl pictured Benny climbing down from his bed in the dark, making his way into her room, clearing the books away from beside her bed, and building a small nest on top of her sweatshirts and jeans. He had never done that before— not even on the nights of his worst dreams or sicknesses— because Diane was always there. Pearl imagined the times when she was little and too scared to leave her bed. She would repeat her mother's name over and over again, conjuring Diane in her doorway, wrapped in a flannel robe. And she would always appear. By some stroke of luck or mercy, Diane would pluck Pearl from her bed. She'd make Pearl hot honey tea or draw her a bath if she were sick or weak from weeping. Reserved for times when Pearl was really upset, her mother would hold her hand and guide her down the dark hallways and into the kitchen—no matter what house or what town they lived in—and pretend they were wandering out of the woods. She would describe the imaginary scene so well Pearl could smell the night-blooming flowers and hear the owl calls. Diane would pretend to pluck apples from the trees. From the ether, a jar of peanut butter would magically appear. She and Pearl would sit at the kitchen table, and Pearl would watch her mother slowly peel a red delicious apple with a small paring knife. Diane could cut away the skin into one spiraled peel, and Pearl would wind the red rind into serpent shapes while she and Diane ate apple slices dipped in peanut butter. And Pearl always felt better.

Pearl shook the memory from her brain and listened to Henshaw's house again. She pressed her ears into the silent echoes of the rooms, and she knew Diane was still not there. She closed her eyes and looked at Benny again. He appeared so small when he slept. His strawberry blonde hair overgrew his ears and brow. His skin was nearly translucent, nearly glowing, like the cold marble of a statue. Pearl wondered if anything so true had ever been carved into stone. Not *David* wrapped in grape leaves, or conquerors atop horses, not curly-haired aristocrats, or broad-eyed smirking women, but something as simple as this: a young boy asleep, both in this world and on the other side of it, his eyelids flinching from the pictures in his mind, his small hands bunched into fists beneath his chin, preparing to battle the monsters on either side of his consciousness.

"Benny, hey Benny, wake up." Pearl shook her brother softly until he woke into blank uncertainty. "Is everything okay?"

Benny ground his face into his pillow and then looked at Pearl from one eye. He pulled his Scooby-Doo blanket closer to his face, the blue cotton setting off the bright clarity of his irises. "I heard something," he finally said.

"What?"

Benny shook his head.

Pearl sat up on her elbow and pursed her chapped lips. "You have to tell me."

Benny pulled the blanket closer to his chin and yawned.

"I heard someone in the living room. I thought it was mom."

"Was it?"

Benny shook his head again.

"When was this?"

"I don't know. It was still dark out."

"Did you get out of bed?"

Benny nodded.

"And went to the living room?"

He nodded again.

"And someone was there?"

Benny shook his head. "No."

"Then why did you think it was mom?"

"The door was wide open."

"The front door?"

Benny nodded.

"But Henshaw locked it. I saw him."

Benny pulled the blanket over his head and peeked out at Pearl. "I think there was someone in the yard."

"What do you mean?"

"I think I saw someone in the yard watching the house."

"Was it a man or a woman?"

"I think it was a man, but he was so still. It could've been a scarecrow."

"Henshaw doesn't have a scarecrow in the yard."

"No—"

"It was most likely a man?"

"Probably."

"Did you get a good look at him?"

Benny shook his head.

"What did he look like?"

"Like a scarecrow."

"He was tall?"

Benny nodded.

"And thin?"

Benny nodded.

"What was he wearing?"

"Black."

"What did his hair look like?"

"Black."

"Was it long?"

Benny nodded.

"Was it the painter from the diner? The one mom has been hanging out with?"

Benny buried himself beneath his blanket. Pearl could hear him yawn.

"Do you think it was him?"

"I don't know," he grumbled.

"What did you do?"

"I closed the door as fast as I could then looked for mom. But I couldn't find her, so I looked for you."

"Why didn't you wake me up?"

"I tried— but you wouldn't wake up. You were crying."

"I had a dream about mom."

"Was it scary?"

"Kind of."

Benny pulled the Scooby-Doo blanket from his face and looked at Pearl. "Don't be scared."

"I won't—it was just a bad dream." Pearl shook the images of the bone trees from her mind. She looked at Benny again and remembered her promise to Rose: she would keep Benny safe—she would protect him and stay by him— until they could destroy the book and send Miss Bessie's demons back to hell. Pearl needed to keep it together. She knew it was the Devil Man at the door last night, watching the house. She knew he could not come in. He was not invited in. She needed to keep it together to even have a chance of everything ending up on the right side of tomorrow. So, Pearl smiled and swung her legs from underneath the blanket. She stretched her arms above her head and said, "Anyway, Bens—Happy Halloween! Let's get on up and see what's happening, then we can figure out what we want to do today. Do you have that list you made at the church last night?"

Benny rubbed his face with his palms and sat up. "I was thinking about being that monster for Halloween and not the skeleton-vampire." He pointed to the *Creature of the Black Lagoon* poster over Pearl's bed.

Pearl rolled her eyes. "What! You were so excited about the skeleton-vampire! It's all you talked about."

"I know, but I don't know." Benny pulled his Scooby-Doo blanket around him like a cape and shivered.

"Well, if you really want to be the Creature from the Black Lagoon, we can figure it out. We still have time."

"I don't have any green clothes."

"I have a green sweatshirt— you can wear it inside out to hide the logo. The gills would be fun to make. We could probably cut up one of those Count Chocula cereal boxes, paint the pieces, then string them on some of Henshaw's fishing line, like a necklace. We could put green color in your hair and paint your face green and your mouth red."

"What about the fin-hands?"

"We can find some kind of green gloves—even gardening gloves would work. Let's see what mom has in clothes and makeup, get your paints and Henshaw's fishing line, then go from there."

"What about the skeleton-vampire?"

"What do you mean?"

"Well, I can't just forget about that costume. Miss Rose helped me plan it all."

"It's up to you, but whichever one you're not gonna be this year, you can be next year."

"That's no good."

"Why not?"

"I'll be different next year. One of the best parts about Halloween is being what you want to be right then and there."

"I never thought of it that way."

"Even yesterday, I wanted to be the skeleton-vampire, but this morning, I feel different. The skeleton-vampire doesn't sound so much like the kind of monster I want to be anymore."

Pearl nodded. "Alright—you be the Creature and I'll be the skeleton-vampire."

"You feel like that?"

"I could think of nothing that suits me better."

Benny laughed. "Thanks, Pearl."

"No prob—" Pearl pulled on a pair of thick socks then stood up. "Come on, it's freezing in here. Let's get some breakfast and see what's going on."

Pearl cracked open her bedroom door and peered through the slim crevice and into the dark hall. She hoped to see Cindy Stewart leaning against the wall, her long limbs stretched straight, still tanned and freckled, still strong. She imagined the other mothers in the living room, outlining the couch, flowers in their hair, their thick braids and mermaid curls stretching down their backs. Outside of Rose, it had been so long since Pearl had spent any time with a woman alive. Not her mother or her mother's old best friend, Eve. Eve used to sneak hamburgers in her purse when they went to the movie theatre. She used to take them to the park down the street from their house when Diane got upset and started breaking things. Eve was the one who watched Pearl and Benny when Diane was off on weekend campouts or trips to the lake, travels the kids were never invited to attend. Eve was the one who was there before Rose and Henshaw. Pearl missed her freckles and green eyes, her big hoop earrings, and how she always seemed to be singing.

"Whatever happened to Eve?" Pearl asked Benny. "Before we moved out here, she was always at the house. Her and mom went out all the time."

Benny shrugged. "They probably got into a fight."

Pearl nodded. That's what always happened. "Maybe that's what'll happen with the painter."

Benny peered around Pearl's shoulder and into the hallway. "You think he's out there?"

Pearl listened. She knew the faucet was dripping into the bathroom sink, the radiator was clanking in the living room. But she heard nothing else: not the television or the women, not her mother's slippered steps, or Henshaw clearing his throat.

"I don't think anyone's here, Bens." Pearl opened the door all the way. She and Benny stood on the threshold before heading into the dark.

"And you're sure you locked the door back last night?"

"Yeah."

"Did you hear anything? Did the knob jiggle? Did it sound like the man was trying to get in through the windows?"

"No— I don't think so. I stood there for a minute, then walked around the house looking for mom. I probably would've heard someone outside, but I didn't. The only room I didn't go in was Henshaw's."

Pearl nodded once and then stepped into the dark hall. With Benny behind her, Pearl silently investigated each room that branched off the hallway before reaching the kitchen and living room. This was easy work, as most of the rooms were tiny. Benny's room and the bathroom were empty. Diane's room—her closet and under her bed, her hope chest—were all full of the things they should be, and none of the things they shouldn't. Pearl tapped on Henshaw's door lightly before entering. The air was musty and dry. The thick navy shades were drawn across the windows. The bed was unmade, and the pillows were lined in such a way that, at first, Pearl thought there was someone asleep in the bed, but there wasn't. The closet was stuffed with women's dresses and hats. High heels hung on the back of the door. There were suitcases lined on the top shelf, and only a handful of Henshaw's shirts hung in the corner. Henshaw's bathroom was damp, the mossy smell of mold in the air. Mouthwash and shaving cream, an old silver razor and a comb were neatly lined on the sink basin. A wet towel hung on the shower rail. Everything was as it should be.

"It's Monday—what does Henshaw do on Monday?" Pearl asked.

"It's Halloween too."

"I doubt that matters much to him." Pearl turned the bathroom light off. "Maybe he's at the diner."

"Or at one of those elder church breakfasts."

"How do you know about that?"

"Last night, Pastor Hall said the church elders meet for breakfast every week to talk about churchy things."

Pearl smiled. "Henshaw would be an elder alright. He was probably born with a pipe in his mouth."

"And boots on his feet."

Pearl circled the room again. "It looks like he'll be back soon, though."

"That's good."

Pearl shrugged and closed Henshaw's bedroom door as she and Benny returned to the hall. "He hasn't been as mad about mom since the other night."

"He said some kind of mean things last night after church," Benny said.

"I thought you were too sleepy to hear all that." Pearl put her arm on Benny's shoulder, and they wordlessly walked the short distance into the living room.

The silver-framed photographs of Henshaw's family were all turned toward the hall. Each set of eyes was trained on the hallway, trained on Pearl and Benny. It was like walking from the wings and onto the stage, a captivated audience waiting for the first word. Pearl shivered. It reminded her of her mother in the moon. Her mother under the bright stage lights, moments before she disappeared.

"The photos are creepier in the dark," Benny whispered.

"No need for Halloween decorations when you have all of Henshaw's family watching you." Pearl drew the curtains open and let the muted morning sunlight into the space.

"Ain't nobody here but us chickens," Benny sang.

"That's alright, we've got things to do anyway. We already missed the school bell, so we might as well go on a scavenger hunt for all the supplies we need to make those costumes, then we'll finish the rest of the list."

Pearl turned on the oven and cracked the door open to warm the house. She made coffee and toast smeared with thick slabs of butter, cinnamon, and sugar. She made Benny hot honey milk and put it in an old Halloween mug she found on the back of the shelf. Benny sat at the table while Pearl wheeled around him, making a list of all the materials they needed for the vampire-skeleton and Creature from the Black Lagoon costumes. And everything was as best as it could have been. Pearl tried not to look at the front door. She did not turn on the news or cartoons. She did not want to know if anything had changed for the worse. Instead, she told Benny scary stories, which was number three on his list. She tried not to think about the dead mothers, who she knew had left the Swallows, as she could no longer feel them tethered to her. She did not anticipate the black jeep in the driveway or the sound of car doors closing. The morning fog burned off by ten, and the world of the Swallows was like a polished mirror. The wet snow glittered under the sun and radiated a white light that made every house shine like a polished stone. Pearl and Benny left the house, wrapped in their coats and hoods. Empty backpacks on their shoulders and the little money they had between them stuffed into Pearl's pocket, they went out searching for costume materials. They talked, and Benny told cheesy Halloween jokes. They took turns telling scary stories when the conversation lulled, and Pearl felt herself thinking about Miss Bessie and the bad men. She said, "It was a dark and stormy night," when she felt herself remembering that one of the bad men had come to the house last night. Pearl tried not to think of the horrible book beneath the choir robes at the church, or the work she would be called on to do by the end of that last October day. She blocked out the immediate future the best she could and spent the day thinking about Halloween and thinking about how happy it made Benny. After their bookbags were loaded with costume supplies, they went to the library and read every book on the Halloween display, then they played in the sun on the playground. They walked across the park and sat with the scarecrows on the porch of Big Bear Grocery. They played checkers and ate hotdogs, and when Clifford Marchand saw them laughing and having a good time— a far cry from what anyone had seen from the children in the Swallows for months— he brought two pumpkins out onto the porch. Together, they carved the pumpkins into the spooky designs Pearl and Benny drew on the bright skins of each. When it was time to go, Clifford Marchand sent the kids home loaded down with Halloween candy and their carved pumpkins.

"Come back around later tonight so I can see your costumes, and I'll get you something special from the bakery," Clifford Marchand called across the parking lot before returning to his store to finish the day's inventory.

That Halloween day, while Diane was still gone and Pearl's fury paced back and forth in her belly, chain-smoking and working himself up into a frenzy, the whole of the Swallows leaned into Pearl and Benny. When they got home, they set their jack o'lanterns on the porch and watched old black and white horror movies while they made their costumes. As the sun went down, Pearl made peanut butter and jellies and found Diane's old camera. She took a photo of Benny in the living room, *Night of the Living Dead* playing just behind him, his face covered in green paint, his cereal box gills a success, his smile too bright to be scary. Pearl shook their pillows from their cases and made trick-or-treat bags; she tucked her ponytail into the collar of her vampire cape, she found the heaviest flashlight Henshaw had in his toolbox, and stowed a few stones away in her pockets. Then Pearl and Benny set out into the night, smiling but staying close. Pearl knew the evening would end at the church with Rose, but she did not know what tomorrow would look like or if she would be around to see it.

†

Benny yawned. The Creature's red mouth was smeared across his earlobes and nose. The cereal-box constructed fins were wind-bent and sat like spikes around Benny's neck. His trick-or-treat sack was streaked with green hair dye as it was slung across his shoulder, rubbing against his head with each step toward Righteous Dei Lutheran. Benny asked no questions about going to the church, about meeting Rose there. Pearl knew that under the green face paint, Benny's eyes were purple-rimmed and heavy. She had run him all over the Swallows, hitting every house with a light on, and when it got too late to Trick or Treat, they went to Big Bear Grocery. Clifford Marchand was not there, but he told Sandy Lane Snyder that if the kids showed up in their monster costumes, to give them each a cocoa and a cookie. Sandy Lane sat on the porch right along with the Creature from the Black Lagoon and the vampire-skeleton, her thin fingers wrapped around a paper cup of cocoa and chain-smoking. She told stories about her Arizona lovers and the hotel where she used to punch in. Each of Sandy Lane's stories ended with the same down-and-out punchline: in the Swallows, the only thing waiting at home for her was a cannibalistic Venus Fly Trap named Buddy. And Pearl did not mind. Listening to Sandy drone on and on about other worlds—dream worlds of cactus flowers and pink moons—was the least Pearl had thought about her own life in what felt like years. When Big Bear turned its lights off at ten o'clock, and Sandy locked the front door, Pearl knew it was time to walk the nine blocks to Righteous Dei. Waving goodbye to Sandy mid-story, Pearl and Benny made the lonely journey to the church. Pearl listened for John-Boy's whistle. She listened for whispers, the movement of a body moving through the trees—but she heard nothing. The steeple of the church was an arrow pointing skyward—a stone symbol between the spires of Bear Mountain and the low rooftops of the town proper. Benny yawned again as his boots pounded up the church steps. The front door was unlocked, and Rose was waiting in the alcove.

"Happy Halloween!" Rose stood up from the bench in the narthex when Pearl opened the heavy oak door. Rose's smile was taunt and eyes worried, but her voice was like a songbird. "And don't you two look scary."

Benny shrugged his sack of candy off his shoulder and yawned in greeting. "I'm so tired, Miss Rose, I could sleep till Christmas."

"I don't know about all that, but I'll make you up a little bed."

"On one of the benches in the church," Pearl added. She hoped he would curl up into a pew and sleep through the night. Close enough that she could hear him but far enough away that nothing bad would happen.

Rose nodded and picked up Benny's candy sack. "Maybe a little closer?" She looked at Pearl.

Pearl shook her head. "We don't want to keep him up."

Rose put her hand on Benny's shoulder and led him into the nave.

The nave was dark. The storied stained-glass windows looked like black boxes, their shades slightly lighter than the stone walls. The carpet was a red sea, the pews thin boats slicing through the cold night. Pearl imagined the bats circling overhead, the pale stars unflinching as they silently projected the small destinies below.

"Maybe this is too far away," Rose whispered.

"It's cold," Benny said.

"You can sleep over here." Pearl led Benny toward the altar. "The rug is thick, so it'll be comfortable."

"And I can find some things to make it better."

As Rose walked into the sacristy, Pearl pulled Benny's creature-fin necklace from his neck and used her own pillowcase to smear some of the green and red paint from his face. "You're gonna need eight baths to get all this off."

Benny took off his boots and sat down. Rose returned from the darkness with a pillow and a stack of black choir robes. She laid one across the rug then covered Benny with the rest.

"You're warm enough?" she asked.

Benny yawned and closed his eyes in response. He fell asleep immediately.

"You're okay with him being where we can't see him?"

Pearl looked around the dark cavern. "It's probably the best place for him. We can hear him, but no one would ever find him here, especially under all this black."

Rose nodded. "Have you seen the mothers?"

"No—" Pearl looked at her hands. "I don't think they're here anymore."

"And your momma?"

Pearl shook her head.

"That's too bad." Rose looked into the darkness by the front entrance. "Well, we better put all this nonsense to bed so we can get some sleep."

Rose pulled a small black pouch from her pocket and tucked it beside Benny.

"What's that?"

"It's a Gris-Gris—a protection charm called The Devil's Fingers." She handed another bag to Pearl as they left the nave and headed down the short hallway into the sacristy. "Devil's shoestring to bind up evil, Devil's nut to scare it off, and Devil's dung to drive it away."

"In the family book?"

Rose nodded. "Auntie August. But talk about an old recipe. I spent half the day trying to figure out what the shoestring, nut, and dung actually were, and the other half of the day searching for them."

Rose pushed open the small, curved door into the scarcity.

"Where'd you find them?"

"A shop near Deadwood."

"That far?"

"It was nice to go for a drive before walking into this. I needed to clear my head. Everything else I had around the house."

The gloom of the scarcity blossomed along the high walls and rafters, but beneath the beams, hundreds of black candles lined the music benches and piano lid, the ornate chests, and low bookshelves.

Pearl had not heard Bessie Rain's book until she entered the room. It said nothing—like a cornered wolf, teeth bared back and eyes hateful—but she could make out its ragged breathing.

Rose had constructed an altar that Pearl would have found beautiful if she didn't know what it was for. The altar was almost as tall as Pearl, but it was composed of only three levels: earth, purgatory, and heaven. Earth was draped in tea-dyed lace, a thick crocheted pattern woven by a steady hand. There was a small plate of sand and one of stones. There were seashells and tall goldenrod flowers in an antique milk jug. There was salt within a clay bowl, bread and tree nuts in separate baskets, and a plate of gold coins. Purgatory was a world in transition. There was a wire basket of eggs and one of gold sewing thread. There was a prismed vase of cotton blossoms, an amethyst geode cracked in half, and rose quartz and bright crystals neatly set in a row. There was a mug of black coffee and small pastel cakes. Heaven made Pearl want to cry. It was draped in white lace and held silver-framed photographs of the dead mothers. There was a silver Saint Christopher charm and an aged postcard of the Virgin Mary draped in blue.

"Why is all the silver black?"

"It's a standard sign of an attack. I've polished it twice since I've been here, but it keeps turning." Rose frowned at the book in the corner. "The eggs'll probably turn soon, all the evil they're taking in. You've probably had some dreams too."

Pearl shivered. She pictured her mother disappearing in the moon, the cliffs of bone trees and soul-eating spiders. The goosebumps on her arms and neck shook awake at the late hour, and blinked in unison. "Too many."

Rose nodded and walked into a dark corner. She returned to the altar with a slim stick broom and began sweeping the rug. She sang low as she went about her work. Pearl watched and imagined that they were living centuries in the past: the wind rattling across the plains and into the Black Mountains, the spires trembling with word from the sea. When Rose was done sweeping, she pulled a Mason jar of salt from a shelf near the altar.

"Stay in the circle, honey, and don't leave it for nothing. We are going to start with meditating, then move on to the rest of it."

"What's the rest of it?"

"We'll get to it in good time. We have to focus on what's right in front of us or it'll all fall apart. We have to keep ourselves right here—right in this moment—or it'll never work. We can't feel anger or hurt when we work this spell, or all that black energy will transfer into the spell and change it right around. So don't worry about nothin'. We can do this, alright?"

Pearl nodded.

"Alright." Rose smiled. "It'll be alright. As I pour this salt, I want you to think about a bright white light in your belly, building like a fire, and when you get up enough energy, I want you to pull that light into your head, your fingertips, and feet, then I want it to get so strong, it cuts into the earth and sky. Now, I'll be doing that too. And I think if we do it together, we'll be alright."

Pearl closed her eyes. She imagined the monster of her fury pausing his pacing and taking a drag from his cigarette. She imagined her mother's name written on paper and stuck within her ribs. She used the monster's cigarette to light the paper and start the white light on its way. She imagined how hot the sun could be in July, sitting on a lakeside beach with Benny, and how each summer freckle on his cheeks were made of all that vibrant energy. Then she imagined all the love she knew: early mornings of dancing with her mom and watching Sesame Street, naming the clouds and catching fireflies with Benny, how the dead mothers imagined their children away at camp, playing hide-and-seek and setting up tents in sun-ripe mountains because they could not face a world without their babies. She felt all the energy course through her and catapult into the earth and sky, melting through lava-rich caverns and hardening into an icicle as it reached farther and farther through lightyears of galaxies. The circle was cast.

Rose bowed her head and grabbed Pearl's hand. They sat down before the altar. From the shelf behind her, Rose pulled three small black boxes and set them in a row between herself and Pearl. The boxes were shaped like tiny coffins— large enough for a blackbird— and the hinges were primitive. The lid of each box was deeply carved with an eight-armed rune, similar to the spiders hanging in the bone trees of Pearl's dreams. After the small coffins were set in a row, Rose held Pearl's hands again. Their arms and hands built a smaller ring within the salt circle. This is the ring where Rose and Pearl were to focus all of their energy.

"From east to south and north to west, I call to Hecate to attend and bless, to brew my spells and honor you well. With hands steadfast, our circle is cast," Rose spoke, eyes closed.

One at a time, she opened each box. Within painted black as well, but every surface where satin would ordinarily be stitched into place was paved with chards of dagger-edged mirrors. And lying within each coffin was a small muslin doll. The first was Bessie Rain with silver braid. The second was the tall man—his long hair and black suit, and the third was the broad-shouldered giant. One at a time, Rose pulled each poppet from their glass coffins. She held them before the black candlelight, and slowly, she wrapped each body in cotton rope as she recited, "I name thee Bessie Rains. I pray you make no more trouble here. For to torment this town for your own interest will bring you nothing but agony of the severest. For I am a child of Hecate, and she is mightier than thee. From this hour forth, all ill resolve shall fall back upon your head twelve-fold. In the name of Hecate, mother, maiden, and crone." Then closed the lid, pressing her palm firmly against its surface. For each of the monsters that haunted the orphans in the house they now shared, Rose pronounced, "I name thee shadow. I pray you make no more trouble here. Leave this town and its children alone and return to the dark place from whence you come. Extend your tortures to those like you or face the wrath of Hecate—she will bring twelve-fold suffering anew. From this hour forth, you will leave this place, in the name of Hecate, mother, maiden, and crone."

Rose returned each rope-wrapped monster to its coffin and pressed her palm heavily against each lid. Pearl could no longer hear the book breathing. She could no longer feel the tense animal in the corner, the wolf with bared teeth and long nails. She imagined Bessie Rains and each monster bound into their mirrored coffins. The scratchy rope cutting into their arms and legs, the glass reflecting all the black rot of each hollow heart. Rose bowed her head and called, "Mighty, Hecate, our hour of need is complete. We thank you humbly for your protection and power. Please accept all we bring. With love, we walk into the world, passing no harm to those who pass before us."

The candles were almost burned through. Rose opened her eyes and smiled at Pearl. "Do you hear the book?" she asked.

"No—not at all. I heard it breathing until the lid was closed on Bessie."

Rose nodded. "As it should be. I'll take these three and the book into the mountains and bury them separately."

"How did you know how to do all of that?"

"I told you about the black crows in my own family grim. Grandma June and Aunt August had written all about banishing—right after those crows. Fullmouth has had evil for a long time, and it only made sense that it'd be in that old book."

Pearl smiled. Her eyes felt heavy. All the white light energy had reached far beyond, leaving her a sleepy husk.

"I still have a lot to do. Why don't you walk Benny on home and get some sleep?"

"We'll come see you tomorrow then. Benny and I can help scrape off the rest of those Halloween paintings from the diner windows."

Rose nodded. "And tell your momma I said *hello.*"

Pearl left the sacristy. She gathered Benny up, who was still asleep under the heavy shadows of the choir robes. She held both of their candy sacks and Benny's hand. As they walked home, the nighttime seemed less heavy, more shades of purple and navy than the weighted black that had painted everything in the Swallows. Even in the late hour, jack-o'lanterns were propped on the porches, their mouths full of flickering candlelight. The windows of houses were shaded in lace and drapes, but behind each, a golden lamp brightened each glass eye. There was no whistling, no birdcalls or beating wind to disturb the two children slowly walking home in the dark.

The searchlight of Henshaw's porch was not on. Their mother's golden Oldsmobile was in the driveway. The blue curtains were pulled closed, but the lamps that lined the end tables were all burning. Pearl felt her belly tighten. She felt her legs move faster, following the steady rhythm of *mom's home, mom's home, mom's home.*

"She's there," Benny whispered and held Pearl's hand tighter.

They eased their bodies between their mother's car and the perils of Henshaw's yard, full of half-buried carburetors and old tires, broken flowerpots, and hand-held garden rakes. Pearl hesitated to let go of Benny's hand to open the door. But when she did, she felt better for having completed the task.

Before she stepped across the threshold, she heard a long, low whistle calling from the kitchen. It was not so much a song or a jingle. It was not the end of a joke. It was more like the start of a horror movie—tinny and low. It signaled something Pearl did not know. Like the terror to come had only just begun the moment the door swung open and a wilted skeleton-vampire with a smeared face and piecemeal Creature from the Black Lagoon appeared on the doorstep. Chair legs scraped back. A boot stomped against the linoleum. A coffee cup set roughly atop the table. There were suitcases stacked next to the front door.

Pearl held Benny's hand and set their sacks of candy on the porch behind them. She pulled the heavy flashlight from her coat pocket and held it in her punching hand. With Benny behind her, she walked slowly toward the kitchen. Waiting to hear her mother's laugh, the sing-song melody of her voice. Every light in the kitchen was on. Her mother sat at the table, a Virginia Slim burning low between her fingers, her other hand traced the scratches on the table's surface. Her knee shook anxiously beneath the table, vibrating the table's surface.

"Hi, mom," Pearl said.

Diane would not look up. She sighed deeply—eyes on the table—her narrow chest subtly expanding the lace dress she wore. Her hair was wild and curly, more beautiful than Pearl had ever seen. It was brushed toward her face, hiding her sharp cheekbones and forehead. Pearl imagined she saw the rose crown, the dark red petals freshly bloomed.

"Mom?" Pearl whispered.

Diane's eyes were frosted in silver glitter, her cheeks glazed in tears. There were blossoms of purple and blue bruises along her jawline and collar, like the pansies that grew wild in the Black Mountains during summer. Across from Diane, the painter leaned back in his chair, a coffee mug at his elbow. He watched Diane—the slumped curl of her shoulders, her hooded eyes. The cigarette embers burned low, nearer and nearer her long fingers. It burned closer and closer to Diane's new ring, the diamond glinting, the band already black as a rotten tooth, tarnished beyond all meaning.

Kristen Clanton

EPILOGUE

The Sound of the Drum is Calling

"Breaking news out of Fullmouth tonight," Chip Gordon spoke in a voice weighted with the gravity of conclusion. His arms were spread wide, framing his navy-suited torso like protection totems. "Four suspects are being detained and questioned about the death of Karen Kelly after new evidence has surfaced. Kelly's body was discovered on the evening of October 28th when a neighbor heard Kelly's daughter screaming and called local law enforcement. Police have reported that Kelly's death—originally listed as a suicide— is now being investigated as a suspected stabbing. The Fullmouth Police Department has partnered with the FBI to reopen the cases of Cindy Stewart, Molly Boutell, Kaia Goodwin, and Maggie Teller. Suzanne Dubray's death is still an open investigation and may possibly be connected to the untimely deaths of the five other women who were citizens of Fullmouth. The Fullmouth Police Department has not released names at this time, though they suspect at least five other members of the community helped orchestrate Kelly's suspected murder. If you have any information on the deaths of Karen Kelly, Cindy Stewart, Molly Boutell, Kaia Goodwin, and Maggie Teller, or Suzanne Dubray, please contact your local law enforcement office."

ABOUT the **AUTHOR**

KRISTEN CLANTON was born and raised on the swamp in Tampa, Florida. She traveled west for a while, earning her MFA from the University of Nebraska. Her poetry and short fiction have been published in numerous journals, including *Arkana, BlazeVOX, South Florida Poetry Journal*, and the *Sugar House Review*, and she has been nominated for a Pushcart Prize. She currently teaches English and writing at a boarding school in Maine. This is her first novel.